Satellite Campus

Sean Boling

Published by Sean Boling, 2013.

SATELLITE CAMPUS

First edition. November 13, 2013.

ISBN: 979-8224236633

Written by Sean Boling.

To Mom, who engineered my first author event by having her book club read this novel and invite me to speak with them.

Chapter One

When she started to forget she owned a cat, she told her son it would be her last one. The cat would appear at her sliding glass door and she would remember it, and recall that she had named him Mr. Darcy. He was a gray cat with yellow eyes, looking as though he was emerging from a puff of smoke that had not yet fully dissolved after some magic words had been spoken. He would eat, demand attention, then leave. She would forget Mr. Darcy existed until the next time he materialized, then she would tell herself again that when he stopped showing up, she would not replace him.

But the cat outlasted her capacity to make that decision. Mr. Darcy continued with the routine while she forgot her role in it. "There's a cat at my door," she said to her son one morning as they spoke over the phone. He asked her to describe it, and when a picture of Mr. Darcy emerged, her son knew that they didn't have much time left, regardless of how long she ended up living.

He hired a pair of live-in nurses, a husband and wife team who each worked a ten-hour solo shift, and spent a few hours in the evening working and spending time together between shifts. They were the type of people who reminded you of what a pleasure it is to watch someone do their job well. Nonetheless, after he had helped them settle into their position and went back out on the road to resume his, he was compelled to call and check in frequently. They would tell him that his mother was doing fine, and that they were happy with the job, which was the main reason why he was calling. The more he started to believe them, the less he called. He asked the wife nurse one morning if the cat was still stopping by. Neither she nor her husband had seen him for weeks, and speculated he must have taken up with some neighbors. Her son hoped that was the case.

He could never be certain he had made the right decision, even as months gave way to years, so he clung to a compliment once paid to him by some friends of his in the Defense Department. They told him he had a strong sense of situational awareness. It was a term he and his colleagues in the scientific community used as well, but he felt the military version had more gravity since it could mean the difference between life and death, rather than just a way to insure a more sound hypothesis. He was therefore quite flattered when those officers applied it to him, even if their assessment had nothing to do with anticipating threats in a battlefield, or addressing his mother's condition for that matter. They were merely referring to his ability to work a room while giving a presentation.

And that ability was coming in handy during the benefit he was vamping for when he received the phone call from one of the nurses. He was the keynote speaker for a five hundred dollar per-plate dinner intended to raise money for an expanded science wing at a small liberal arts college trying to reinvent itself as a place suitable for lucrative research grants. Even though their plans for the department had nothing to do with Astronomy, they still invited him to speak, since being able to invoke the term "heavens" tended to be a bigger draw than inspiring people to wonder about the microscopic worlds surrounding us on our own planet, as though we'd prefer to keep our familiarity on the surface level; keep our distance and leave enough space to speculate on our place in the universe.

There was also his name recognition, of course. He had neither discovered nor invented anything, but had been the spokesperson for a host of scientific organizations, most of whom appreciated his ability to communicate their activities better than any of the true geniuses could. The ones who didn't appreciate his contributions considered him a shill rather than a legitimate astronomer. Even his name, inspired by his mother's love of literature, had a stagey quality to it: Twain Henry. His mother would joke that she named him in the hope he would grow up to be a 19th-century newspaper reporter. And while he ended up pursuing a career in science, she prized the element of journalism that had crept up on him. A friend of his from the National Science Foundation confided that some of their colleagues referred to him as "the press secretary". He found it funny, and his laughter was sincere. Any insecurities he may have harbored were easily assuaged by an appearance on The Daily Show, or hosting his own show on The Discovery Channel, or posting an interview on his blog with a brilliant fellow astronomer who was too consumed and passionate about his work to be consumed with jealousy over anything Twain was doing to promote that work.

But this crowd, at this benefit, wasn't buying into the hype, at least not at first. His situational awareness was processing a host of people staring blankly at the silverware or at him. They seemed to find the two interchangeable. He resisted the impulse to ask why they would pay five hundred dollars only to allow themselves to be bored, but didn't want to lose the room, and any future gigs at this school, which had a long haul ahead of it as they tried to make their reimagining of the department a reality. There was always a certain number of people at these events who just wanted to say they had been there, and met him, and didn't really care what he had to say, but he had enough love for his field and pride in his work to lead him to believe that what he was saying was important. Or maybe it was just ego. Regardless, he at least needed them to pretend they cared.

He got out from behind the podium and started to glide amongst the tables as he spoke, turning his lecture into a series of intimate conversations between him and whomever he felt needed some attention, all the while staying within range of the data projector so that his remote would work when he needed to change the image on screen.

It was a presentation he had used several times before, designed to give him an opportunity to transition into a more philosophical angle of astronomy should he find himself in front of an audience that was not intrigued by the nuts and bolts of the science. He suspected that was the problem with this group, given the school's historical lean toward the Humanities, and he was about to find out. He pushed on the remote and an image of the Horsehead Nebula took its turn on the screen. That was his cue. He heard some impressed grunts, which was a good sign, as it reminded him of the kinds of reactions people gave at art openings and book readings. So he pressed forward into their territory by remarking that it looked to him like the black knight piece from a chessboard.

"Made of smoke," added a voice from the corner of the darkened room.

"Charcoal smoke," said someone in the opposite corner.

"And it's riding through the Northern Lights," raised another voice. And the contributions kept coming.

"It's as though a wizard was concocting a magic potion in a cauldron and then tapped the surface for the finishing touch, and this beautiful swirl of shapes and colors rose from it," said a bookish woman at the table he hovered beside.

"And the potion had something to do with horses," added another person outside of the light and his vision. "To make them run fast or something."

"To make them fly," said the bookish woman's partner, who appeared to live even deeper within the books they loved. They beamed at one another.

Twain smiled at them, appreciating both their connection to each other and the connection he was now making with the audience. He reminded everyone of the enormity of what they were looking at, as pictures of stellar bodies were apt to diminish their scope, making them no less beautiful, but smaller than people realized.

He leaped to the front again and ran his hands along the neck of the horse, informing the now-captive crowd that ten thousand of our solar systems could fit inside that curve, then utilized the conference room they were dining in as further perspective, claiming that our planets would amount to a napkin ring in the room-sized nebula. He almost compared the earth's home system to a stain on a tablecloth, but caught himself thanks to the awareness honed over the years of how easy it is when talking astronomy to make people feel insignificant, which is far from the best way to hold their interest. To provide even more insurance against any collective self-doubt infecting this crowd, he called even more attention to the earth by exploiting the horse figure as a metaphor for the early days of human exploration, and the subsequent imperialism that followed in many cases, and encouraged the attendees to think about whether space exploration will pose similar moral and ethical questions. This allowed the History and Social Science folks to speak up, a diplomatic move given that the Art Department had been provided their chance when describing the smoky horse.

As Twain expected, they seized the opportunity, and his pride in his situational awareness swelled. While a professorial type in relaxed-fit jeans stood and provided a short dissertation on how naïve it is to think that we will be the imperialists rather than the subjects of domination, Twain felt the phone in his back pocket vibrate. His phone was constantly receiving messages during the day regarding professional matters, so the less-frequent night call always intrigued him, as it usually signaled either something personal, or international, often an invitation to speak or consult in a part of the world far enough away as to make time change calculations moot.

He let the audience members debate a little while longer, or more accurately, take turns lecturing, before segueing into his concluding remarks. He had prepared a statement that encouraged them to persist in their journey to create a new section of campus, and to join those whose persistence had revealed worlds beyond our galaxy and in our own backyard. Within a few sentences, however, he ditched it in favor of an ad lib that played off the horsehead riff that had held their concentration so effectively, informing them that portions of the nebula will become stars in the future, as will their science wing should it take flight.

The rest of the lights came up and the applause that followed seemed to brighten the room even more. Considering the sleepy reactions to the initial phase of his exhibition, he was very happy with the end result, and felt a current of adrenalin he often appreciated in moments like this that he imagined a pitcher must feel when he strikes out a fearsome hitter on three pitches, a sense of domination that was the nerd equivalent of being a stud.

As often happened during the question and answer sessions that followed any given visit, especially ones such as this that catered to a roomful of scientific dilettantes, the questions were wont to be more personal than astronomical. They asked him how well he knew certain celebrities with whom he had been photographed, if he had any anecdotes about the president he could share from his time as the face of the President's Council of Advisors on Science and Technology, what his favorite cities were to visit (and how their hometown ranked, which was usually the real purpose of the question, like a date asking about past relationships). They asked about his name, too, and he rolled with it and mentioned his mother's thirty-year career as an assistant to the chair of the Literature Department at a competing university. The rival school's name elicited some playful boos and hisses, but in the event of any genuine animosity amongst the playfulness, he quickly followed up with Mom's joke about how his name reminded her of an old-fashioned muckraker. The fellow literary acolytes loved it, and proceeded to contribute their own takes on what someone named Twain Henry should do:

"Work on the Illinois Central Railroad."

"Lead a slave revolt."

"Manage a lumber mill."

"Run for governor of Missouri in 1898."

"In other words," Twain cut in, "nothing related to science."

He got his laugh and thanked them for the invitation and their contribution to the future of science. He glanced back at the architect's rendering of the building that now filled the screen. The glass walls that encased the hallways separating the offices and classrooms caught his eye, as they not only revealed some faceless people figures walking on each of the several floors, but a central courtyard that looked like an atrium, filled with trees and various flora.

"One more thing," he said as he continued to look at the picture. "Please remember to stick some falcon and owl decals on those glass walls. Otherwise the perimeter of the building will be littered with dead birds who tried to reach those trees and were interrupted by the glass."

The room seemed unsure how to react, which was oddly satisfying since his advice was genuine, and their confusion indicated to him they were listening, and not assuming everything had settled into a series of laugh lines. He was feeling so triumphant that he even considered hanging around for an impromptu meet-and-greet, which he had not been contracted to do.

He exited the podium to one more round of applause as the master of ceremonies retook center stage to wrap up the program. Twain lingered by the door and checked his phone, figuring a solicitation for another engagement would add to the momentum. Or maybe it was the woman who had organized the wrap party for the most recent season of his show, which completed production a couple of weeks before. That would really inflate the air he was walking on.

There were actually two messages: a text and a voice mail. The text was simply the name of a doctor and a phone number. He recognized neither, but saved it in case the voice mail offered an explanation.

"Hello, Dr. Henry..." he recognized the voice of the husband live-in nurse. "Uh, this is Oscar, the LVN for your mother. Uh, your mother is in the hospital. She's okay, but, uh, Esther was working today and she found your mother really shaking, real bad, and, uh, she called 911. Uh, like I said, she's okay, but the doctor wants you to call him. I sent you his number in a text. But she's okay. Uh, like I said. Okay. Good bye."

Now the doctor's name rang familiar: Mom's primary care physician. She had been going to him for years before her Alzheimer's started to reveal itself. Twain had never met him, but his name had been on some forms he filled out in securing the services of the LVNs.

Between the doctor's request to talk and the number of times Oscar said "okay", Twain decided to stick to the contract and skip the meet-and-greet.

He slid out the door and strode to the parking lot. He re-traced his path to the row in which he had parked the rental car, but could not remember what it looked like, his mind drawn to bigger pictures. He took a chance that the number on the text was the doctor's personal line. Plus it was a few hours earlier out west.

"Hello, this is Dr. Walls."

Twain hesitated. He wasn't sure if it was a voice mail message or the doctor himself.

"Hello?" the voice questioned.

"Oh, hello Doctor," Twain finally answered. "I wasn't sure if you would pick up at this hour. This is Twain Henry. My mother's LVN said you wanted to speak to me."

"Yes. Thank you for calling, Dr. Henry. How much do you know about what happened today?"

"Not much," Twain started to pace in an imperfect circle under one of the light posts. "Oscar told me that she was shaking, and his wife called 911, and that she's okay."

"Physically, yes," Dr. Walls said. "She has pneumonia, and they'll knock it out of her in the hospital."

"That's good," Twain said, knowing full well there was more to it.

"On the surface, I suppose it is. But her state of mind is making her stay in the hospital a difficult one. To put it mildly."

"I see," Twain said.

There was a pause, which surprised him. He had pegged Dr. Walls right away as someone who valued truth over tact, but here he seemed to be gathering the right words to express the situation.

"As you know," the doctor found his direction, "she never spent much time in a hospital before. She once told me that the only time she was ever in one was the day she gave birth to you."

Twain smiled. "It's true."

His expression must have come across in his voice, as the doctor joined him in a moment of levity. "If all of my patients were as healthy as her, I would go broke."

Since Twain had already surmised that such a moment was rare for Dr. Walls, he also reckoned the doctor wouldn't quite know how to press on, so he decided to be the one to get them back on track. "And now?"

"Now," Dr. Walls sighed. "Now that her physical health is coming down to the level of her neurological condition, I'm afraid it's going to be a very bad combination. Potentially very lucrative, in other words, to anyone willing to take advantage."

Twain processed where this conversation was headed. "One case of pneumonia and her health is deteriorating? Isn't that a rather large inductive leap?"

The doctor put his armor back on. "Not in my experience, and not according to the research."

Now it was Twain's turn to hesitate. Dr. Walls filled it in.

"The cycle is very dependable, Dr. Henry," he continued, now very much back in his element. "In her stage of life, once the respiratory system is compromised, days like today become more common. And for someone with Alzheimer's, those days are terrifying."

Twain stopped pacing and massaged his forehead. "Are you asking me to make a decision of some sort?"

"Of course not," Dr. Walls backed off while still maintaining his professional grip. "She's already in the process of making it through this round. I've requested that she be released in the morning. They want her there for a few more days, naturally, but at this point, now that she's on antibiotics, the infection will go away, and I'm convinced staying in that hospital would kill her, given how agitated it makes her."

"That bad?" Twain asked.

"She has nothing that connects her to a hospital room, or the inside of an ambulance. It may as well be a torture chamber. She doesn't understand who the people are and what they're doing to her, these people restraining her and sticking needles and tubes inside of her. It's a living nightmare. The kind that keeps you from getting back to sleep after you have it."

Twain imagined his mother clawing at the sides of a hole she was sliding down. He felt awful, and fell silent. Dr. Walls again exploited the gap.

"It's going to be the same thing every time, Dr. Henry. Those LVNs will keep calling 911, and she will be rushed back into her nightmare again and again. I don't have the authority to stop it."

The night sky had always been a reliable source of comfort and inspiration for Twain, but as he looked up for it, he found it hidden behind the stooped lights of the parking lot.

Back when his mother still claimed much of her brain's territory, but could feel the ends of her neurons losing ground, she was very resourceful about her future, helping Twain interview LVN candidates, and composing a living will that stipulated she was not to be kept alive "if her quality of life becomes pitiable, or if caring for her becomes a depressing burden or financial drain."

He continued to look skyward, despite the interference of the fluorescent glow that made everything in its beam appear as though it was being reflected in a public restroom mirror.

"And if I exercise my authority," he prefaced his question to the doctor, "what does that look like, exactly?"

"Next time she gets pneumonia, you don't call the ambulance. You call hospice."

Twain's gaze plummeted to the ground. The gray pavement appeared even more ashen beneath the lights that hunched over him and cast his shadow across it.

"How long before that happens?" he managed to ask.

"It could be a couple of weeks, maybe a couple of months," Dr. Walls answered. "You have some time to think about it. To think about her."

This time the pause was left unfilled. The doctor allowed the silence to linger for quite a while. Twain took some slow, deep breaths and looked around the expanse of empty cars without really looking at them, just trying to clear his mind. He accidentally spotted his rental car.

"I should come out there," he said.

"That's a good idea."

Twain wanted to wrap up the conversation since he wasn't sure he could generate any more words for the night. "Thank you, doctor."

"Call me when you get into town. I'm sorry to have to saddle you with this."

"Just doing your job. Good night."

They hung up and he heard voices. Some people were starting to emerge from the benefit, from the room he had been manipulating just minutes before. The string he had used to lead them around was now unraveled. His control had vanished. He jogged to the car and ducked inside.

The street taking him away from the event was dark. He appreciated the chance to focus on his immediate surroundings, to be vigilant for any hazards that may appear in his headlights. He muttered "situational awareness," and laughed callously at himself.

Chapter Two

His mother lived in a farm town in name only, a once-struggling enclave that had re-invented itself decades before from "middle of nowhere" to "agritourism destination"; a place where people went to feel closer to the land while staying in a coiffed hotel room with a wine buzz. She had kept an eye on it during the last few years of her career after vacationing there with a Cabernet enthusiast. That weekend was the last she would spend with the man, but she fell in love with the area, and retired there before it started to rise in prestige and price.

Twain touched down at the regional airport closest to his Mom's home and called his agent, asking her to make him unavailable for the next month, maybe longer. He would keep her posted. She was very understanding, though the fact it was a time of year when he usually didn't have many engagements booked may have enabled her thoughtfulness. He wouldn't need to start promoting his show until after the holidays, the couple of appearances she had scheduled could be easily postponed, and he could post to his website and blog in the meantime to keep his name circulating. His agent mentioned that he may even want to look into doing some pieces about aging or Alzheimer's, but Twain wasn't sure he was ready to use his Mom's circumstances as a platform.

"Just putting it out there," she said.

"I didn't say no," he reminded her.

"You rarely do."

"Good bye, Sherry."

He hung up, a decade of working together providing them with the ease to jab at one another regardless of the situation.

Last Christmas he had given Mom's car to the LVNs as a bonus, since she didn't need it anymore and he wasn't in town very often, so he needed to rent one. He asked the clerk if they happened to have any pickup trucks available, figuring a native vehicle would be a good way to get into the spirit of the area if he was going to be spending a fair amount of time in it. There was a compact with a short bed, and he snatched it up. He'd fit right in with the retirees who tended to buy just such a truck when they arrived, so they could still get good gas mileage while being prepared for their trips to the home improvement store as they meddled with their gardens.

He drove from the airport and out of the city that had always served as the economic hub of the region, which had grown and industrialized accordingly, out toward the small town that had surpassed it in hipness. After forty minutes of kneaded hills and grazing land tanned by the late summer sun, the landscape started to streak with leafy vineyards and tasting rooms vying for attention, with the occasional renovated farmhouse serving as a Bed and Breakfast. Fifteen minutes later, the outer rim of the town presented some more thrifty and mundane options for food and lodging, and then the structures once again grew more photogenic in the downtown area.

His Mom's house occupied the space between: a tract built in the relatively early days of the hamlet's modern boom, a fairly small development that did an effective job of camouflaging the uniformity of the floor plans, helped by a generation of growth in the landscaping. He pulled onto her sleepy street and was surprised to see a bus stop had been built in front of her house. It was a simple one, just a bench and a short sign mounted on a wood post that wasn't even planted into the ground, instead supported by a couple of crisscrossed two-by-fours.

He had called Oscar that morning to give him his flight information, and when Twain pulled into the driveway, both Oscar and Esther appeared from behind the front door to greet him, as though they had been waiting offstage for their cue. They were dressed in casual clothes, as though dressed for an office job on a

Friday. The last time Twain had seen them in anything other than their nurses' scrubs was during their job interview.

Each smiled uncomfortably, and Twain got the impression they somehow felt responsible for what had happened. He got out of the truck and hugged Esther, who bawled as soon as his arms were around her. He held her for as long as she needed, glancing over at Oscar, who remained stoic, but with moist eyes at seeing his wife so distraught.

"I'm sorry, Dr. Henry," she said into his shoulder as she tried to catch her breath. "I had to do it. She was shaking so bad."

"I understand, Esther," he assured her. "You did the right thing."

"Don't let her die," she pleaded. "Please don't let her die."

So they were aware of what Dr. Walls had suggested. Twain wondered how. He looked to Oscar for an explanation.

"She heard Dr. Walls talking to the Emergency Room doctor," he informed him.

Twain separated from Esther and stood in front of her with his hands on her shoulders. "I haven't decided anything yet."

She nodded repeatedly, calming herself down.

"Can I see her?" Twain asked.

"She's awake," Esther wiped her eyes with the back of her hand.

The outside of his Mom's house may have been suburban, but the inside was decorated like one of the countryside farmhouses or downtown Victorians, only with smooth stucco walls instead of wood paneling.

"Are your bags in the back of the truck or the front seat, Dr. Henry?" Oscar asked.

"I'll get them later. Don't bother."

"No, really," he insisted. "It's no trouble."

Twain realized Oscar was looking for a place to hide for a few moments, so he accepted his offer with a thanks, told him they were in the front seat, and followed Esther down the hall to his Mom's room.

Her bedroom was her primary residence at this point, the place where she felt most at ease, and it was easy to see why; everything was soft to the touch, and anything hard, such as the side tables and bookshelves, were made of soft wood stained in warm colors that glowed. And while the television was an exception on the surface, what it played fit the sense of relaxation: videos designed to entertain infants and toddlers with footage of wind-up toys and plush puppets set to kid-friendly arrangements of classical music. Oscar and Esther discovered how much she enjoyed them when they were looking after their granddaughter one day and turned on a channel that streamed such videos all day, commercial-free; Twain's mother was drawn into the living room by the sounds of the music and started watching the screen with keen interest alongside the three-year-old girl.

She wasn't looking at the screen when she noticed Twain; she was sitting in her plush recliner in the corner, set in the upright position, looking into a distance only she could measure, perhaps listening to the music. She smiled at her son, but it was not a smile of recognition; it was a polite gesture extended to someone who has just sat down at the table next to you at Starbucks.

"Hello," Twain said, stopping short of calling her 'mother', as that confused her. "I'm Twain."

"I'm Paget," she said, which was true. She had not forgotten her own name. "Can I help you with something?"

"No," he hemmed, thinking of a suitable reply. "You just have a such a lovely home, I wanted to see what it was like inside."

Now some recognition surfaced. "You saw my home?"

"Well...yes."

"Was there anyone living there?"

"Sure."

"Did they let you inside?"

"No."

"That's too bad. Next time I'm there, please come by and I'll show you around."

"I'd like that," Twain said. He looked over at Esther, who was grinning as though her granddaughter was still in the room.

"And I'd like to tell you something," his Mom said in a confiding tone, as a parent might with their child.

"What's that?" he indulged her.

"Don't ever go to the hospital," she said to him gravely. "Promise me you won't go to the hospital."

"I promise," Twain said, as he caught sight of Esther now starting to fidget and look like a talent agent standing off camera whose client just went off script, or forgot the words to a song.

She decided to burst onto the set and turn up the volume on the synthesized Beethoven floating from the television.

"Why don't you look at some pictures, Paget?" she cooed as she grabbed a big coffee-table book of bird photography from a shelf and opened it on Paget's lap before guiding Twain into the hall.

"She's very tired," Esther rationalized.

"Fascinating," he said to himself, barely noticing that she was leading him down the hall.

"Fascinating?" she halted him in the living room and faced him with her hands on her hips.

"She actually remembered something that happened yesterday, not fifty years ago," he continued to take mental notes out loud. "Just how much does something have to freak her out for that memory to make its mark? Is that the key? Trauma? All the good stuff gets lost and the scary stuff pokes through?"

"It wasn't that bad," Esther interrupted him.

"Then why aren't you wearing your nurses' scrubs?"

Her hands remained on her hips, but the rest of her body slackened. Oscar entered through the front door with the luggage.

"You're looking for an excuse to kill her," Esther said.

"Esther..." Oscar gently warned her.

"It's okay," Twain held up his hands. "It's an emotional time."

"And so we should make it a science project so we can make a good decision," Esther quivered.

Twain took a deep breath. He looked at Oscar, who seemed convinced they were about to lose their jobs.

"Like I said," he maintained. "It's an emotional time for all of us."

He took a step toward Esther and repeated the last line. "All of us."

Esther wouldn't look at him. Her face was upright, but her eyes stared down at the floor, pointing in the same direction as the sides of her mouth.

"I'll put your bags in the spare room, Dr. Henry," Oscar moved the situation along.

"Thank you," Twain answered, still checking to see if Esther would look him in the eye. After several seconds, he started to feel as though he was bullying her, so he backed off and followed her husband to the spare room across the hall from his Mom's door.

"I'll buy dinner tonight," he said loudly enough for Esther to hear as he joined Oscar in wanting to move on. "Is that Thai place still around?"

"Ooh, I love that place," Oscar overcompensated.

Twain hesitated before going into the room. "I hope both of you can join me." He looked down the hall at Esther, framed through the opening in the defiant position she still held. She turned her eyes up from the floor and nodded. He nodded back.

Oscar greeted him as he entered the room with frantic, hushed apologies, which Twain waved off.

"I appreciate that Esther loves her that much," he assured him.

"You're not going to fire her?" Oscar asked. "Or us?"

"Of course not."

Oscar exhaled and thanked him.

"Though if we're being realistic," Twain ventured, "you may want to start looking around, planning for the future."

He was pretty sure that Oscar wouldn't be as quick to react as Esther, but nonetheless he held his breath for a moment.

Oscar gave him a single, solemn nod and said, "It's the job. It's part of what we do."

He then moved to leave and give Twain some privacy, but stopped and added, "We've just never had a job last this long."

Twain smiled and told him to call in the dinner order, whatever they wanted, and he would pick it up. He liked the same things they liked.

Meanwhile, Twain had a call of his own he couldn't put off any longer: his aunt, whom he felt more comfortable referring to as his mother's sister.

She didn't answer, much to his relief, but he also wasn't prepared to leave a message. He staggered through an assessment of the situation, and made a cryptic remark about big decisions to be made. As soon as he ended the call, it occurred to him how much fretting his message would inspire in her. But he realized that didn't really bother him, so he let it go and fetched dinner instead.

"Does Mom still imagine she's dating Montgomery Clift?" Twain asked both of them after everyone had moved past commenting on the food and settled into satisfied silence.

Esther nodded, "She calls him Monty. Did he get in an accident in real life?"

"Yes. Is she referencing that now?"

"Oh yes. She's very concerned for him. She always wants to make him feel better. She says he is still beautiful, says it all the time. Well, I don't know about now. She hasn't talked about him since..." she stopped short, apparently afraid that she would provide evidence for hospice if she mentioned the hospital.

Twain barely noticed, anyway, but played even more dumb, as he continued to ponder what was going on inside his Mom's head.

"And she still talks about her childhood home? Wanders off looking for it?"

"That's why Oscar built the bus stop," Esther beamed.

"The one in front of the house?"

She reached out and grabbed Oscar's hand. "It was his idea, too."

Oscar shrugged. "I got tired of chasing her, and she always would say that she was going to the bus station to go home, so I gave it a try."

"And it works?" Twain asked.

Now Oscar appeared to be just as proud of himself as his wife was. "It catches her, she sits there, and then forgets why she's sitting there."

"Could I have hired two better nurses?"

He was about to remark that it would be interesting to see if she starts using it again, or if the hospital knocked the wanderlust out of her, but decided against it, as he had visions of Esther dragging her out to the fake bus stop in the middle of the night and pretending Mom had gone out on her own.

"It's strange," he said instead. "Mom never had a nice thing to say about her childhood; the people, the place. And now it's all the reality she has left. I imagine she's embellishing it, rewriting it. But they seem to be her only memories based on lived experience...besides the hospital."

"And that might go away, too," Esther jumped in.

"It could," Twain agreed, trying not to smile at how predictably she reacted to his ploy. "But even her fantasies have this tragic angle. I mean, why Montgomery Clift? All the old movie stars she could have chosen, and she goes with the torn-up soul who died too young.

One of the quotes about him that I read was that his death was 'the longest suicide in Hollywood history'."

He looked at Esther and Oscar and recognized he was bringing down the conversation, so he tried to lighten it up.

"Hey, maybe he's my father."

"You think?" asked Esther, taking him seriously.

"No," Twain quickly diffused any misunderstanding and wondered how he could have possibly thought his ridiculous attempt at levity would work. "He died a few years before I was born."

"It sounds like you really did your homework," she followed up, a touch of mischief evident that Twain was relieved to see.

"When she started talking about him, I couldn't help but wonder," he admitted.

"I always listen for clues," she said, with a genuine warmth that signaled they were on good terms again.

"Thank you, Esther."

"She should have told you," she pressed the issue without turning cold. "That's the only thing I don't like about your Mom."

"She had her reasons. At least now we know whomever he was, and whatever happened, it came after the part where her memories end and her life gets better."

The three of them ate quietly for a while, and Twain noticed that Oscar was not so much lost in thought, as he and Esther were, but concentrating on his food. He wondered if he knew something, if Mom had blurted out some evidence in his presence that he didn't feel like sharing at the moment. If that was the case, questioning him was out of the question. He would share when he felt like it. Then Twain wondered if maybe he was reading more into Oscar's body language than was really there, so intriguing was the mystery he had lived with his whole life.

Mom had always been willing to give him information, but no name. According to her, his father was a brilliant academic who had given a talk at the university. She had helped organize and promote the event, along with some of the other assistants from the other departments, and was very flattered when he took an interest in her, when he looked past the faculty members and grad students who clamored about him as though he was a pop star, and focused on her, if only for a few days.

She had resisted identifying him, she claimed, because he was not a good father. Initially she based her assessment on instinct, which is why she never told the brilliant academic about Twain; but whenever she debated contacting him, she would first do some research, which faithfully confirmed her suspicions. By the time she stopped checking in for updates, her sources told her that he was on his third marriage, with the previous two ending in large part because when it came to the child borne of each attempt, technically he couldn't be referred to as a bad father, because that would imply he actually tried to be one. Paget wanted to spare her son the hurt of being rejected, and encouraged Twain to capitalize on the natural gifts his father provided without risking a trip to discover the natural defects.

Or so went the official version of her rationale. Twain always suspected that maybe she just figured life would be more interesting with a never-ending mystery for him to contemplate, as if studying the cosmos wasn't enough. And he had done his share of investigating, starting at a young age.

Since "dad" had merely stopped by for a visit to Mom's campus, rather than serving as a guest lecturer, there was no record of his presence in the class schedule or archives, and any announcements on the school website concerning special events for that year had long since been buried deep in the queue or faded from existence entirely by the time Twain was old enough to commence his research.

When adulthood officially arrived, he thought he could convince Mom to relent, just as someone who's adopted can unseal their birth records at age eighteen, but she held firm. For a time it seemed to be the only source of friction between them, which she claimed was part of her motivation at that point; that it was unnatural for parent and child to maintain such harmony; that in order not to disturb the fabric of the universe they needed to craft some conflict. This was complete crap, obviously, but he appreciated her creativity and embraced the uncertainty, the excuse to remain in pursuit.

So as his career came to fruition, he incorporated his quest into his travels. Twain was pretty certain his father wasn't involved in the sciences, as he had spent the last couple of decades casually asking older, luminous male colleagues about their marriages and children, and in the likely event they weren't being completely forthright, he would find a way to sneak in a second-hand query while in conversation with others who knew them. He didn't have the contacts to conduct much of a search with regard to aging hot shots in other disciplines; occasionally he shared the stage or served on a board with someone from the Humanities or Law, with whom he would have a rigged conversation about some of the elder stars in their field, but mostly he had to rely on the thin biographies offered on the backs of the likely suspects' books, or the even thinner content he could conjure up online, as he discovered early in his investigation that the private lives of academic celebrities don't inspire much interest compared to actors, singers, athletes, and politicians.

"Things have to end at some time, Dr. Henry."

He heard Esther's voice and spun his attention back to the table and the take-out Thai food. It wasn't hard to deduce that he had been thinking about his father, based on where they had left the conversation, so he assumed she was picking it up.

"Probably when we're not looking," he went with it.

"Well..." she apparently wasn't referring to his father-quest. "It's getting close, no matter what your decision."

"Oh," he realized this was about Mom. "Indeed."

"So I just want you to know I have the name of a good funeral home here in town."

"Thank you, Esther," he accepted her peace offering and sighed quietly.

"She makes people look so beautiful, like they are still alive and just sleeping there."

He imagined the sound of an olive branch snapping as he inhaled.

"When the time comes, I'll keep that in mind," he said as patiently as he could, not interested in switching the label on their argument to *cremation vs. burial*.

"Does the cat still come around?" he asked, changing the subject.

"Oh, not so much anymore," Esther said. "We are not the cat people like your mother. So even though we fed him, he wasn't getting attention like he did, so I guess he found someone else in the neighborhood who likes him."

"We see him once in a while," Oscar said. "Looking in the window, or passing through the yard."

"Cats are too rational," Esther shuddered.

Twain suppressed a laugh by performing an exaggerated stretch and yawning an announcement about what a long day it had been. Esther and Oscar started to clear the dishes while Twain gathered up the take-out containers and brought them out to the garbage can in the garage. Rather than head back inside right away, he detoured through the door leading into the backyard and finally got the unobstructed view of the night sky he had wanted since taking the call from the doctor. He found a couple of familiar constellations to get his bearings and let a thousand more stars reveal themselves as his eyes adjusted to the darkness. As the complete spectrum settled into his vision, he caught sight of a satellite gliding along its orbit, and was reminded that Esther would be heading home soon, her shift complete. He didn't want to appear obstinate by standing outside when that happened, so he glanced back at the window looking into the kitchen. Oscar and Esther had finished putting the dishes away and were embracing. Oscar said something to her, and they gave each other a familiar peck good night. Twain went back inside to catch her before she left. They exchanged pleasantries and a hug, and when she said that she'd see him tomorrow, he sensed, or maybe hoped, that her tone of voice carried a promise of less tension in the days that followed.

He and Oscar watched some sports highlights on the television in the living room before deciding it was time to go to bed. Twain followed him to Mom's room as he checked on her. She had fallen asleep in her recliner, still in the upright position, her reading lamp still on. Oscar went over and pressed a button on the remote control, the chair responding with a hum and a slow stretch. He covered her in a blanket while her feet rose and her head descended, as though she was levitating as part of a magic trick. He grabbed the plate of half-eaten peanut butter sandwich and leftover carrot sticks from the table next to her before pushing the stop button, then headed for the kitchen with it.

Twain stood in the room alone with her. He felt oddly shy about going over to watch her sleep for a moment. He couldn't recall if he had ever seen her sleep. It wasn't something a son would see his mother do. He took a few steps forward as he heard Oscar clattering with the dish in the kitchen. The lamp was still on, and her head was tilted in his direction, so he saw her quite clearly.

She looked more familiar than she had in years. With her eyes shut and the lack of recognition hidden, she seemed capable of waking up in the morning and greeting him by name. He whispered a question to her, asked her what the name of that wonderful little restaurant is that she loved to take him to when he was in town. He remembered it, and it was easy to imagine that she had told him.

He stood up and turned off the lamp. Oscar reached her doorway the same time as Twain. They looked back at her, half visible in the light streaming from the hall.

"You and Esther do a great job," Twain said.

"Thank you, Dr. Henry."

Twain recalled Oscar's demeanor over dinner when the subject of his father came up. He didn't want to pry, or more to the point, be obvious that he was prying, but that was always the way he had handled the great mystery.

He closed the door and turned to Oscar, looking at him with what he hoped was the right combination of appreciation and vulnerability. "I don't know what people do in this situation who don't have the means to hire some help," he told him.

"They do it themselves," said Oscar.

There was no malice or condescension in Oscar's tone, just the same straightforward note he always played, but Twain felt he had been scaled nonetheless. He nodded and Oscar said good night, as sincerely as he said everything else, then retired to his room.

Twain lingered in the hall for a few moments. He regarded his mother's closed door, then went to his room as well.

Chapter Three

He had not visited his mother's social networking site for a while. She used to post links to his promos and blogs, and then after a few dozen of her friends had voted to like it and provided their exclamation-mark-laden comments, she would make a comment of her own to thank them all and mention how proud she was.

He would feel proud too, and the next morning, as he faced his first full day of the final days of her life, it dawned on him that the very reason he had failed to visit her site since she was rendered unable to use it was because it no longer lured him in by his ego.

So after skimming some news sites and his own website while drinking from the pot of coffee Oscar had made, he visited her page for the first time since the postings had stopped. And while she had not been able to contribute anything, he discovered it was still a very active site.

Many of her friends were loyally sending her messages telling her how much they loved her and missed her. The most recent one was from that very morning:

"Sitting here looking at the finches on my birdfeeder and thinking of you, my dear friend. There are dozens of them fighting for a spot, like all the memories I have of you."

Most of the names were unfamiliar to him. He recognized a few from the university, but it was clear she had made a lot of new friends in her new home. And these more recent friends were good writers, or at least had a knack for the quick online hit ("Happy Birthday, Paget. On the bright side, you have no idea how old you are"); more so than the crew from her days at the university, who tried too hard to be profound and grand in their sentiments ("Missing your luminous presence and reconciling ourselves to the realization we will never be able to replace it").

He checked the photo collection to see if he remembered any faces, but very few people were pictured. Most of the shots were of landscapes taken on her drives through the country, or of specific moments she observed: a dog standing on a gravel driveway looking up to her for attention, an entrée she thought looked delicious that she was about to enjoy, a glass of wine she was recommending placed artfully in front of her garden in full bloom, the branch of an oak tree that extended outward in a unique twist. And most of the people featured were connections she made and appreciated along the way rather than close friends, such as the ancient woman smiling in a doorway whom the caption declared as Julie, her favorite Meals on Wheels client, or the cheery young man standing in a field with his gloves and boots caked in mud, identified as Clark, the farmer most likely to go out of business for being too generous. There was one shot of a half-dozen friends gathered in her kitchen drinking wine and chatting while she was trying to cook, as the caption claimed getting them to pose for a picture was the only way to shut them up, but there were no photographs that displayed any friends from her more distant past, and none of herself.

Some of the current generation of friends mentioned how much they missed her at Book Club. Twain thought that must be one hell of a book club, and was inspired to get to know the town better than he had in his previous, relatively brief visits.

He started with his Mom's favorite downtown restaurant that he had imagined she reminded him of the night before; it boasted of all-organic ingredients from a nearby family farm, and occupied an interior patio that one accessed by passing through a deliberately quirky coffee house. Twain adopted the layout as his daily starting point and end point.

The coffee house provided a rich place to start, as it was filled with plenty of likewise time-wealthy patrons pretending to look busy, laptops open, every so often tapping a burst of productivity into their keyboards; but they were much happier, it seemed, to offer recommendations on wineries once Twain engaged them in conversation. Sometimes his fellow time-spenders would take the initiative if they recognized him. He appreciated the level of fame he occupied, as it led to recognition only by those who genuinely liked his work for the most part, and they usually weren't the types who wanted to pose for pictures.

He wouldn't have minded attracting more single women. Not that he wished his circuit had a groupie culture, but the maturity level of his fan base meant most of the best were already taken, and the ones still single or left for single frequently found themselves in that place thanks to some rather baroque histories that made for interesting visits, but he didn't want to live there. Twain's was not the most stable situation, either, he readily acknowledged. The inside of his apartment looked as though it was still available for rent. It was essentially a mailing address and a way to help maintain good credit.

During a heavily-booked era in the burgeoning stages of his notoriety, he had spent almost an entire year homeless, renting just a P.O. Box and conducting all of his business online as he traveled from venue to venue, making a point of disclosing his situation at each stop, claiming it was an experiment to test a hypothesis he held about the future: that we would ultimately return to being nomadic, as wireless communication became wholly ubiquitous. When he did find himself on a promising date, he would mention the possibility of becoming less of a pioneer in the nomad movement, and conform to the sedentary present, but neither he nor any interested parties had been motivated enough to take that idea beyond the realm of wine-inspired dinner conversation.

As for the winery suggestions he fielded at his Mom's old haunt, Twain decided to filter out the downtown tasting rooms and focus on the ones in the countryside. For while he enjoyed beginning and concluding the day downtown, he had no interest in spending an entire day there. The civic pride was justified; the building renovations and business revitalization plans were worthy of the praise heaped on them; but at a certain point hanging out on its brick-inlaid sidewalks started to feel like being with someone who wouldn't stop talking about themselves, as every sign seemed to incorporate the name of the town, and the shirts and bumper stickers that synchronized the name with heaven-on-earth did so without a hint of irony.

Plus he found that the wineries outside of town gave him the feeling of going right to the source, and discovered that if the winemaker or owner was on the premises, they enjoyed giving him a tour of the operations and emphasizing the science of the process, once they found out who he was (either due to familiarity with his work, or because Twain just happened to mention it during the small talk in between pours at the tasting bar).

By the end of his second full day he had several people accepting his invitations to meet him at the wine bar in the restaurant part of his headquarters, ordering enough hors d'oeuvres for his end of the bar as to make dinner unnecessary. He knew he was sublimating for what was happening with Paget, that the coffee and conversation and wine and the rush of driving away from town into the countryside and wrapping it up with woozy reflections on life in the universe with people he barely knew was all a head fake, but he excused himself. He told himself that he was allowing Esther to work her day shift without his presence compelling her to either pick up the argument about end-of-life decisions or try so hard to avoid it. To the people he met, he would simply say he was visiting family in the area. If they knew Paget, he assumed they would know why and ask about her.

So far no one had. Most of the brewing circle of acquaintances he met on the wine trail were from out of town, anyway, which he initially found comforting, as whatever relationship they concocted with him, it was guaranteed to end, and on a high note, no depth required. But as the second day blended into the third and the third day wound down, and his affinity for the geography of the area fortified, he started to grow even more curious about who some of these people were who continued to post messages on his Mom's site.

After that nice pre-elderly couple from Reno hugged him good night and teetered out arm-in-arm to find their downtown Bed and Breakfast, Twain was left with only his wistfulness as he sat at the end of the bar. He decided he may want to contribute some content to Paget's page as well. He borrowed a pen from the bartender, a tightly-manicured young woman who referred to herself as a sommelier (even though you could order other drinks besides wine from her), then grabbed some cocktail napkins to start brainstorming some possibilities.

He decided specific memories would be best; moments her new generation of friends would appreciate hearing about, which would also prevent him from lapsing into the pretentiousness that sometimes marked his early drafts when scripting a presentation or an article. He didn't want to appear as though he was trying to upstage any of them, so he was determined to be as direct and detailed as possible, avoiding any commentary on the events.

The first note he jotted down read *marshmallow test*, as he recalled the most memorable of the many childhood cognition studies he was subjected to at the university, since one of his Mom's favorite colleagues was a research assistant in the Human Development Department.

Maybe he remembered it because it seemed as though every university in the country had conducted a version of it over the years. He was led into a room by an adult and sat at a table with a marshmallow perched on top of it; the adult said they would be back in five minutes, and if he could resist eating the marshmallow, he would get another one and therefore double his pleasure. The researchers would keep track of who could resist and who could not, then turn it into a longitudinal study by checking in on the kids later on as they matured into adulthood, and compare indicators of success such as graduation rates and income levels, and reveal that in general the kids who could resist, who ostensibly understood the benefits of delayed gratification, performed much better in life than those who couldn't wait. He prided himself on being an exception to the trend, having eaten the marshmallow but hitting most of the metrics used to judge success (except the one about stable relationships). Part of the reason he remembered this study more clearly than the others is because the division filmed each kid through a two-way mirror as they tried to avoid the temptations of the gooey cylinder by contorting themselves into all sorts of mind games to make it to the end of the five minutes. Paget had savored her son's performance, in which he had turned his back on the treat only to tilt his head back onto the table and look at it upside down for a wobbly couple of minutes before giving in just as time was about to expire. The fact that he was so close to being in the "patient" group somewhat usurped his status as an outlier, but he maintained his pride in it nonetheless, more as a running joke than anything else.

Not long before his Mom first started her forgetting, he read about a study that demonstrated the results could be manipulated by conducting a pre-marshmallow ritual of promising each child a chance to draw before the test began, then following through on that promise to half of the children by returning with the crayons and paper, while the other half were told that the art supplies weren't available after all. The children who got the impression that the adults in charge were good at following through on their promises invariably resisted eating the marshmallow, while the ones who saw that the adults were unreliable ate it almost instantly. Twain sent a copy of the article inside a Mother's Day card to Paget with the message, "See? Success had nothing to do with me, and everything to do with the home you provided."

He smiled as he thought about that card, sitting there at what had been her favorite place up until favorites no longer existed for her. But he wasn't sure how he could squeeze that memory into a couple of sentences. He wrote down a few other potential subjects:

doing homework in middle school with college basketball team, helping them with theirs

research for 5th grade state project by interviewing former governor of that state who taught in Political Science Department

lab tech from Zoology bringing Sonia the Orangutan to 3rd grade show and tell

asked to befriend child prodigy who was in college at age eleven, but girl genius wanted nothing to do with me

He chuckled as he finished penning that last one. She had told him it was nothing personal, that it was because she would have preferred a girl her own age, that boys "had nothing to offer" (to quote her directly). So Twain was unable to collect on the McDonalds gift certificate he had held out for in agreeing to be her ambassador of normalcy. And as his giggling subsided at the remembrance of that arrogant child who cost him a month's worth of fries, he also realized that not only was it going to be hard to translate any of these musings into a post that didn't take up half the page, but that he shouldn't bother taking up even a single line. It was the territory of his Mom's friends. He had plenty of platforms to broadcast his memories; he would leave theirs alone.

"Did anyone throw in some money for the check?" a voice jostled him out of his scribbling on the paper napkin.

The voice belonged to a woman who worked the patio at the restaurant, but she had delivered some of the food he ordered to the bar over the past couple of evenings. Twain had been glancing at her whenever he could, and she was around his age, but he had not bothered to strike up a conversation. She struck him as part of the local faction who resented the growth spurt of their town, and the people like Twain who were responsible for it. She had left some of her beauty at a few too many parties, but seemed to carry no regrets over it.

"I told them it was on me," Twain said.

"Did they at least put up a fight? Play the game?" She was leaning by the register behind the bar, waiting to be cashed out for the night.

"No," Twain smiled. "But I find that refreshing."

She smiled back at him, but her eyes could not quite play along.

"So I guess Paget doesn't have much time left," she said.

His expression started to match hers before he turned his attention back down to the napkin.

"Probably not," he finally said. "Thank you for noticing."

"She's too young."

Twain was about to agree and commiserate with her, but she was on to the next point she wanted to make.

"I've read these articles," she said. "They talk about how if people keep their mind active, if they exercise their brain, they can keep away Alzheimer's. She totally did that. She did everything they said."

"Those are trends. They're not absolutes."

She sighed and nodded.

"Paget was always an exception to the rule," she said. "So I guess it makes some kind of warped sense."

Twain was convinced she must have contributed something to the website.

"What's your name?" he asked.

"Marina."

He mentally scanned what he could remember of Paget's website to see if her name conjured up any hits as the manager arrived to cash her out. After they were finished conducting business, Marina turned back to him and appeared ready to say good-bye. But Twain was hoping for some more information.

"I know she came in here quite a bit, but she seems to be more than a regular customer to you."

"She worked with the farm we deal with."

"Really?"

"Not as like a farmer or a driver, but she got them to donate to the Food Bank, and they would drop off her orders here, so she wouldn't have to drive out to the farm every time. Sometimes she drove out there to pick it up, though, because she loved the scenery. I went out there with her a few times."

He imagined the two of them driving through the countryside that he was starting to love, too, the more familiar with it he became.

"I'm Twain."

"I know."

"Just wanted to make it official."

"Nice to finally meet you," her smile was more genuine now. Twain picked up on it.

"She didn't talk much about me, did she?"

"She didn't want to brag."

Marina removed her apron and twirled it around her wrist before making her way out from behind the bar.

"See you, Twain."

"Nice meeting you, Marina."

He was left alone again, but less so thanks to his satisfaction at having made a local connection, and having learned a little bit more about the life his Mom had led. He folded his napkin full of memories and carried it with him to his rented pick-up truck.

Esther had already gone home by the time Twain arrived back at the house. Oscar was folding towels on the kitchen table.

"Need a hand?" Twain offered.

"Almost done," Oscar assured him.

"I could tell. Why do you think I asked?"

Oscar smiled politely.

"Everything okay?" Twain asked.

"Bad day today."

"How so?"

"Your mother had some accidents," Oscar gestured toward the towels.

"Sorry to hear that," Twain said, though he also felt like thanking him for his honesty, as he couldn't imagine Esther would have told him.

"She still knows how to go to the bathroom," Oscar explained, as if realizing Esther would disapprove if she found out he said anything. "But she gets things backwards. You know how sometimes she puts the cap back on the water bottle and tries to take a sip? "

Twain nodded.

"Well, sometimes she puts the lid of the toilet down before sitting on it."

They looked at the number of white towels he had washed, dried, and folded. Twain thought of Oscar's simple declaration regarding people who couldn't afford help, how they have to take care of their own, and he wondered if he could handle it.

"And then she gets upset," Oscar said as they held their gaze on the towels. "Like all of a sudden she knows there is something wrong with her. Then she forgets, but the bad feelings stick around, she just doesn't know why she's feeling bad. We try to settle her down, make her feel relaxed, but it's hard when she isn't sure who you are. So all we can do is watch her and make sure she doesn't do anything to hurt herself or damage anything. She paces and talks to herself and all we can do is watch."

Twain kept meditating over the neat, clean stack and came to the rare conclusion that he shouldn't say anything. He did thank

Oscar, however, as he so often felt compelled to do since arriving, and offered to put away the towels.

The closet in which Paget had always stored her towels and linens was in the spare bathroom down the hall amidst all the bedroom doors. After putting them away, Twain briefly considered checking in on his Mom and telling her that he had met Marina, and what a great first impression she left, and what a great circle of friends Mom seemed to have, but he didn't want to risk opening the door to find her still awake. From what he gathered about her day, the last thing she needed was a stranger poking his head in as she tried to go to sleep.

He decided instead to have that conversation in spirit, as he went into the guest bedroom and sat on the edge of the guest bed and spoke to her as if she was there. When he was done he toppled backwards and laid there on the hard mattress with his feet still on the floor. He considered heading back out to watch television with Oscar, but the wine and rich food caught up with him and put him to sleep before he could make up his mind.

Chapter Four

From the day that Twain had taken up temporary residence, Esther and Oscar had taken to ringing the doorbell or knocking when they arrived, even though they had keys to the house. But Esther had already arrived when the doorbell rang a second time the next morning. Twain barely heard it through the windows as he sat in the backyard with a cup of coffee, and by the time the sound registered, Esther was announcing that she would answer it.

A rush of guilt made him think that maybe it was Dr. Walls stopping by on his way to work, since Twain had yet to stop by his office. But then he heard a female voice talking to Esther, and the rush turned to excitement as he thought maybe it was Marina. But the voice was too clipped and the conversation too much of a standoff. He sighed and lowered his mug as he arrived at the correct answer.

"Hello, Aunt Grace," he said as entered the house and walked toward the front door.

"Hello Twain. I can't remember the last time you put an 'aunt' in front of my name."

"Feeling a little sentimental these days, I guess."

Esther stood to the side looking peeved.

"I see you've met Esther," he angled himself into a position where he could assess what had transpired between them.

"Yes," Grace said as pleasantly as she could.

"Esther, this is Mom's sister, Grace."

"Pleased to meet you," Esther managed to be a shade more sunny than Grace.

"Come on in," Twain cleared a path and gestured her in. "Join me in the backyard for some coffee. It's a beautiful morning."

Esther saw a chance to break away and seized it.

"She isn't going to offer to get it?" Grace asked as they walked through the house toward the sliding glass door.

"She's a nurse, not a maid," Twain said. "I'll get the coffee. Milk? Cream?"

"Do you have any non-dairy creamer?"

"Yes. Oscar likes it. He's the other nurse. Esther's husband."

Grace nodded and maintained her pace to the back as Twain veered into the kitchen.

"You go find a place in the sun," he bid her as their paths split.

Twain used his time in the kitchen as much to prepare himself as he did to prepare her coffee. After a long exhale, he brought her cup onstage with him.

"How is Richard?" he said as he served her and took his place on the other side of the table.

"He's Richard," she took a sip and gave no indication as to whether she liked the coffee.

"And Mark? Mary?"

"Mark got a divorce. You might get along with him now. Mary had another baby, a surprise. She's actually happy about it. She always liked babies better than kids. Not sure how her husband feels about it. Did you ever meet Kyle?"

"I was at their wedding."

"Oh. Right. I always imagine you and your cousins never speaking again after that weekend in New York."

"It wasn't that bad. I don't know what they told you."

"I'm sorry if they played the Hand of God card too heavily. I only brought them up religious to guarantee some stability. I didn't intend for them to use it as a science book."

"We were all adults. Everyone minded their manners. I left the planetarium for another job, not because of anything they said."

They retreated into their coffee for a few moments before Twain decided to address the reason for her visit.

"Thank you for coming," he said.

"I didn't want to just return your call, talk to you on the phone. You're so good with words."

Twain wasn't sure what she meant by that.

"I didn't want to get all twisted up in your words," she responded to his expression.

"I still don't get it."

"You said there are big decisions to be made about Paget."

"Yes."

"Which means you've already made up your mind and are going to try to convince me you're right."

"I barely remember leaving you a message, Aunt Grace."

"I would have come earlier, but I've always wanted to expand into this territory, so I set up some meetings before I came out."

"My point is that it's a very unstable situation, hardly settled."

"Well, don't worry. I've got my own hotel room."

Twain leaned back and gathered himself. "That's not what I meant. Good Lord, it's like we're speaking a different language."

"It's rude to think out loud."

He gave up and drank his coffee. She was welcome to take this conversation wherever she wanted, as far as he was concerned. It took her a while to decide on a direction.

"What exactly is her condition?" she asked, with a softness so subtle as to go unnoticed if not for the coldness that had preceded it.

Twain provided her with a summary of what had been reported to him over the phone by Dr. Walls and what he had observed over the last few days. As he reached his conclusion, a thought occurred to him that he risked sharing out loud.

"I'm curious how she'll react to you. In her mind, life seems to have ended once she hit her late teens. And you're the only person who knew her back then who's visited since her illness."

"Her illness?"

"Is there a word you think is more appropriate?"

She shrugged. Twain found her dismissiveness breathtaking, far exceeding even her own chilly standards.

"I know how hard you had it growing up," he eased into a point that was going to be difficult to make without raising his voice. "And I admire you for overcoming your circumstances. But I admire the way Mom handled it a lot more."

"Do you now?"

"Much, much more."

"There's a surprise."

"Know why?"

"Tell me, Twain."

"Because she didn't rub everyone's face in it every chance she got, and she felt bad for people who had a hard time overcoming their own tough situations. She didn't toss them off as useless or weak. She tried to help people, not scoff at them and wonder why they couldn't be as strong as she was."

He braced himself for some blowback, but Grace just smirked, first down at the table, then in Twain's direction.

"And pretending nothing happened," she finally said, "that's strength?"

She shook her head, and it seemed in part involuntary.

"Let me guess," she pressed on, "her version of the past that she's reliving now inside her mind sounds pretty great, the little bits and pieces you get, that you can understand."

"Some of it is clearly made up," Twain answered, though he wasn't sure Grace actually wanted him to reply.

"All of it is made up," she snapped back. "Unless she's crying herself to sleep and screaming in the middle of the night, she's lying. Did she ever tell you how many times we moved?"

"She said it was a lot."

"Sixteen times!"

She caught her breath, and while she did so Twain felt as though he was holding his. Upon regaining her composure, she forged ahead.

"But then again she didn't get the worst of it. She had someone five years older than her running interference, taking the brunt of everything. So maybe she really did have a good time. She sure did when she got older."

She looked away, down to the ground off to her side, and Twain wondered if he was going to see her lose control for the first time in his life. Instead she started to laugh, and when she looked back up at him her expression was far more caustic than amused.

"I can sum up her life's philosophy in one word," she paused for effect. "Wheeee!"

She held the note as long as she could, then cackled again as she ran out of breath.

Twain waited until she quieted down.

"Why are you here?" he asked.

She looked as though she wanted to get defensive again, but at the same time seemed to realize she had either forgotten her purpose for coming, or never really had one, and had just traveled on instinct.

"Would you like to see her?" he offered.

The stress sailed from her face, and she nodded peaceably.

Twain got up to slide the door open, assured her he would take care of the coffee cups later, and led her to the back of the house, toward the master bedroom. The sound of baby Mozart music grew quietly as they approached, and the volume rose to its usual murmur as he gently opened the door.

Paget was seated upright in her recliner, looking at a heavy book of Grand Canyon photographs spread across her lap. Esther kneeled beside her and read the captions aloud. None of the earlier tension was apparent as Esther greeted them with a smile. But Twain was paying closer attention to his Mom, looking for signs that she recognized her sister.

All she provided was the customary polite nod before returning back to her book.

"Well," Grace noted the lack of acknowledgement, "I don't exactly look like I did fifty years ago."

Twain reached out and patted Grace on the back. They watched Paget for a little while as Esther read to her. Grace appeared to relax for the first time since she entered the house. She seemed to appreciate the opportunity to look at her sister without Paget being able to sense it, without the typical sisterly moment of her younger sibling glaring up from her book and lobbing an accusatory "What?" in her direction. Grace grew so pensive that Twain started to wonder if maybe it was about victory, the satisfaction of outlasting the little girl whom she claimed had it so much easier than she did.

He was startled when Grace finally broke her meditation, as he had just turned his attention back to his Mom.

"You, on the other hand, look great, Paget," Grace called over to her. "I want to know who your doctor is."

She meant it as a dig at Twain, looking his way after she said it. But instead she inspired Paget to slap her book shut and scowl at Grace.

"They didn't do anything," she said.

Grace wasn't sure how to reply. While she hesitated, Paget repeated it a bit louder.

"They didn't do anything."

"Okay," Grace shrugged.

"You don't need to call them," Paget insisted. "It doesn't matter."

Esther tried to put a comforting hand on her shoulder, but Paget swatted it away.

"It doesn't matter what they do," she stood up.

"We're sorry," Twain steered Grace toward to the door. "We didn't mean to upset you."

"They didn't do anything."

Esther tried again to provide some relief, and this time Paget shoved her to the ground. Twain left Grace at the door and sped over to assist Esther. Paget came at him and pounded the bottoms of her fists into his chest and shoulders. He grabbed her forearms to stop the blows. Her strength stunned him and he had to try harder than he expected to keep her at bay. Her grunts gave way to a frustrated howl.

"It's okay, Mom," he tried to sound as soothing as possible while exerting the energy to hold her. "Nobody is making any calls."

Esther had regained her footing and was standing behind Paget rubbing her back. Twain could feel her resistance slacken.

"It's okay, Mom," he said one more time, now that he could say it with less effort, now that he was thinking about it, and not blurting it out from instinct. He said it out of curiosity as much as he said it in an attempt to calm her down.

It stopped the assault. She slumped into her chair and looked up at him, but without remorse or recognition, just paralyzing confusion. Esther's backrubs now had room to work on her. They were clearly more helpful than anything Twain could follow up with, so he left her to them and walked out of the room, taking for granted that Grace would follow him.

He walked out the front door and stood in the driveway. His goal was just to get some air, and the front door was the closest one to the outside. But when his aunt joined him in front of her rental car, she wondered aloud, "Are you trying to tell me it's time to go?"

Her levity surprised him, and he laughed in spite of the circumstances.

"We're gonna need a bigger boat," Twain contributed his own humor.

"A boat?" she didn't get it.

"You never saw *Jaws*?"

"The shark movie?"

"When they realized what they were up against?"

"I don't know anything about that."

So they stood there for a while, and now Twain had to recover from a failed joke in addition to what it was he was joking about. In the process of staring into various spaces looking for peace, he spotted the decoy bus stop, and thought maybe explaining its purpose would help them move on to wherever they needed to go next. He told Grace how it was designed to catch her sister, often late at night, to extend her a place to sit and start fresh yet again, until Oscar could discover her missing and come out to get her.

"And you're thinking that's not the way she would want it," Grace responded.

"I'm just telling you some of what goes on here."

"Is she a financial burden?"

Twain shook his head. "I don't make as much as a lot of people probably assume I do, but aside from eating a little too well and not being able to find a bottle of wine I like for less than thirty dollars, I have no other major expenses besides paying Oscar and Esther. If she was a financial drain, her living will would be a very clear guide. As it stands, the quality of life clause is a bit more vague."

"Probably written very poetic, though," she sneered.

If she was joking again, any sense of touch was missing. But he could respond well enough without an accurate interpretation of her aim.

"The only input a lawyer had was a signature."

His aunt sighed. "Not to sound like my children, but just be careful about playing God."

"Why do people only use that cliché when it comes to death?" Twain threw aside his manners. "Seems to me when God really wanted to flex some muscle, someone was brought back to life. That's when imitations of God happen, when someone is kept alive who should have died."

He settled down and figured that the ensuing silence was a product of anger that Grace wasn't sure how to express. But then she lapsed into an impressed pucker.

"I'll have to use that one on my kids some time," she said.

Twain was caught pleasantly off-guard. "Really?"

"I've always stuck with 'if heaven's so great, why are people so afraid of going there?' But I'm getting tired of it, and so are they."

"You argue with them about faith?"

"Be that as it may," she pretended his question didn't exist, "you have some time to think about your decision, obviously. Her mind might be gone, but she's strong as an ox."

He nodded ruefully.

"Oh..." Grace burst into a glow of recognition. "That's what you meant when you said we need a big boat."

"A bigger boat."

"Whatever it is. I get it."

She made a move toward her car, deciding that her insight was the right time to adjourn their meeting.

"I'll be staying at the Hampton Inn for the next couple of days before heading home if you need me," she said as she ducked into the driver's seat. "I wish you well, Twain."

"Likewise, Aunt Grace," he respected her wishes and kept his distance. "This town could use some Amway products."

"I don't sell Amway."

"Whatever it is. I'm sure it's necessary."

She glared at him, but mustered a wave after she shut the door and started the engine. He waved back and watched her drive away.

Twain drifted back toward the house and was pretty sure he saw some movement in the narrow window next to the front door. Upon entering, he found Esther concentrating a little too intently on a spot she was pretending to clean on the kitchen counter.

"I need something else to do while I'm here," he announced while she maintained her ruse. "Or else I'm going to gain fifty pounds and become an alcoholic."

She stopped and smiled, happy that he was acknowledging the physical condition of his mother rather than the mental.

"You should teach at the college," Esther said.

"There's a college here?"

"A community college. The main campus is out by the airport, but we have a campus here. It's where me and Oscar took a lot of our nursing classes."

"The semester probably starts in a couple of weeks."

"So there's still time," she was getting more excited about the possibility.

"No, what I mean is, they have all the classes staffed by the previous spring, or early summer. It's been a while since I've been a faculty member anywhere, but I remember that much."

"Maybe not all of the classes."

"It's an intriguing suggestion, Esther," he tried not to laugh, "but even when I was a faculty member, a teaching assistant at that, it was only for a semester. I'm sure they'd prefer someone with much more experience."

"Oh, but you're teaching all the time," she swatted him with the dish towel. "On your show, and those speeches you give. They would love to have you."

"You seem really interested in keeping me busy," he teased her. "Am I that annoying to have around the house?"

She waved him off. "Keeping busy is good. Just call them. Give it a try."

"I'll call my agent," he said. "I'm sure there's something she can arrange that doesn't involve traveling."

"Whatever," Esther said in a tone that implied how sorry he would be for not taking her advice. Even her body language as she exited played up the superiority of her idea.

Twain stood in the kitchen facing another day of feeling useless.

"At least I hope there's something she can arrange," he said to himself.

Chapter Five

His agent told him she would check to see what was available and call him back later, but only after bragging that she had won the intra-office bet on how long it would take him to call in looking for work. The next lowest estimate was one week, and she had beaten that by a few days.

She called a few hours later just as he was about to case one of the downtown tasting rooms that one of his new wine enthusiast buddies from the other day had told him had a great Rhone blend. He saw her name on the screen of his phone and answered before sampling the first pour, preferring not to wait until later and wind up accepting an offer that was only appealing due to a satisfying backdrop of drinking and discussing wine with the like-minded and likewise buzzed.

It was a voiceover job, providing the narration for an educational film produced by a textbook company. They were hoping for a famous actor to do it for free, "for the children" as the pitch would go. But so far nobody on their list had offered, and the project was nearly complete, so they were excited at the possibility of Twain falling into their laps.

He liked the idea of being part of a project aimed at a young generation of potential scientists, but the working title was *The Future of Space Exploration*, and he was wary of that topic. For as much as he liked to tempt people into wondering if any of the remote likenesses of earth being discovered hold life, and to speculate on the ethics of interacting with new worlds by noting the growing tally of these exoplanets, Twain preferred to stop short of delving into the business of actually reaching them. The technology exceeded our capacity to develop it, the political and financial willingness to get us there. Finding a way to synthesize the dreamy quality of the ideas with the frustrations of putting them into practice was a maneuver he never felt he could pull off. He noticed a lot of colleagues and science journalists simply focused on the exciting part and pretended the arduous part didn't exist. Twain was sure this would lead to disappointment. Audiences, particularly young audiences, would get all jazzed about riding into deep space, and then start to wonder why it wasn't happening. Besides, his biggest neurosis concerning his career was that he excelled at exalting, and struggled with hard facts. A project on space exploration that followed the typically disingenuous path would highlight his most dubious quality. He was going to call back his agent and decline, but got a whiff and mouthful of a reserve Syrah that inspired him to buy a half case of it.

As he loaded his latest tribute to leisure time onto the passenger seat floor of his pickup truck, his sense of purposelessness swelled and he called to accept the offer while still standing next to the parking spot. By the time he reached his next stop, a winery just off the city grid he had visited two days earlier where the star-struck winemaker had practically pleaded with him to return for an extended barrel tasting, one of the producers of the film called to thank him. They would overnight mail the script to him and he could start the next afternoon. The broadcast center that hosted the local television affiliate had agreed to let them use some studio space to record his tracks.

He enjoyed his barrel tasting all the more knowing that he had something to do tomorrow besides more of the same. Perhaps the script would even surprise him, he started to convince himself. Meanwhile the young winemaker scaled to the top shelf of the barrels and dipped his wine thief into a young Zinfandel, suspending it over Twain's head so he could lap at it like a baby bird being fed by its mother. The wine was sweeter than something sucked out of a juice box through a straw. He lied to the young man, telling him it was sure to make an excellent bottle in another year.

The script was about what he expected. It had several names ascribed to it, most of whom he recognized, and the product indeed came across as written by committee. The technical aspects were very well-crafted, written in layperson's terms that the kids would be able to understand, and it was even somewhat genuine when it came to the challenges that earthlings posed in completing any plans to get off earth, but it had no vision when it came to where these ships would be traveling. Not that it didn't try, but the extent of its efforts were strings of hypothetical questions, all imagination thus dropped into the lap of the audience: "Where will our travels take us?" "What strange new worlds will we discover?" "How close will our expectations match our findings?"

At one point as he read it over breakfast on the back patio he responded out loud, "I don't know, you tell me! Any ideas on the subject?"

Which prompted Esther to come out and ask him if he needed something.

He chuckled and explained the situation.

"Maybe they really want the kids to think about it themselves," she said.

"As they should," Twain acknowledged. "But I'm sure some of them would appreciate at least a little inspiration. And the questions are so broad."

"What should they ask?"

"Why do we leave?"

Esther looked puzzled.

"Why would we want to leave earth?" Twain clarified. "Will it be dying? Will it be necessary? Or are we just curious? Do we have something to prove? Will it be expensive to move somewhere else? Will space colonies be status symbols? A community of people who can pay the fare? Or maybe it's the other way around: space will be a string of labor camps, filled with people mining resources to send back to earth, to those who can still afford to live here."

"Maybe it will be punishment," she added, "a place for criminals."

"I had never really thought of that," Twain appreciated her contribution. "See? This is what the right questions can do."

"I just can't imagine wanting to leave."

They shared a moment preoccupied with life on earth. He was fairly certain she had intended no metaphors, but just in case she was planning on bringing up his mother, he guided the conversation back to where it started.

"Well that settles it," Twain declared. "I'm checking to see if I can do some re-writes."

"You're welcome," Esther smiled as she turned and went back inside.

"For what? Helping to prove my point?" he called after her, then called the lead producer.

He was also one of the writers, and claimed to speak for the others when he said he had been hoping that Twain would offer to inject some life into the script. They weren't expected to get it into classrooms until the following school year, not the one about to start, so there was no great hurry. Though if production went past the holidays, people would start to get nervous. As a sign of good faith, Twain told of his plans to go ahead and record the passages that were already sound later that afternoon, which amounted to roughly three-quarters of the narration. Any trepidation in the producer's voice subsided. Twain also felt some relief, since voicing those portions would attach his name to some stable science and logistical realities before engaging the re-writes that would play to his strengths.

After each assured the other that they'd keep in touch, Twain asked what kind of tone and energy they would like to hear in the voiceover.

"Wonder," the producer said in what sounded to Twain like a Carl Sagan impersonation. "Awe."

The broadcast center was in the industrial part of town, amongst the corrugated metal buildings and truck loading docks and rail yard that made it possible for the other side of town to be so quaint. The hospital also occupied the area, with complexes of doctors' offices orbiting it. On one of the signs listing a roster of MDs, he noticed the name "Dr. Humphrey Walls."

He couldn't remember if he had said he would stop by when he got into town, or if Dr. Walls had invited him to stop by. Regardless, he felt guilty for not doing so. He vowed to check in after the recording session was over, consoled by the assumption it would likely extend past the doctor's business hours.

But the studio time took wing. He rarely needed more than one take, as he established a strong connection to the desired sense of wonder and awe by thinking about his Mom, and the mysteries inside her head that were physically just inches away from him when he sat beside her, but which remained as distant as the edge of the universe. The sound engineer sent some samples of the cuts to the various producers, each of whom responded within minutes. Their approval was uniform, the only variations were in how they expressed it.

Which also meant he had time to visit Dr. Walls.

He introduced himself to the receptionist and explained the situation, quickly adding that he understood perfectly if the doctor didn't have time to see him. There was, after all, a patient still sitting next to the fish tank.

"I'm just waiting for my wife," said the white-haired man as he looked up from a Sports Illustrated that may have been older than him.

"And she's our last appointment of the day," the receptionist interjected, apparently rooting for the meeting to take place.

The man's wife entered the lobby soon after, escorted by Dr. Walls, whose appearance offered no surprises in terms of how he looked versus how he sounded on the phone. He seemed to have heard the preceding conversations, giving Twain a nonchalant nod and inviting him backstage upon sending the last patient of the day on her way. He kept the greetings brief and the tone professional as they walked to his office.

"So what's your assessment now that you've seen her?" he asked Twain, who was still half-expecting some questions about the weather and the wineries at that point.

"Well," he shifted in the chair which sat facing the doctor's nameplate on his desk, "she's much stronger than I expected."

"Strong enough to sustain at least a year's worth of hospital visits, maybe more. Over and over again. Bouncing back every time."

"Have you been to that organic restaurant on Park Street?"

"I know I'm being rather aggressive in pushing my point," he acknowledged. "But I have a great deal of respect for your mother."

Twain took a deep breath. "It would be a lot easier if she looked bad."

Dr. Walls nearly smiled. "You know who has it the hardest when it comes to making these kinds of decisions?"

"Please tell me."

"People who have a poor relationship with the person they're considering letting go. People who have unresolved issues."

"Well, I do have some of those," Twain cracked.

"But none that make you especially angry."

"You seem so sure."

"She was my patient. I got to know her. And it was clear you two got along quite well."

Twain nodded for a few extra moments. "And that makes it easier?"

"Absolutely," Dr. Walls maintained. "No less sad, of course. But without the anger. At times I've felt like some people keep their parents alive out of spite. Especially considering the inevitable deterioration. Their mind completely disconnects from any life they've lived or imagined they've lived, so they become more confused and scared, then the mental trauma starts to exacerbate their physical condition, which is already pretty feeble, of course. And if they're a man, they try to hump everything that walks in the room."

"That must be of great comfort to the angry daughters."

"It does provide a good excuse to yell at their father."

Twain disguised another deep breath with laughter, and it occurred to him that almost every breath he had taken since he sat down was a deep one. He wanted to express something more about what was happening, but wasn't sure how to do so. He finally decided to just dive into his thoughts and see if he could sort them out as he went.

"I guess, because I wasn't expecting her to be very strong, I also wasn't expecting to have to stay here for very long."

"I seem to recall I told you that it could be a couple of months," the doctor defended himself. "I apologize if I didn't make that clear."

"No, no," Twain shook off any indicators that he was making accusations. "I just got that call and jumped."

"Understandable."

"And now I feel guilty, because I cancelled some arrangements, put things on hold, and within a few days started to wonder how much of that I could undo, how much I could go back to my life."

"You've read your mother's living will."

"But it's not about that," Twain felt as though the doctor's chair was becoming a psychiatrist's. "It's not about her being a burden. The nurses take care of everything. At a price I can afford. What is it that I do, exactly? Wait for her to die while I look at my watch."

"And if you left," Dr. Walls seemed to adopt the role that Twain was imagining for him, "would you trust the nurses to do the right thing once the time came? If you decide you want to let her go, will they respect that?"

"I think they would try."

"But you can't be sure."

"Oscar would probably follow through. Esther, I don't know."

"And maybe you won't even be able to make that decision until the day comes. Maybe you need to be there so you can look into her eyes, and then make the call."

Twain had a hard time imagining how that day would play out, but the dread over having to face it was quite clear.

"Your time here is not wasted," Dr. Walls continued. "You have a vital purpose, and the opportunity to see it through. Be thankful, not guilty."

He stood up and extended a hand toward Twain, who rose and shook it.

"Keep me posted," the doctor said in lieu of good-bye.

Twain said he would and walked out of the office appreciating how highly Dr. Walls assessed the value of his time, but no less anxious over the duration of it. Indeed he had an important decision to make and to see through, but there were still weeks, possibly months leading up to it. It wouldn't take him that long to re-write the necessary bits of the script. Even at his most obsessive, he couldn't overthink something that much.

He stopped by his favorite restaurant for dinner, but realized he was more interested in seeing Marina than he was in the menu, as when he saw that she wasn't working that evening, he changed his plans and headed for a burrito in one of the narrow, fluorescently-lit spaces in a shopping center on the bargain fringe of town. And since the reason he was intrigued by her, aside from any opportunity to look at her, was her first-hand link to his Mom's life before Paget found herself surrounded by strangers, Twain got an idea. He ordered his burrito to go so he could catch Esther and Oscar before their shift exchange.

They were swapping good-byes and reminders when he arrived.

"No need to stay, Oscar," he interrupted them. "Take Esther out to dinner, and then both of you take the day off tomorrow."

"There's an agency we go through when we need a substitute," Esther said, no more surprised or delighted by his offer than Oscar appeared to be.

"Don't worry about us," Oscar added voice to his indifference.

"Well..." Twain regrouped. "You deserve a break."

"It's not that hard," Esther said. "Your mother is a good patient."

"So then I should be able to handle things easily enough."

"We're okay. Have you checked to see if they need teachers at the college this semester?"

"I'm still going to pay you. It's a paid day off."

Esther waved her hands dismissively. "We weren't even thinking of that."

"Then let me do this," Twain firmed up his tone. He startled them slightly, so he followed up with a soft "Please."

Oscar and Esther looked at one another and seemed to figure out what was going on.

"Of course," Esther said. "A day off would be nice."

"Thank you," said Oscar.

They all stood there fidgeting for a moment before Esther gave him some parting instructions and advice about meals, toilet lids, the shower that wouldn't be necessary since she took one earlier that day, and to call them for any reason at any time.

When they left, Twain couldn't recall being in a more quiet place. It was like being in space, as though gravity would give way and he would start to float. And as obvious as that parallel was for someone in his profession, he realized how rarely he found himself able to make it. His head may have been devoted to the heavens, but his body was deeply immersed in the currents of earth, and all of its noise and movement.

He listened so long to the silence that it started to go away. The sound of a car passing by on the next street made its way into his space, then an occasional creak or tap as the house relieved itself of some pressure, and finally his Mom's kiddie classical music.

He peeked into her room and she looked over at him from her chair.

"Are you here to play left field?" she asked.

"No."

"All those rocks," she shook her head disapprovingly.

"I know," he agreed.

"I don't think we can find a hat, anyway."

"Probably not."

She turned her attention back to the screen. A red plush octopus puppet with a happy human-like face was wiggling its arms playfully to the tinkling of a xylophone in front of a black velvet backdrop.

"Can I get you anything?" he asked.

"Tell Monty where I am."

"Monty Clift?"

"He gets lost sometimes."

"Will do."

He eased the door shut and remembered his burrito was still in the truck. The script was underneath it on the passenger seat, so he decided to work on the re-writes after dinner.

Doing so reminded him of what a fine editor his Mom had been, how much he had relied on her opinion as he fought through his doctoral dissertation, and early in his career when he had to make presentations or try to get articles published with no access to professional editors, with no need for her to consult the English professors in her department because she was so good. She knew very little of his subject matter, but knew how to communicate thoughts clearly, how to spot when a touch of flair was contributing the right feel and when it was becoming heavy-handed.

Out of curiosity, or perhaps masochism, he decided to read her the passage he had been working on.

Along with the marked-up script, he brought her the bowl that Esther had prepared: mashed potatoes with carrots and chicken mixed in; the food groups combined in a manner that made it easy to eat, but still looking like a meal rather than something gurgling through a feeding tube.

"This is a good place," Paget said to him as he handed her dinner.

"We aim to please."

"No parking, though."

"No?"

"I had to parallel park and it took me five times."

"Sorry."

"That's why nobody's here."

"Can I read you something I wrote?"

"It has nothing to do with the weather."

"It's about exploring outer space."

"It's a nice day and people still aren't here."

"Oh," Twain realized she had not paid attention to his side of the conversation. "Can I read you something I wrote?" he tried again.

"What is it about?"

"Exploring outer space."

She laughed and started eating.

He waited for some sort of nod that it was okay for him to start reading aloud, but she just kept digging her spoon into the potatoes and looking at him as she chewed. No permission appeared to be forthcoming, but neither was a refusal, so he sat on the edge of the bed near her chair and launched.

"Images of the earth no longer capture our imagination as much as images of the people who live on it. We are still brought to tears or wonder at the sight of the conditions in which people live, or the way we treat one another, but the land itself is somehow familiar, even if we've never visited the setting that provides the backdrop to the human drama or comedy unfolding on our screens or pages. It's difficult to imagine a time when reports of places that would eventually become national parks may as well have been sent from a robotic research vessel roving the surface of another planet, and how strenuous the journeys were to reach those uncharted places, journeys perhaps even more daunting than anything we will encounter in our expeditions to space."

He glanced between the page and her face. She wore a pleased expression. The potatoes were apparently quite good.

"To cut into an unmapped jungle, or a forest filled only with animals; to finally cross a desert that people had only stared at for generations; to be the first one up a river to see where it comes from or down that river to see how it ends, or to head straight out to sea rather than along the shore; to do these things was to die in many cases."

The toddler orchestra music changed to something that sounded as though it had been inspired by looking into the night sky. He didn't recognize the composer, but it was the kind of piece that played at planetariums while patrons watched animations of the solar system projected onto the domed ceiling, and a glance at his Mom's television screen revealed a similar vision on a smaller scale, as a mobile suspended from a dark ceiling with a few cartoonish planets dangling from its strings spun slowly around to the spacey tune. Twain was not one to believe in signs, but maybe this reading would lead somewhere.

"Was your curiosity so great that you were willing to risk being struck down by disease in a fit of cramps, chills, and dehydration? Was your greed so insatiable that the possibility of finding treasure took precedent over the possibility of being burned alive by inhospitable

natives, eaten alive by a shark or a bear, or skinned alive by traitors in your own crew? Did you need to show off badly enough that you were not dissuaded by the thought of spending months at a time soaking wet and cold, or sweating until your clothes disintegrated and your digits rotted? Were you so zealous to spread your religion that you were willing to walk through hell to do so? Was your need to escape your circumstances, to start a new life, so intense that you would take the chance of every door you opened becoming unhinged, your life as it was before the voyage disappearing into insanity, your connection to the earth you were exploring severed by throbbing delusions?

Twain was now immersed in his reading and not paying attention to his Mom.

"It was like going to war. The likelihood of dying and the guarantee of trauma insured that only so many would find what they were looking for, or return home, and even if they did, it was often with a touch of madness. Aside from the same motives that have always driven humankind to explore unfamiliar terrain—curiosity, greed, or neediness; enthusiasm or disenchantment with what earth holds for them—is there anything that connects our space explorers with those who braved primitive earth? In spite of the greater distances we will travel, and the likewise inhospitable environments, we will be able to engineer the conditions so they are less fraught with danger. Even when our destination is an earth-like planet, we know from experience with our own home that conditions which make life possible include hostile forms as well as nurturing ones. So we will guard against those lives; we will wrap ourselves in plastic and build glass boxes. Could it be the feeling of isolation that binds the ancient explorers with those of the future? We will be able to communicate with earth; we will see the places and people we left behind; but they won't really be there; they will be sound and vision, touching none of our other senses. And we will know exactly how far away they are.

He stopped and looked at her. She seemed to want to say something, but was too confused to know what it was. For a moment, he imagined it was something profound that she just needed time to articulate. She always used to choose her words carefully when offering a critique.

But she wasn't trying to formulate a response. Like someone who has just been spoken to in a foreign language with which they are only vaguely familiar, she was trying to remember how to say "I don't understand."

"I'm sorry," Twain sat up. "I'll let you eat."

The tension in her jaw dissolved, and she smiled at being able to use it for chewing again.

He retreated to the dining room table and worked on the script for the rest of the night, receiving feedback from his Mom in a more ethereal manner. He would ask himself as he tweaked a passage, "What would Paget say?", elevating her to a deity whose earthly body was left behind, the body he would check on periodically to take away the bowl and spoon, and to make sure she went to sleep. There was no need to change her into a nightgown or pajamas. Her clothes were as steady as the chair in which she spent her days: always a sweat suit, changing into a different color after a bathing. It was the kind of outfit people appreciate slipping into after a long day at work, or when deciding to stay in for a weekend and relax, and think of how great it would be if that's all they had to do all the time, just hang out in their sweats.

He actually would have liked to provide some sort of assistance, to seek the beauty in simple tasks that he had heard so much about. But those moments of grace were not available. When he sensed that his Mom may need some help, she would grow suspicious and fearful of him if he moved too close to her. He couldn't even treat the situation as lending aid to a stranger, since she was not aware that she needed any support, and therefore saw him as a threat rather than relief. So he kept his distance, limited his offerings to food service, and hoped nothing happened that would force him to come to her rescue.

Twain brought her breakfast in the morning and took a seat on the bed after he turned on the toddler symphony channel, positioning himself in her blind spot slightly behind her, experimenting with the idea that maybe being in her presence while writing would key inspiration, that seeing her would help answer the question "What would Paget say?" each time he asked it.

But it obstructed the answers rather than facilitated them. To actually see her rather than imagine her undermined her sway. At least it reminded him to keep the text simple, that his audience would be children.

There was little to do in terms of caring for her. He just had to make sure she didn't put herself in any precarious situations during those interludes when she would stray from her chair toward the bathroom or other household destinations. By the afternoon of his first full day as caregiver, the situation started to feel less sad and more tedious. The realization of how quickly tragedy can turn to drudgery, though, did supply its own low hum of melancholy.

He was grateful for the re-writes, for something to do, and projected his day onto the script, wondering in writing how prepared people would be for their new circumstances in another part of the ether, and if anyone should be allowed to reside on a space station or a new planet without specific duties to perform. Merely lingering in a distant galaxy would likely enhance people's worst fears about the universe, that it is unmoved and pointless.

The middle of the night wrinkled the tedium, as Twain awoke to the sound of a door opening and closing inside the house, and then the same sound coming from the front of the house as he got out of bed to see if he had dreamed the noise. He pivoted to the bedroom window and peered through the blinds. He saw Paget shuffling in the moonlight up the driveway toward the street. He put on a sweat suit of his own and some slippers, hurried outside, then slowed down when he saw her silhouette sitting at the bogus bus stop.

He stood to the side of the bench. Holding still made the temperature drop and he shivered.

"You're cold," she noticed.

"Aren't you?" he asked.

"I want to get home."

"And this bus will take you there?"

"I'm going to ask the driver."

He nodded and they held their positions in the dark for a while.

"Do you know where this bus goes?" she asked him.

"No, I don't."

"What are you doing here then?"

"Well, you seemed like you could use some company."

She leaned away from him. Twain searched for a way to make her feel less leery.

"You remind me of someone I used to know," he said.

"Really?" she smiled. "I hope she was nice."

"She was. Smart, too."

"And you don't know her anymore?"

"No."

"What happened?"

He considered explaining the situation to her, telling her about Alzheimer's just to see what sort of reaction it would elicit.

"We lost touch," he decided to say.

"You should look her up."

"Actually, that's why I'm here at this bus stop. I'm going to visit her. And why are you here?"

She looked around as if for a visual clue.

"I don't know."

"Why don't we go into this house," Twain gestured back down the driveway.

"Do you know the owners?"

"Yes I do."

He extended a hand in her direction, but she didn't take it.

"I must be here for a reason," she said.

"You can figure it out inside. We'll be able to hear the bus if it comes."

"It's a strange place for a bus stop."

"It is."

"So exposed. What if it rains?"

"Then I guess no one waits here. Come on," he extended his hand further. "It's cold."

"Where do you want to take me?"

"This house right here. I know the owners."

She looked around and fidgeted.

"It is cold," she seemed to be talking herself into going with him.

"I mean you no harm," he assured her. "You remind me of a very good friend of mine."

He hoped that she would say something similar to him, now that he had invoked familiarity a second time. But she just studied him, and he wondered if his face was that unwelcoming.

"Please," he said. "I don't want you to get sick."

He nearly mentioned the possibility of a hospital stay, but visions of wrestling with her in the street at this hour convinced him to keep pursuing a less drastic strategy.

She got up, but didn't take his hand. They walked side by side to the house, and once inside, she appeared to be soothed by the warmth and started to look more drowsy by the second. He escorted her to her room, to her chair, and as he settled her in and was waiting for her to fall asleep, he glanced at the clock and saw that Esther would arrive in a few hours to relieve him.

His Mom's breathing soon turned into a light snore. When he closed the door behind him, rather than go back to bed, he went to the dining room table and turned on his laptop.

He didn't know the name of the community college Esther had been mentioning, so he conducted a quick search that combined the name of the town with the word *college*. He found their website, then found the Human Resources page on their website.

Chapter Six

He was inclined to see the world as full of coincidences into which people crafted meaning. But discovering an unstaffed astronomy class available on the local satellite campus almost had him believing in totems.

Almost. Because if there was to be a class that the school was looking to staff the week before the fall semester started, astronomy was a likely candidate, as the applicant pool of teachers would be much smaller than for subjects like Math or English. And it made sense that the class would be offered on their satellite campus. Paget's retirement haven may have been reputable wine country and a magnet for talented restaurateurs, but from an academic standpoint it was the boonies. As if to offer proof, the interview was scheduled on the main campus. So Twain had to drive back to the county seat with the airport in it and resist the temptation to jump on the next flight out.

He had been given no indication that anyone recognized his name so far, as the only phone call was from a woman in Human Resources who gave him the date and time of the interview, and the topic of his teaching demonstration: an introduction to the solar system intended for students in a lower division survey course.

Twain had no concerns about the demo, given his background. It was the interview that concerned him, also thanks to his background. For as many groups of people that he had spoken to over the years, some of them college classes, he officially had no teaching experience. All of the professional references he submitted on his application were faculty members at prestigious universities (all of whom found his pursuit hilarious when he contacted them for permission to drop their name), but he himself had never been an instructor of record, not even as a guest lecturer. The closest item on his curriculum vitae was the one semester as a teaching assistant back when he was in graduate school. Otherwise, his times spent in front of a class had been for a day, for an hour or two.

The main campus was impressive, comparable to many of the state universities he had visited, if not the private ones. Its land grant was probably outside of town when it first opened, but since then it had been swallowed into the city limits and blended seamlessly, the surrounding blocks apparently ordered to comply with its architectural style when approved for development. The parking lots were each maybe one quarter full. A sparse herd of students were on hand to register or visit the bookstore, while Twain assumed the rest of the vehicles belonged to administrators and staff, along with some faculty members preparing for the following week.

As with the voice over the phone, nobody else in the Human Resources office took notice of him, either. He could tell they were truly not part of his audience, and not just being polite. This disappointed him a bit since his mission was to bring astronomy to the masses. Or at least that was what he told himself, since it sounded a lot better than the anonymity being a blow to his ego. He was finally recognized after he was escorted to the Science Building and offered a seat outside the door of what seemed to be a conference room.

A young man wearing a business dress shirt that still had creases in it from the packaging backed out of the door, nodding humbly and saying "thank you" to the voices inside who likewise sounded grateful to have met him. The interview seemed to have gone well, too, at least according to the young man. Until he turned to see Twain sitting there. His look of recognition went from excited to devastated as he processed who he was, and then what he was very likely doing there. Clearly hoping for a different answer than the one he had surmised, he asked Twain if he was there for an interview.

Rather than simply say yes, Twain answered, "It would just be for one semester."

The young man sighed and gloomily said, "I'm a big fan."

"Thank you," he responded, as though consoling him.

The competition wandered off, leaving Twain to sit back down in the chair against the wall in the empty hallway. He heard voices on the other side of the door, and preferred not to try to make out what they were saying.

When the door opened, a large woman in a pants suit untraceable to any particular fashion era surged into the hall, her forehead spritzed with perspiration.

"Two things," she said with a nervous warmth.

"Okay."

"First, we normally do the teaching demo in front of an actual class, but since this is an emergency hire and classes aren't in session, no can do."

"I wouldn't have known."

"Second, we're a state institution and have to be real careful about keeping the interviews uniform and equal."

"Why would you apologize for that?"

"Well, we're very excited that you applied to teach here, it's a stunner to say the least, and I'm afraid our enthusiasm may not have a chance to come across. I'm probably violating some law by even telling you that."

She extended a hand to introduce herself. "Stevie Evans, Dean of Sciences"

"It's a pleasure, Dean."

"Stevie."

"Stevie."

"Come on in. Let's meet the rest."

Stevie had barely turned to lead him into the room before stopping to face him again.

"I wish there was some sort of visiting professorship we could offer you, something where we wouldn't have to go through all of this song and dance, but we don't have that kind of thing here. We're not a university. We just teach."

"Sounds good to me," Twain assured her.

She smiled and held the door open for him.

There were a half dozen others sitting around the far end of a conference table. They each introduced themselves, and Twain was surprised to find he immediately forgot their names, as remembering names was a forte of his. They were a mix of faculty and administrators, he managed to remember that much, and they all greeted him with a similar mix of zeal and deference, except for one of the faculty members, who clearly considered Twain's application an intrusion.

His name was Robert Wheatley. The fact he remembered his name above the others, who were so obviously pleased to meet him, made him think of how his mother was stuck recalling an unhappy era in her life. And when he found himself keeping an eye on Professor Wheatley during the teaching demonstration to see if he could get a positive reaction from him, it further reminded Twain of the happy re-writes she was applying to that painful time. That dour face helped him focus, though, as the others were overreacting: laughing a bit too heartily, raising their eyebrows a bit too high.

He started his lecture on the solar system with that old mnemonic he first learned back in middle school to help remember the order of the planets, My Very Energetic Mother Just Sat Us Near Pluto, with the first letter of each word representing the first letter of the planets' names (Mercury Venus Earth Mars Jupiter Saturn Uranus Neptune Pluto), except in the case of Pluto, of course. He acknowledged the debate about whether Pluto was a planet or not, and divulged his opinion that it was, because why ruin a good mnemonic? While repeating it one more time before transitioning to the next phase of the lesson, he paused slightly after "My Very Energetic Mother", thinking of just how energetic his mother was, and how it was only thanks to the depletion of her energy that he found himself applying for this job, which probably would have been her ultimate wish, her dream job for him.

In providing more detail about the system, he used Earth as the building block rather than the sun, and expanded in each direction from there. Making people the cardinal point of any concept being discussed was the best way to keep their attention and give them a chance to understand it, at least according to his experience. He referenced and explained the "Goldilocks Zone" that was common in describing Earth's location amongst its neighbors, Mercury and Venus being too hot, Mars and the gassy planets beyond too cold, Earth just right, but took the additional step of describing each non-Earth planet in the context of a bear, and how its characteristics would kill you if you wound up in its clutches. He was afraid it may have been too low-level, but the committee members' nods and humpback whale-like moans of approval seemed to compliment his efforts in making the information accessible. His touchstone, the resentful Mr. Wheatley, continued to serve his purpose by remaining sullen and silent.

As he suspected, his experience with public appearances allowed him some wiggle room when it came to providing examples of teaching experiences, but in handling a question about dealing with a hypothetical student who was dissatisfied with their grade, he had to reach back to his teaching assistant days in grad school and embellish the one incident he could barely remember. It had been a polite conversation that was probably no more than a minute long, and now he was trying to infuse with as much drama as he could summon.

Wheatley pounced with a follow-up question: "Any more recent examples?"

Twain looked right at him and smiled. "No."

They all jotted down some notes. He suspected most were writing excuses on his behalf. His nemesis, however, made a point of underlining what he wrote three times, with enough of a flourish to nearly tear the paper.

Twain had vowed not to name drop too heavily, but after being called out on the previous question, he put the full weight of his contact list behind his answer to the next question, which asked about influences and mentors. He also capitalized on the chance to mention his colleagues' involvement with the books, articles, and shows he had produced, since he assumed that publishing would not be a consideration for the position, and would not be the subject of any remaining questions.

This proved to be the case, but one of the last questions stumped him.

"What motivated you to want to teach at a community college?"

It was such an obvious question, and he had not necessarily failed to anticipate it, for he certainly had his reasons for wanting to be there. But it only occurred to him at that moment how misaligned his inspiration was with the community college mission. Tired of spinning yarns and suspecting he had the votes necessary to get the gig, he decided to be forthright.

"My mother is ill," he said. "She may not have much time left. I came here to be by her side, but discovered I'm not very good at that. I need something to do."

Even Wheatley broke eye contact and stared down at the table for several moments, along with everyone else.

"Well," Stevie half spoke and half cleared her throat. "There's another question. I'll do the honors."

Everyone was relieved to have a handy excuse to move on. Their eyes slowly rose from the table and their smiles softly returned.

"The course you would be teaching is offered on our satellite campus. Are you willing to accept the position regardless of the location?"

"I prefer that campus, actually."

Stevie voiced what all of their incredulous looks were thinking: "Really?"

"It's where Mom lives, where I'm staying."

That appeared to explain everything and appease them all. Stevie once again served as their spokesperson.

"It is becoming quite the town, apparently."

"It's lovely," Twain declared. "And the opportunity to teach what I love while I'm living there is a chance I wouldn't take for granted. This is not a gimmick. I'm not here to do a feature or conduct research. I just want to do what you do as best I can."

The faces beamed. Wheatley, meanwhile, took his turn reading from the list of questions.

"Do you have any questions for us, or anything you would like to say that the interview did not allow you to express?"

"Oh," Twain matched his flat tone. "Now I really wish I had saved that previous statement."

All but Wheatley appreciated his line. Everyone shook hands again, and now that the interview was over, Twain started to remember their names. He summoned each one as he grasped each hand and told them what a pleasure it was to have met them.

He had not even completed the walk back to his truck, and was still arriving at a conclusion as to why he had been more nervous for this appearance than any of the last one hundred or so, television included, when he got a call on his phone from Stevie, telling him he got the job.

"We understand it's most likely just going to be for one semester," she continued after breaking the initial news. "But we couldn't possibly pass up this chance. I'm not sure who should be getting the congratulations, you or us."

"Me," Twain said. "Absolutely. I'm very grateful."

"Oh," Stevie seemed to remember something thanks to the relief in Twain's voice. "And the committee wishes to express their thoughts and prayers for you and your mother in the upcoming days."

"Even Mr. Wheatley?"

"*Doctor* Wheatley," she chuckled. "Careful. He's the senior full-time faculty member in Astronomy. Then again, there's only two of them."

"So let me guess," Twain reached his truck and switched the phone to his other ear in order to reach for his keys. "He's going to be evaluating me this semester."

"You still want the job?"

"I've had worse reviews than whatever he's going to say."

"There's some forms Human Resources needs you to fill out, of course. They'll notify you and you can do most of it electronically. They may need you to stop by and sign some of it."

"Will do," he settled into the driver's seat.

"Meanwhile my assistant will send you the link to download your roster and access the class website. You can load files onto the site for the students to download, so you don't have to worry about making copies of everything."

"Perfect."

"One thing that needs to be done the old-fashioned way, though, is if you haven't left yet, you should stop by the bookstore. They won't be able to get your order in by the first day of class, but the sooner you submit your text request, the earlier it will get there. If you need any recommendations..."

"I wasn't planning on using a book."

"Sure, I imagine you've got all sorts of materials you can use."

"And I promise none of it will be my own."

"Well, that's okay with us. There's no rule against that."

"It's more of a promise to myself, really."

"Ah, got it. And hey, while I've got you on the line here, Dr. Henry…"

"Twain."

"Twain. Thank you. Would you mind if we ran a story or two about you teaching with us? A press release, maybe? A little promotion?"

Twain was about to start the engine, but paused and leaned back in his seat. He took a deep breath and almost exhaled out loud, but didn't want to hurt the Dean's feelings.

"It's got nothing to do with the school, Stevie," he let his words surf on the escaping air. "I'm truly proud to be associated with it, with you. But part of why I'm here is to blend in for a while, to forget myself."

"I understand," she said quickly and loudly, overcompensating for the possibility of an awkward gap in the conversation. "Perfectly. Just thought I'd ask. Anyway, don't hesitate to call me if you need anything. Thanks again for looking us up."

"Thanks for having me."

"Wheatley will be in touch to set up a classroom visit."

They both mixed in a laugh with their good-byes, and Twain finally started the engine.

He found himself growing more giddy about his new job as he drove, and when he reached the outskirts of Mom's adopted hometown, he marked the difference in his perspective compared to when he had approached it the previous week. He thought it would be a great time to have a celebratory glass of wine and catch Marina before the dinner rush, but decided to first be a good employee and check out the satellite campus to get a sense of where he'd be working for the next few months. Plus the detour would put him at the bar at a slightly later and more respectable time.

He had seen the signs directing people how to get there. It was in the direction of one of the wine trails outside of town he had followed before, but reaching the campus required an additional turn before reaching as far into the countryside.

It appeared after a couple of slight bends in the road. Unlike the main campus, it had yet to be surrounded by any other development, and was confined to a single cluster of buildings that was one structure short of enclosing the central square, which was resourcefully landscaped in the manner of a front yard in a new housing tract. The utilitarian architecture made the compound look like the storage and operations facilities for the land around it that was still being farmed, that had yet to be donated or sold to the college.

A few cars dotted the small parking lot in front of the campus, while the larger lot that wrapped around the side was empty. On the building nearest the side lot hung a banner that proclaimed "Late Registration". Twain wondered if his class was full enough, or if his adventure would end before it began. He imagined they wouldn't have gone to the trouble of hiring someone if the course hadn't filled, but he had yet to check the schedule for the room number, either, so he pulled in and parked amongst the cars in the small front lot in a space marked "staff", and pulled out his phone to look it up.

With a few taps and swipes of the screen, he found it: the only offering of Solar Astronomy on this campus, filled to capacity, as there were several on the wait list, and marked as being taught by "staff". He cracked a joke out loud to himself about already having his own personalized parking spot, and decided to get out and walk around, perhaps get a feel for the classroom if he could.

All he had to do to find the right building was stand on one of the gravel paths in the central area and scan the numbers on the walls. He identified his target and found the main entrance open. The room, though, was locked. He peered through the slender window along the side of the door, but it was too dark inside to see anything.

"Can I help you?" a voice startled him.

Twain turned and saw a security officer about the same age as him who was sincerely asking if he needed help, rather than accusing him of anything.

"Just trying to get a look at the classroom I'll be teaching in."

"Good idea," he said, and took out his keys to unlock the door.

Twain offered his thanks. The officer assured him it was no problem as he led him into the room and turned on the lights.

"This is one of nicer rooms," he announced while Twain started to wander. "Seems like it should be in a university."

"It does," Twain agreed, noting the arena-style seating that rose above the lecture area, which contained not just a dry erase board and a screen, but a tech station on the podium that allowed for anything you could fit under the document camera or call up on the computer to be projected for all to see.

"That's something people forget when it comes to the different campuses," the officer narrated as Twain surveyed the equipment with the fascination of a car buyer who had come upon a vehicle that interested him. "Our buildings are newer, so they had the bells and whistles built right in during construction. The main campus has to backtrack and upgrade all the time, and sometimes it doesn't work real well. So what class are you teaching?"

"Solar Astronomy," he replied, and sprinted up the steps to the back of the room to get a perspective from the top.

"That's Astro 1A, right?" the officer seemed to be cooperating by saying something so that Twain could test the acoustics.

"Yes it is. Could you talk some more while I walk around? In a normal voice, just to see how much I'll need to project."

"Sure," he agreed as Twain started to make his way down by switching back every few rows and walking along the aisle of seats. "You know, when you said you teach Astronomy, it hit me. Are you that guy on TV?"

"You've seen the show?"

"I've seen some commercials for it. And saw you on some other show."

"That's me," he confirmed as he turned another corner.

"Wow..."

"So what am I doing here?" Twain finished the thought that the officer seemed hesitant to verbalize.

"Well...yeah."

"A change of pace," Twain offered as he made his way across the third row from the front, getting closer to the ground floor. "Something to keep me honest."

"Great idea. I guess."

Twain reached the end of the seats and walked down the last few steps. They faced each other from opposite ends of the floor.

"Are we alone?" the officer asked.

"Excuse me?"

"In the universe?"

"Oh..." Twain smiled and drifted toward the center. "I don't think we are. There's a telescope, the Kepler Telescope, named after the first astronomer to accurately chart the flight path of the known planets, or at least he came real close, and this thing, this telescope has discovered a number of Earth-like planets, called exoplanets. And that number is going to grow, because we find distant planets by looking for dips or wobbles in the light of a star caused by a planet passing in front of it, and planets can take hundreds of days to make it around their sun, so the data can take quite a while to compile and confirm. But it's getting better. We used to just find big old gassy planets like Jupiter and assume there may be some Earths in the vicinity, but now we know. And they're getting closer. A couple of the ones discovered recently are only 120,000 light years away from us."

"And space stuff is usually in the millions and billions, right?"

"That's right. So even though it's still a long way away, and we may not be able to reach it, we could still reach out to it, communicate with them. We'll know they're out there. Whoever they are."

The officer nodded and looked around the empty room.

"What's your name?" Twain asked.

"Ed."

"Nice to meet you, Ed. I'm Twain Henry."

"Ah, that's it. I couldn't quite remember."

Twain laughed and leaned back on the front desk. "How would the discovery of other life make you feel, Ed? Would you feel bigger? Or smaller?

He thought about it, then answered "Bigger."

"Why?"

"Well, because space is really huge, and we're really small, but if we found some more life out there, we could be, like, fighting the loneliness together."

"You've taken some classes here, haven't you?"

"Got my A.A. degree. Took me most of my twenties to get it, but I got it."

"I take it you grew up here, then?"

"My family has been here since the nineteenth century. I'm fifth generation."

Twain extended his hand. "Thank you for letting me in, Ed. I'll see you around."

"Likewise," Ed shook it. "And thanks for teaching here. We deserve it."

En route to the parking lot, Twain considered exploring some other parts of the campus, but thought it may be more productive to do so when school had started, so he could get a sense of the energy and the people who inhabited the place, rather than just the place itself. Besides, he was anxious to regain his path downtown and check in with Marina over a glass of Syrah, and expand on the initial contact he had made with her.

She was working, it wasn't yet busy, so she did have time to talk as she waited for the first wave of customers to arrive. Twain at first stuck to saying hello and sipping his wine, feeling self-conscious about bothering her, but she lingered near his spot at the bar rather than the servers' station by the patio, so he gathered she was granting him permission to start a conversation.

"I'm celebrating a new job."

"Congratulations," she said.

Now that he was able to focus more on her, now that he was speaking to her, he was pleased to notice that her edge had softened.

"Where is it?" she asked.

"Here, at the college."

"You're giving a speech or something?"

"I'm teaching Introduction to Solar Astronomy."

"Seriously?"

"Would I joke about teaching Introduction to Solar Astronomy?"

"How did they find out you were in town?"

"They didn't ask. I applied."

She smiled, and it was more broad and more unguarded than any previous smile of hers he had memorized.

"I used to take classes before they had the new buildings," she said. "Back when it was all evening classes at the high school."

"Any tips you can offer? Insights into the local student population?"

"Not only was it a long time ago, it wasn't for very long."

"No?"

"Having a kid sort of got in the way."

"You have a kid?"

"A son. He moved to Los Angeles with a buddy this summer after they graduated high school. Couldn't wait to get out."

"Good for him. Kids should want to get out and see the world."

"Tell that to my family. They think I'm letting him go on a suicide mission."

"They'll get over it."

"Maybe. We're fourth generation in this area. They're probably more offended than scared."

"You're the second person in the last half hour to tell me how long their family has lived here."

Marina shrugged. "Small town."

"So you know Ed?"

"Ed?"

"He was the other one."

"Not that small."

"But you could be two of the elite families. Local royalty."

"I can't speak for Ed, whoever he is, but mine certainly isn't."

"Perhaps in a few more generations."

She laughed. "If your family didn't make it in the first generation, they're not making it."

Twain raised his glass. "Then may your son return a conquering hero."

"Well, he made the first move," she scanned the establishment as she spoke. "The only way to conquer this place is from the outside."

She excused herself for a moment to check the patio. Twain waited and sipped and did not plan his next move. He was enjoying himself too much.

"Coast is clear," she stated upon returning.

"I have this vision of you and Mom trading single-parent war stories."

"How do you know I was single?"

"I'm stereotyping."

Marina puffed out a laugh. "We didn't do that very often. She seemed to have a very different experience than I did."

"She loved to tell stories."

"Like when she had her own place, when you were a baby, a little apartment with just you and her, she thought that was one of the best times of her life."

"Stories, like I said. Fiction."

"I believed her. I could see it in her eyes. It sounded so cozy, and so exciting to be on your own."

Twain appreciated what he could see in Marina's eyes. "And what about your experience?"

"Terrifying," her eyes cooled off. "I wasn't out on my own. I mean, I was, I had my own place. Dad kicked me out. But I was younger, and my apartment was in the same town that I had just blown my chance to escape from, a town where pretty much everyone else lived in a house."

She was very forthright and didn't seem angry with him for asking, but he still wished he hadn't done so. He tried to redirect the conversation.

"I wish I could take care of her as well as she took care of me," he offered.

"It's not the same," she assured him.

"Thank you for allowing me the gender excuse, or the career excuse, but I'm afraid it's deeper than that, a genuine flaw."

"I mean the situation."

She crossed over to the bar at which he sat and leaned toward him, narrowing the space between them.

"A baby's going to grow up," she continued. "An old person's going to die. That whole thing where people compare babies to old people? Wrong."

He liked the feeling of being closer to her, and relished it for a few moments.

"You're brilliant," he told her. "Please spend some time with me someplace where you don't have to run away and check on other people."

"How do you know I'm not seeing someone?"

"You would have referenced him in the conversation by now."

"Give me your phone," she held out her hand. He obliged and she tapped in her contact information.

"Hicks are good with technology," she said as she passed it back to him. "Keeps us connected to the big, scary world out there."

They grinned at each other.

"Now finish your wine and go," she nodded toward the exit. "That was a great closing line, and if you hang around, you'll ruin it."

Chapter Seven

Esther hovered over him as much as she did his mother in the days before class started, as he spent more time in the house preparing: designing a syllabus, assignments, exams, and loading videos and articles onto the website. Twain attributed most of her doting to her pride in recommending the job, but another motive emerged the more time she spent toggling between him and his mother.

She started to use the word "son" more often when addressing Paget. "Can you believe your son?" she'd say to her. "A college professor, just like where you used to work." She would frequently ask if she was proud of her son, or state that she must be proud of her son. Paget would look suitably baffled and then ask if Montgomery Clift had called.

Esther was undeterred, taking Paget's momentary confusion as progress. "If I just keep saying it," she would claim, "then maybe she will remember, even a little bit."

Twain had withheld comment the first several times, but as she repeated her hypothesis while making lunch one afternoon, he decided to finally respond from his spot at the table as he took a break from his laptop.

"Did you read something about this technique?"

"No," she chirped. "I only started to think of it because now you're around so much."

"So you have no evidence that it works?"

"I have a feeling."

He leaned back and wondered if he should pursue the matter.

"Not everything needs evidence, professor," she merrily piled on. "You can't get everything from a book."

He sighed and decided that he should indeed pursue the matter, thinking of the best way to do so.

He imagined he might say "People wrote those books," while trying not to sound pompous. "People with experience. They felt something, too, then decided to see if what they were feeling was true."

And when she said, "Okay, I'll stop," he would say, "I'm not asking you to stop, necessarily. I'm just wondering if you value what happens at a school, or if you just used it to get a job, because people herald education all the time, and then in the next breath dismiss it as nerdish and out of touch with 'the real world', whatever that is. Apparently the real world is some place where nobody ever takes the time to figure out if what they believe is true."

He thought that may be a good way to put it.

But instead all he said was "Thank you for the turkey sandwich," as she placed his lunch in front of him.

And upon walking into the lecture hall on the first day of class, he started to have his own doubts about college.

At first they merely revolved around his own disappointment and fear. It was the first time in over a decade he had entered a room full of that many people without receiving applause. He only realized how accustomed he had grown to the cheers when greeted by the silence that was made all the more silent by his epiphany. Then he saw the disinterest on the quiet faces as he nodded in their direction on his way to the lectern, and it occurred to him that all of his earlier encounters with former students of the college had been with people who were predisposed to be enthusiastic alumni: people employed in jobs they enjoyed, or at least didn't mind, and who would have been good at whatever they decided to do, no matter where they went to school.

But here were the majority, the people for whom this campus was a test to see if college was a sustainable plan: young men wearing gaudy basketball jerseys of no discernible team and baseball hats brandishing free advertising for the company responsible for the logo on it, young women flashing more skin in a single day than most generations of women throughout history had bared in their lifetime, and the smattering of older students who were future projections of the young ones, dressed more modestly for the most part, in clothes a decade out of date, their faces besieged by forces that had yet to tug on the junior versions surrounding them.

By the time he reached the front table, Twain had decided he appreciated the desperation transmitted by the older students, as at least it indicated an interest, whereas the young seemed so easily bored, with their stab at college being the latest thing that bored them.

Which is what led him to question the purpose of the whole enterprise, not just his place in it. And he hadn't even started.

The school never did bother to put his name on the schedule, as the class was filled by the time he was hired, so while he shuffled through his belongings on the front table he decided to sublimate his snap judgments of the student population and instead look for signs of anyone starting to recognize him. A few in the front far corner to his right had clearly made the connection and were delighted, which made sense because they looked like they already had some opinions on whether Pluto was a planet or an asteroid, but most of the rest didn't even seem to notice that he had walked in, much less recall where they may have seen him before.

He had grabbed the most practical tote bag he could find from his mother's closet, which had the logo of his show on one side. In the interest of avoiding self-promotion he had been careful to keep the logo facing his body, and had also placed it on the table with the logo facing away from the gallery. Now faced with an audience who had not been primed for his appearance and trying to negotiate his disappointment without resorting to blatant name-dropping, he discreetly nudged the bag around in subtle spurts as he retrieved its contents, so that by the time he had fetched everything he needed from the bag, or at least pretended to need, the logo was positioned squarely outward, as though he was standing behind a table at a media networking conference to advertise the show.

The visual cue did not appear to jog any memories amongst the heedless. The small crew who already assumed they were aware of the situation now had confirmation, and stared at each other in disbelief while mouthing amazed exclamations. The rest were more interested in their screens in the palms of their hands than in him, and even their screens didn't seem to inspire much of anything. He internally sighed and put off the introduction just a little while longer, moving instead to turn on the equipment, giving them one last chance figure it out before he provided the answer.

A couple of the unconscious majority approached the lectern. He looked up and was pleased to see them with pens and paper in tow. Twain was ready to tell them that yes, he was that guy, but that they would have to wait for autographs.

"Could we get an add code?" one them asked.

"I'm sorry?" Twain replied.

"We're trying to add the class, but we need this, like, number to do it."

"Oh...yes. Well, let me take attendance first and see if anybody didn't show up."

They sagged and retook their seats. He opened his binder and flipped to the roster he had downloaded and proceeded to call out the names, taking advantage of the process to further scan the room for signs of life. With each name, an arm would blithely rise and fall, or a distracted "here" would provide a blip on the motley radar. A couple of people corrected him on the pronunciation of their names, he assumed a couple of others would but they didn't bother, and upon tallying up the number of no-shows, he found there was enough space to add all those looking to join. He called them up to assign each of them one of the numbers listed on the final page of the attendance roster, which finally elicited some enthusiasm from parts of the room besides the fan club to his right, as each of the new adds returned to their seat greeted by a high-five from an awaiting friend.

Twain tried to seize the moment of energy for his own use, grasping it to pull himself from the sinking feeling that he should have let the Dean flaunt his hiring.

"Good afternoon, everyone. My name is Twain Henry."

An awkward sort dressed as though it was winter rather than early fall raised his hand. Admitting that the young man's type also occupied a fair-sized segment of his followers, and thinking this may finally be his chance to modestly own up to his identity, Twain called on him.

"Do you prefer Mr. Henry or Dwayne?"

"Actually, it's Twain."

"Twain?"

"As in Mark Twain."

"Who's Mark Twain?"

At least he didn't know him, either.

The ensuing low-level laughter was also somewhat soothing, as it assured Twain that a fair number of the rest, on the other hand, did in fact know who Mark Twain was. Not wanting to embarrass the kid any further, the laughs also prevented him from snapping back with a clever rejoinder.

"He was a great American writer," he started to answer as best he could. "He wrote *Huckleberry Finn*."

"Ohhhhh," the kid dressed in layers said. "Yeah. That book."

"So you've read it?"

"I think so. In high school."

"But you don't remember."

"I never read the books in high school."

Twain tried to make sense of their exchange while a new, louder wave of laughter repealed any comfort established by the previous one, as they were now laughing with him rather than at him, indicating to Twain that they were complicit in not reading.

"How did you graduate, then?"

"With everyone else."

He said it with utter sincerity, as surprised by the peak laughter he created as Twain was disheartened by it. He took no pride in it, nor was he embarrassed by the inadvertent laughter. It was just something that happened to him, and probably not for the first time. Thanks to this quick deduction, the kid with all the layers who was hard to understand and had inspired all of the discouraging howls was the least annoying person in the room, as far as Twain was concerned. He decided to keep talking to him.

"Didn't you have to write essays on them? Take quizzes?"

"We mostly just talked about them," the kid seemed to appreciate the effort Twain was making to learn more about what he had said. "But if we did have to write an essay, you could go on a website and get some ideas for it."

Twain nodded with a sustained, soft grunt as the laughter paled.

"So what was *Huckleberry Finn* about?" the kid asked, igniting the room all over again.

He and Twain maintained eye contact and waited for the noise to subside.

"It's about going on a journey," Twain said to him as the opportunity presented itself. "Huck floats down the Mississippi River with a runaway slave named Jim, and there's all kinds of danger and adventures they get into. That's the story. But the big picture, the things we're supposed to relate to even though we haven't taken the same journey, is how we come to learn about the world we live in, and discover our place in it, what we feel is right and wrong, and whether we have the courage to follow our convictions once we make these discoveries."

The students were mute. But as Twain scanned the faces, he didn't see a whole lot of appreciation for his impromptu summary. He saw confusion.

"But you're an astronomy teacher," the kid seemed to speak for them all.

"So?"

"How do you know so much about books?"

"Because I read them."

He earned a little bit of his own laughter on that line, particularly from his fan club. But their minor contribution had a smug tone, which inspired Twain to explain himself.

"I'm not necessarily calling you out on not reading the books you were supposed to in high school," he offered. "What I mean to say is that this is what an education is supposed to be about. It all fits together. If you want to work in your field and always answer to someone else, then by all means narrow your focus as much as possible on just that subject. If you want to be an innovator, if you want to get noticed, then go big. The more things you're interested in, the more interesting you'll be."

The room was hushed, but he couldn't tell if he had stumbled into an inspiring moment or into a tangent that further tranquilized them. They mostly stared, with but a few giving him the small, satisfied nod and smirk of approval so common to students in movies who have come to realize that their teacher, the star of the movie, is actually kind of cool.

But as he pressed on through the first day's lesson plan, he wanted more of that, more of what he was used to: one hundred percent approval, or close to it. Thanks to his customary high marks, he had developed a habit of seeking out the random dour face in the midst of all the beaming ones, of scrolling through the comments section at the bottom of an article he had written to find a naysayer amongst the compliments, and searching the web for a negative review of his show while taking for granted the positive ones. And now in this present crisis, with a room split between yay and nay, this penchant to sift through the good in search of the bad had him flustered, as he was unaccustomed to having as much of one as the other for any sustained amount of time. With every tepid response to one of his asides or observations concerning the syllabus projected onscreen, he had to keep reminding himself that failing to tip the balance in his favor was not the same as losing the room completely.

By the time he was introducing them to the articles he wanted read for the following class, he had decided to forego even trying to break the deadlock and simply deliver the material.

As they filed down the aisles and through the door, the appreciative bunch in the front right corner held their position and made their move once the room was empty. Twain spent a lot of effort placing objects back into his promotional tote bag so as not to greet them with too much gratitude.

The mostly male band featured one young woman, a girl who was probably too enthusiastic about too many things to have been very popular in high school. She was the first to speak.

"So is this some kind of hidden camera show?" she asked, looking around the room for effect.

Twain smiled. "If it is, I don't think it's going the way the producers had hoped."

"They can just focus on us," offered the male who seemed closest to being the alpha in a collection of betas. "And we'll be all like..." he completed his thought by making exaggerated astonished faces.

"No," Twain made it official. "It's not a hidden camera show. I'm just...here."

"Why?" asked the alpha beta male, his astonishment now genuine.

"Family matters," he answered, wondering how to follow through on that statement without being too indulgent or too enigmatic. "My mother lives in the area, and she's having some health problems."

"Oh, I'm sorry," said the young woman. "I hope she's not suffering."

Twain meditated on the word she had used, suffering, and how exactly it applied to his Mom, if at all. He noticed the teacher's pets were waiting for an answer.

"Well," he tried to supply them with one, "she's definitely not herself."

The young woman, who revealed herself as the true alpha each time she spoke, took that as a cue to change the subject.

"I can't wait to tell my friends going to universities who my Astronomy professor is," she said.

"Check us out, bitches!" chimed in a boy who appeared to have beat out some stiff competition for the role of group clown, thanks to a hint of lunacy in his eyes. "We got us some Twain Henry, and for one-tenth the price, y'all!"

Twain wanted to smile politely, but couldn't get past a smirk. He noticed some movement to his left, some people in the hall looking through the skinny window by the door, and he used it as a diversion.

"We need to clear out for the next class," he announced, then realized that he wasn't prepared to let go of their admiration just yet.

"I could use a bite to eat," he said as he slung his bag over his shoulder. "Anyone want to join me?"

Half of them went slack-jawed, and the other half slack-shouldered.

"Dammit," one of the disappointed half blurted. "I have class, and I can't be a first-day drop. I need it to transfer."

"Where you going?" asked another whose shoulders were melting. "Maybe we can catch up with you later."

Twain shrugged and looked to the available half for suggestions. "I'll rely on your local knowledge."

The young woman, faux alpha male, and court jester traded ideas and settled on a local grill nestled amongst the ring of fast food abutting the town.

"Perfect," Twain approved. "And can I get some names before we go, so I'm not dining with strangers?"

The possible late arrivals introduced themselves first before heading to their next class, then his lunch dates took their turn. The young woman's name was Alice. He couldn't remember the names of the two young men, and hoped lunch would provide opportunities to pretend that he did.

The restaurant had clearly once been a fast food franchise as well, and the new owners tried their best to destroy the evidence and imprint their personality on the décor.

Alice was already there when Twain arrived. She waved him over and told him Gavin and Blake were driving together and would be there soon. He sat down and briefly calculated if hearing their names helped him recall which one was which, but came up with no solution. He settled for the fifty-fifty chance, and after soliciting some ideas from Alice on what to order, asked her what she was considering for a major.

"Because isn't that what you're supposed to ask college students?" he added.

"Not sure," she laughed. "Something in the sciences. Maybe astronomy, but probably something more broad, so I have more options when it's time for grad school."

"Grad school," Twain was impressed.

"A bachelor's is like a high school diploma these days," she said. "Especially for the kinds of things I'm interested in. I'm not even sure you can get a bachelor's in genetics or biochemistry or molecular engineering. Can you?"

"Beats me," he held up his hands. "I'm not much of an authority on colleges. Until this fall, they were just venues for me to perform in. I can tell you what the educational landscape was twenty years ago."

She laughed and caught the boys' attention as they walked in. Twain greeted them by name, taking a chance by eyeing the self-appointed alpha as he said "Blake", and saying "Gavin" while looking into the loony eyes of the other boy. His guess was incorrect. They looked at each other, wordlessly trying to decide if they should tell him, and who would break the news. He saved them the trouble.

"Sorry," he said. "Now that I've got them down, I won't forget them."

The boys relaxed and smiled. Twain added "probably" to his statement as they sat. He was kidding, but they lapsed back into discomfort.

"I was just telling Alice how long it's been since I was on a college campus for more than a few hours," he incorporated them into the conversation. "Which got me to thinking, is this appropriate?"

Now the boys appeared to become protective of Alice. Twain managed to keep from chuckling at their misunderstanding. His jabs had been inadvertent up to this point, but he was starting to enjoy keeping them off balance.

"I mean, we used to hang out with our professors after class," he continued. "But that was then, and it was grad school. Maybe I should call the Dean before we order anything."

"We'll never tell," Alice whispered playfully, which didn't put the boys any more at ease.

"It's just lunch," said Gavin.

"For real," added Blake, still the wacky sidekick, but with some exposed nerves.

"Just lunch," Twain agreed. "A for-real lunch. So let's do it."

He led the way to the counter to place his order, then stood to the side as the students placed theirs, instructing the cashier that he was paying for all of them. They expressed their gratitude with polite protestations followed by thank-yous once Twain completed the transaction.

The boys seemed more relaxed as everyone arrived back at the table by way of the drink filling station. Blake planted their plastic order number on the table.

"Lunch on Dr. Henry," he crowed. "Can we get a picture together?"

Alice and Gavin clutched their foreheads.

"What?" Blake asked. "Too soon?"

"It's okay," Twain chuckled. "But the end of the semester would probably be better."

"Ah, I get it," Blake agreed. "Motivation."

"I was thinking more of a perceived conflict of interest," Twain considered his perspective. "But, sure. We can go with the motivation angle. And speaking of motivation..."

"Oh my God," Alice looked out from under the hand on her forehead. "I know what you're going to say."

"What am I going to say?"

"The students," she said. "Those drips."

"I wasn't going to call them drips. I was just wondering what inspires their lack of inspiration."

"Alice already said it," Blake offered.

"But I've got some ideas on why that's the case," she added.

"You do?" Blake said, as both he and Gavin reunited with their distrust, but aimed it at her this time, as though wary that she was showing them up.

"I call it the 'Get Me The Hell Out Of Here' Theory."

"It's probably a hypothesis at this point," Twain kidded her, which the boys enjoyed.

Alice hopped over the obstruction and proceeded.

"My mom took classes here like twenty years ago, and she said the students were really dedicated, pretty much across the board."

"Are you dumping on our generation?" Gavin probed.

"I'm not attributing it to generational differences. That's so boiler plate."

Twain delighted in her response, while the boys sunk a little deeper into their insecurities.

"Twenty years ago is before the wine industry started to dominate..." she continued.

"So now everyone's drunk?" Blake cracked, which drew no response.

"...and once the industry established itself, the nice places to work followed. Twenty years ago there were no jobs at gourmet restaurants and luxury hotels and tasting rooms. It was still a cow town."

"It's still a cow town," Gavin said.

"But not as much as it was," she defended her hypothesis. "Back then, the only work for a student, besides on a farm, was at Foster's Freeze and Arby's. People couldn't get out fast enough. And college was a good way to do that."

"I see your point," Twain engaged her. "But these new jobs don't pay that much more than the old ones, do they? They just look nicer, smell better."

"Exactly," she said. "They lull you into complacency. They make you think you're doing okay, that you've got some sort of career, but all you're doing is wearing a pressed shirt and talking to rich people. Now my aunt, she teaches part-time at a couple of junior colleges out in the valley, where it's still a cow town, just a much bigger one, and she says her students are great. They want to get out, so they throw themselves into their studies."

Twain nodded, intrigued by her ideas but unsure what to do with them. The boys, meanwhile, looked unsure of what to do with themselves.

"Damn wine industry," Twain muttered.

"You sound like my grandpa," Blake hooted.

"People need to adapt," Alice said. "I'm not blaming the industry for anything. If somebody can't work at a Bed and Breakfast and pull a 'C' in their Econ class, that's their own fault."

"And here I thought it was the cell phones," Twain kidded.

"Now you sound like *my* grandpa," Gavin laughed.

"To your grandpas," Twain raised his glass and the boys clinked it with theirs before they all took melodramatic swigs.

Alice rolled her eyes. "Blaming cell phones is as tired as blaming generations. People bury their faces in their phones for a reason, and they'll look up from them if you give them a reason."

"Was I that bad?" Twain barely managed to say through a gulp of his iced tea.

"No," they all said more or less in unison. Then Alice provided further explanation.

"You got more out of them than most of my other teachers. Just those little reactions every so often, those are like bringing down the house compared to the rest. But why settle for comparatively bringing down the house when you can actually do it?"

"So what you're saying is..." he didn't bother completing the thought.

Alice shrugged and grinned.

Twain exhaled. "I want to really give this a shot. I want to teach, not name drop."

"But dude..." Blake started to plead.

"Dude?" Alice chided him.

"Doctor," Blake corrected himself.

"Twain" Twain corrected him.

"Twain," Blake finally continued, "you heard Alice, and she makes some sense."

"Some?" she got on him again.

Now was Blake's chance to ignore her. He pressed his point forward. "You've got what they like. You're the kind of person they serve and suck up to, a famous one even. They just don't know it yet."

Gavin joined in. "You merge the cult of celebrity with astronomy in your regular job. Why not do it here, too?"

"You're doing them a favor," Alice said. "Getting them interested in the class is a good thing, no matter how you accomplish it."

"That last part of your statement is demonstrably false," Twain noted.

"True enough," she acknowledged, "but the way you're going to get their attention is harmless enough."

"Bribing them with stories of Emmy Awards after-parties..."

"Absolutely," she maintained.

"It's the medium, not the message," Blake backed her up.

They all looked at him. Blake smiled modestly.

"I took a Media Studies class at State before I dropped out. The professor said that all the time."

"And he's right," Alice kept up the momentum. "They don't realize how interesting the class is because they're used to it being taught by people like Mr. Lundquist."

"I like Mr. Lundquist," Gavin interjected.

"I like him, too," Alice agreed. "But would you like him if you weren't such a nerd?"

"Probably not,' he admitted.

"Is Mr. Lundquist one of my new colleagues?" Twain asked. "Should I be defending him?"

"No," Alice explained. "He was our high school science teacher. He dabbled in some astronomy."

"He used some of your articles," Gavin mentioned.

"Well then lay off Mr. Lundquist," Twain said.

"He liked using your work because he thought it was easy for the kids to read," she added.

"I do tend to strive for accessibility," he acknowledged, "but there's something about the way you said that…"

Alice laughed and suggested that Twain should visit Mr. Lundquist while he was in town. Blake leaned back out of Alice's peripheral vision and shook his head in Twain's direction while excessively mouthing the words "Don't Visit Mr. Lundquist".

Twain tried not to laugh as he fidgeted for the right response, and was relieved of coming up with one as their orders arrived.

They shared brief reviews of the food after their first few bites, then Twain shepherded the talk in their direction, and learned how each of them ended up at that table on that day thanks to their interests and their choices. He was proud of himself for listening almost as intently to the boys as he did to Alice, but their stories were all so similar, the three of them, that he may have just processed everything through her version. They each felt a little out of place, as though they should have been born in a big city, maybe even to different parents, though they didn't say so in angry fashion. They fancied themselves too smart to rebel too hard, finding overt displays of mutiny just another version of conformity, and liked to think that they were able to see the broad scheme, able to understand how short childhood and young adulthood really are compared to the rest of a life, barring accident. They even gave themselves credit for acknowledging the possibility of an accident, having witnessed so many bored locals die young with their last words mostly likely being a rebel yell just before hitting that final bend in the road on which they had just felt so invincible.

They continued the exchange long after their plates had been cleared, inhabiting the table without remorse since the lunch rush was over and they weren't staving off any other customers. Twain felt better about his decision. Even if he couldn't manage to capture much of the imagination of the rest of the class, he was glad to know these people were there, these bright young people who did not intend to make him worry less about the apathy of the masses, but who were doing so by their very presence.

He arrived at his mother's house and decided to talk to her about his day in spite of her disconnect with the person she used to be, that person with all the experience working at a college who could relate to his observations, or at least compare them to her own.

She looked at him with a flimsy courtesy, as though Twain was the one who had lost his mind, some crazy person who approached on a subway platform or at a sidewalk café, babbling on about something indecipherable to anyone other than himself. Eventually she decided that the crazy person was harmless, and turned away from him to lean back in her chair and look out the window above the television, at the small section of sky framed by the tips of tree branches bowing in the breeze that was new to her every time she saw it.

He continued to share the details of his day with her, anyway. It felt like praying, talking to his creator, wondering if he was being heard.

He wasn't sure how much of Alice and Company's advice he was going to embrace, but knew he didn't have enough talent for teaching to completely ignore it. After dinner and a few innings of a baseball game that Oscar was watching, Twain concluded the day by working on the script, at something he knew he was good at, or at least would be appreciated for. Something in which he knew where he stood.

Chapter Eight

"Now even the young people around here are getting all sentimental over the old days?" Marina questioned the heavens as she and Twain sat high on a hill overlooking the place they had come from, the elevation shrinking the town down to size while expanding the land around it in spectacular fashion.

They had decided to start their date with wine tasting, so if it wasn't going very well, they could quit before spending any money and anxiety on dinner. They chose a winery that touted itself as having the best view of the valley from its deck, and the boasting was warranted. The town occupied a rather small plot in the distance, its signs of convenience overwhelmed by the swirl of beautiful challenges grounded in the farmlands and pastures. The wines they sampled tasted like afterthoughts, but Twain and Marina found a pleasant-enough Zinfandel that was priced appropriately for the grape, and had bought a bottle to take with them onto the deck, along with some cheese and crackers purchased from the gift rack that cost almost as much as the wine.

"Just one young person," Twain qualified her statement, "and I wouldn't say she was longing for the old days, just offering an explanation for why the students on the satellite campus were better back then."

"See, now there you go," Marina gulped the last sip from her glass and re-filled it. "Who says they were better? Her mother? Grandmother?"

Their date had actually gotten off to a fine start, the mediocre lineup of wines providing a chance to share their tastes and prime them for slightly deeper conversation later on, part of which involved Twain recapping his first week of teaching, and sharing Alice's ideas on the root of the droopiness that reigned over most of the students.

"I believe she said it was her mother."

"Ha!" she raised her glass. "There it is."

"There what is?"

"When people talk about what this place used to be like, they're really talking about what they used to be like. The place wasn't any better back then. It was a dump if you ask me. But the people telling the stories, they were better. They were younger, stronger, hadn't made their mistakes yet, or at least hadn't paid for them. When that girl's mom tells her about how great the students were, she's talking about herself. She doesn't remember the rest. I do."

"Oh, really?" he challenged her.

"You bet I do," she accepted. "I took classes twenty years ago, or maybe a little earlier, whatever...same general time frame. And half the campus was tweaking."

"Half?"

"Maybe a quarter. And then a quarter were drunks, another quarter illiterate, or some combination of the above, and the rest were okay, I guess. They could stay sober most of the time and seemed to know their multiplication tables."

"So what gives you such a sharp recollection?" Twain filled his glass to a level that matched hers. "Why should I trust your assessments over dear old Alice's mother?"

"I was never under any illusions about this town. Oh, my family chatted it up, too. And if you think twenty years ago was paradise, well you should hear about forty years ago, sixty years ago. Heaven on earth. But at some point I just had to ask, then why all the losers? Half the members of my family who made any money got ripped off by the other half. For every happily married cousin I have, there's one more who married a child molester or a meth lab assistant. My grandma prattles on about the great times she had with my grandfather, who I never met since he drank himself to death before he was fifty. She lives in a version of this town that never existed. Pretty much all of them do, and not just in my family."

"Maybe they did have some good times," Twain said, offering a sincere suggestion, but also trying to keep the discussion buoyant.

"I'm sure they did," she agreed. "There were great times, great people. But it's like listening to an oldies station on the radio. All you hear are the best songs from a certain time and it's easy to think 'Wow, they sure had great music back then.' Nobody remembers the one million crappy songs that were written at the same time."

Twain refrained from contributing anything more for now. He just stared out at the valley, which looked even more lovely than when they had arrived, as the late afternoon sun lowered itself into sunset position. She followed his gaze, and they kept quiet for a while.

"It is beautiful," he said.

"It is," she granted. "Always has been. No matter what's going on inside, it's always been gorgeous from a distance."

Twain almost seized the moment to parlay the word 'gorgeous' into a line he could use to kiss her, something that compared her to the view of the valley, but held back. She seemed a little too vulnerable, and he didn't want to feel as though he was taking advantage of the situation.

"Why did you stay?" he asked.

She clearly could not believe he asked that question.

"Why couldn't you take your son with you?" he followed up.

"Free child care," she tempered her disbelief only slightly as she answered. "Plus his father and his family would have sent a bounty hunter after me."

Twain blew air through loose lips. "The father..." he said. "I suppose we have to have that conversation now."

Marina laughed. "Maybe it would be easier to have it over dinner."

"So we're doing okay here?" he gestured back and forth between the two of them.

"You know that French restaurant around the corner from my work?" she asked, not even bothering to answer his question about the status of their date.

"I do."

"Tried it yet?"

"I have not."

"Second best restaurant in town. And no corkage fee." She stuck the cork back into the bottle they shared and hammered it gently with the palm of her hand. "Give me a head start and I'll see you there."

"Why the head start?"

"I'll end up racing you down the hill," she said. "Us natives tend to get weird on the back roads."

She handed him the bottle of wine. "You should probably take this, too."

He accepted it and looked at her with the kind of curiosity that she had affixed on him earlier. "I'm beginning to wonder why everyone is more afraid of the city than the country."

"We've got better sunsets," she said, cueing him to take in the landscape as she left. But he preferred to watch her instead. She turned back as she reached the door and told him to give her five minutes. He waved back and set his sights on the valley only after the door closed behind her.

He focused on committing the sight of it to memory, and the feeling of knowing who would be waiting for him inside that vision once he took his turn going there. He was hoping that if he was attentive enough, he would be able to remember this moment if someday he should be afflicted with the same condition as his mother.

Taking his turn driving down the hill, he could see Marina's point about the temptation to race. Trees lining the road would open up sporadically to reveal yet another stunning outlook, and encountering no other cars inspired fantasies of owning the road. He imagined being seventeen and doing this, with little sense of having much to lose, accompanied by the restlessness that comes standard in those years, and how liberating a drive on such a road would be, and how dangerous, how easy it could turn out to be like a brief light rain that leaves your car dirtier than it was before.

The traffic thickened as he reached the valley floor and made his way into town. The closest parking spot he could find was a couple of blocks away from the restaurant, so he had a few moments to mull over the day thus far as he walked to meet Marina with their half-drunk bottle in hand, swinging in time with his stride.

She was waiting for him at a table in the corner, talking to one of the servers whom she introduced as a fellow member of the town's hospitality sisterhood. He took his seat, and her friend took their table, making a good-humored show of removing the cork and emptying the bottle into their glasses. After she shared the specials and left them to decide, Twain posed a question to Marina:

"Why no country rap?"

"There is country rap."

"Why haven't I heard of it?"

"Because you're old."

"Don't make me say 'so are you.'"

"I didn't say I listened to it, I just know it exists. Was there a point to you asking about this?"

"Do country rappers sing about gritty stuff?"

"From what I've heard, yes. At least more so than most country music."

"That's what I'm getting at," Twain leaned in. "So there's all these people on welfare and drugs and dying too young and having babies too young in the country, just like the city, but no one sings about it. It's all prom queens and football players."

"As I was saying," Marina quipped.

"I'm just picking up where we left off," he said.

"We left off talking about my son's father."

"Right," Twain conceded. "So what was the attraction? A nice car? A bad-boy attitude? A mustache?"

"Allow me to get defensive for a moment," she smiled.

"Please do."

"What kind of area did you grow up in?"

"A college town, not too far from a big city," he obliged.

"So you had, let me see, a cool independent movie house, and one of those bookstores that was hip to hang out in even if you didn't like to read."

"Yes."

"Because it wasn't frowned upon to be smart, it was something you could take pride in, and even pretend to be until you really were."

He nodded.

"And the university had really interesting people show up to share their work, and had a theatre where they'd put on plays, and have operas and Broadway shows come through, and even if you didn't have a Mom who worked there to get you in for free, there was probably a student discount."

"I'm pretty sure there was."

"Oh, and the clubs! I'll bet there were at least a couple of places to catch some music, some bands who were maybe on the verge of being famous, and the ones that did make it big, later on you could talk about how you saw them before anyone else."

"I wasn't that into music."

"But it was there, wasn't it? And you could always hit the big city if you were feeling bigger than your college town. Was there train service of some sort?"

"There was."

"Perfect. Because who doesn't get fed up with their surroundings when you're growing up, right? Who doesn't get frustrated? Now imagine all of that stuff you got bored with wasn't there. No bookstore, indie movie house, clubs, university productions, no outlets to the big city, none of it. Now how restless would you be?"

"I'd like to think I'd find a way to occupy myself."

"We'd all like to think the best of ourselves."

"I get it," he said. "Then along comes...what's his name?"

"Cody."

"Cody. Of course."

"And now you've got something interesting to do. You finally feel like you're a part of the world. You've joined the club. It's not a concert or a good film or a book, but it's the subject of those things."

"It's performance art," Twain said, hoping it sounded as he intended, in full support of her point.

Much to his relief, Marina clearly liked that idea.

"What did you name your son?" he asked her.

"Jesse."

"Is his middle name James?"

"No," she barked.

"Is Cody still around?" he asked.

"Always will be," she nodded. "He's really not such a bad guy. Never quite got over being a restless kid. Still has to spend his free time riding anything with an engine, and needs to know how many women in the room are attracted to him, but he seems to be making peace with holding still a little bit more often as he gets older."

Twain laughed softly to himself.

"What?" she asked.

"He's one step ahead of me," he admitted. "Even when I want to lay low, nobody will let me. Alice and her buddies recommend that I utilize my D-list celebrity stature to win over the class."

"You still have a choice," she said. "You're just using them as an excuse to do what you want to do, anyway."

Twain confessed with a moment of culpable silence.

"It would have been nice if they had all just recognized me on their own," he said at last. "Self-promotion gets exhausting."

"Self-promotion," she grinned. "Sure. That's the reason you're disappointed they didn't recognize you."

Twain looked her straight in the eye and slowly raised the menu the menu in front of his face. She rapped it with her knuckles.

"Seriously, though," she talked to the menu as Twain kept it up. "I agree with the kids. Use what you've got while you still can. Fame fades."

He lowered the menu.

"Only if you let it," he said.

"I was afraid you were going to say 'not as fast as beauty fades.'"

"Why would I say that?"

She looked at him and recognized the authenticity in his words. They spent some more time looking at each other before deciding on two different appetizers and main courses to trade, and a different glass of wine each to replace their bottle from the hilltop. And though the conversation resumed, it was mostly just opinions on the food and wine they shared, as they kept returning to looking at one another. Marina's friend in charge of their table would tease them during her visits, waving her hand between them and asking if they heard anything she was saying. They decided to skip dessert and have it at a nearby wine bar that had an outdoor seating area that was great for people watching, but again they were more content to watch each other. Twain ordered coffee instead of wine with their dessert.

"But we're at a wine bar," Marina reminded him.

"I want to be perfectly aware of my surroundings when I kiss you later on," he said.

She cancelled her wine order and joined him in a cup of coffee and a glass of water.

They held hands and walked a few laps around town before deciding to take his truck back up into the hills and lie in the bed to look above the valley this time, up at the stars. He promised he wouldn't talk shop and start pointing out too many things in the sky, and it was easy to keep that promise because they hardly spoke, each enjoying the feel of the other now that they had enjoyed what they had been seeing.

A vague notion of time grew more crisp as the moon rose to erase most of the stars, and they lifted themselves out of the truck bed groaning in rhythm to the creaks of their joints and muscles, laughing over being a little too old to fool around on hard surfaces.

He drove her back to her car, which was one of the last two still parked on the street by the restaurant. A note was stuck under the windshield wiper from her friend who had waited on their table. Marina read it aloud ("You're a gutter slut"), and they laughed before kissing some more.

"I'd invite you to my place," Twain said, "but I live with my mother."

She smacked him on his arms repeatedly but giggled nonetheless.

"Besides," he added as he defended himself against her punches, "Esther would be appalled."

"I thought Oscar worked the night shift."

"He does. But you'd still be there in the morning."

"Do you want to stop getting hit at some point?"

"If I said no, would you think that's odd?"

"There are no surprises here," she said, ceasing her swings and coming in for another kiss. "Remember, I knew you before I met you."

"You think Mom really knew me that well?"

"Are you really asking me or just making a point?"

"Making a point," he admitted.

"I suppose she knew you as well as anyone can know a person."

"Exactly."

They kissed a while longer until Marina groaned with frustration and pushed away.

"My living situation isn't as tragic, but much more lame," she said.

"Are you in your parents' house too?"

"I have roommates."

"That's okay," he said. "But you should really pledge a sorority when you transfer next year."

"Stop it."

"Can't we put a hanger on the door? What's the signal for when you're gettin' some?"

"After Jesse moved out, my folks said they wouldn't chip in for rent on the house anymore, and I couldn't bear to go back to that dismal apartment complex. It took me so long to mend fences with them and get out of that place the first time around."

"I'm glad I rented a truck," he pulled her back in for more kisses. "It's going to save me a fortune in hotel rooms."

They finally managed to say good night and drive their separate ways. Twain realized it was awfully early to be thinking of such things, but he couldn't help but wonder if the college would have any classes available for him next semester, if it was viable to manage his media work from this location long term, and just how old was Professor Wheatley, anyway? Close to retirement?

As he turned onto Paget's street, his headlights swept across two figures sitting at the fake bus stop. The beams focused on them as the truck straightened out and drove forward in their direction. It was Oscar and his Mom.

Rather than turn into the driveway, he pulled over just before reaching them. Paget glared into the light rather than squint, looking as though she was already dead.

"Sorry, folks," Twain announced as he stepped out of his truck. "The bus isn't running tonight."

"See, Mrs. Henry?" Oscar said.

"Why not?" she asked Twain, who had not prepared a reason.

"Well...there was an accident."

"Oh my," she clutched her chest. "Was it Monty?"

"Mr. Clift?" Twain picked up on the reference. "No, ma'am. No. He already had his accident."

"There you go, Mrs. Henry," Oscar gently grasped her elbow and guided her up off the bench. "Let's stay in this house, like I said. I know the people. They won't mind."

She consented. "As long as they don't mind."

Oscar escorted her down the driveway and looked back at Twain with a grateful expression and a lip-synched "Thank You".

Twain stood outside his truck with the engine still running and watched them all the way. Just before the door closed and he could still see her, he said to himself, "You're right, Mom. She's quite a woman."

When he estimated they had reached her room, he climbed back in and finished pulling into his spot. He noticed some movement in the rearview mirror caught in the red glow of the brake lights. A pair of yellow eyes shone back from just above the ground at the top of the driveway. The body behind the eyes came into focus. It was a cat. He released the brake pedal and doused the light. When he got out of the truck and looked back, it was gone.

"Mr. Darcy?" he asked.

Of all the questions he had recently pondered, this was the least likely to be answered.

So he listened instead.

There was the sound of small footsteps on dried leaves in the bushes. He held still and tried to discern where the noise was coming from, but the clues stopped, and the mystery ended in silence, unsolved.

Chapter Nine

Twain looked into the gallery of unreadable expressions and told himself for at least the tenth time since that day's class started that people fall into a similar face for the most part when they're enjoying a movie or reading a book, a blank stare with an occasional smile or laugh, so he shouldn't assume the students were dissatisfied with him.

The article he was discussing with them had been projected on the screen for several minutes and so far only Alice and her friends had offered any response to the questions he posed. She would also bulge her eyes after each of her contributions as a plea to plug into his relative fame. So in an effort to involve the rest of the class and avoid her glare, he found himself drifting stage left, away from her crew, to search for answers from the silent majority.

Frustrated with the dead air on that side of the room and having to still rely on the stage right gang to carry the load, he decided to wade into the territory Alice and everyone else who knew him had encouraged him to exploit.

"The author of this piece is actually a friend of mine," he said, moving behind the media console to type in a web address. "I recorded a podcast with him not too long ago, and he made a few points in the interview that I think might help explain what he's getting at in the article."

He clicked away from the article and into the section of his website that listed his podcasts, then scrolled to the photograph of him and the author seated at a table positioned behind their respective microphones, smiling at the prospect of talking about the subject at hand. He tapped the photo and it enlarged, with the audio player controls appearing in the lower quarter of the screen.

Twain glanced up and noticed a few eyebrows raised amongst the heretofore slouched. He cued up the interview to the point he thought would be the most relevant, and as they waited for the file to load, a few more took notice.

"You have a blog?" someone said whose voice trailed off before he could trace the source.

"Yes I do," he responded, pleased with the signs of life until he spotted Alice making a whoop-de-doo twirl of her index finger.

He asked her with his eyes what her problem was, but before she could pantomime a reply, the audio kicked in.

His voice boomed over the room in mid-question and he apologized while lowering the main volume on the computer.

"...so we've found two exoplanets in the Kepler 62 system, and three revolving around Gliese 667c. Any chance we could find a star surrounded by four planets capable of sustaining life?"

"I believe so," said the author.

"And what would the conditions have to be?" he followed up.

The author then launched into a stammering and roundabout explanation concerning the temperature of the star they would have to orbit, the heat such a sun would project, how far away from it the Goldilocks Zone could be in relation to the size of the star, and how close together the planets could spin without their gravitational forces flinging each other into oblivion.

The pulse that Twain had detected when he first introduced his website became faint. As his colleague's recorded answer droned on, their smiles in the photograph that hovered above him on screen no longer appeared to be fixed in time, but instead forced and tense the longer they lingered.

He peeked over at Alice while he listened helplessly.

"See?" she mouthed with an agitated flourish.

He exhaled slowly and let his friend's voice finish his thought, as if he'd somehow know if he cut him off, and said feebly as he clicked the Stop button, "Does that help?"

The bite on the end of his line had indeed broken free of the hook. Any excitement, however mild, was gone, and now drifted unseen below the steady current of indifference.

"I guess you had to be there," Twain salvaged a joke from the misbegotten attempt to impress, which garnered a few laughs, and some movement from the fan club corner. It was Alice, raising her hand. He called on her and held his breath.

"Do you think your answer was better when Jimmy Fallon asked you pretty much the same question on *Late Night*?"

His first impulse should have been to rebuke her, given the intent he had brandished over the last couple of weeks to conduct the course without relying on the most non-academic features of his background, but he found himself relieved, somewhat grateful that she forced his hand. And this sudden awareness of his passive aggression kept him from being even more grateful.

"Well..." he sheepishly embraced the moment as he noted a genuine stir in the audience this time: practically every student either traded looks, some from across the room, or leaned forward in their seat, a position they all ended up in eventually by the time he answered.

"The *Late Night* appearance was actually before that podcast interview, but when you're just trying to get a somewhat curious public to understand some information that's fairly common knowledge in astronomical circles, you sometimes switch roles, and ask questions you may already know the answer to out of curiosity as to how your colleagues articulate it, so you can maybe borrow some of their ideas, or more to the point, borrow their metaphors and analogies, how they present it, since the ideas are pretty standard fare by the time they reach me."

"You didn't answer my question," Alice reminded him, looking sunny at achieving the double whammy of coaxing him into using his assets and catching him in an evasive reply. "Whose answer was better, yours or his?"

"Mine was shorter," he said, and the walls shook with laughter.

He took a moment to assess what just happened. It was like discovering a super power: falling from a bridge and realizing you can fly, trying to lift a car out of desperation to save someone and finding you can actually do it, or in his case, stumbling into the awareness of being able to control minds with the power of celebrity.

"Can we see it?" a young woman asked.

"I can't imagine anyone posted it to their YouTube account," he answered. "I was the last guest that night, the one who gets bumped if the A-list star runs long."

"Like you don't have it on your website," Blake called him out from just over Alice's shoulder.

Twain gave him a comically blank stare, then looked down at the floor as the class became a boisterous chorus of voices demanding to see the video. The cacophony turned into a unified cheer as he walked back to the console without a word or gesture, and tapped his way over to the "Media Appearances" section of his site.

A different kind of hush fell upon the room as they watched him sit in the same seat that some of their favorite butts had sat. It was not the disengaged silence of the first few classes. They were captivated.

When it was over and he minimized the window on which the video had played, the list of links to his other appearances was revealed, and the demands started again.

"Put on the Colbert Report one!"

"Let's see the Tonight Show!"

"You're the host of a show, too?"

He held up his arms and asked for silence.

"You can look those up on your own time," he told them. "Meanwhile, did you notice anything similar or perhaps different between our answers to the two-planet question?"

Dozens of hands went up.

"Excellent," he said, nodding with satisfaction at being able to use the moment as motivation rather than a distraction. He called on one of the young men up in the back row who usually spent much of his time making sure his baseball hat was placed on his head the right way.

"So what's Fallon like?" he asked.

"I didn't really talk to him for long," he answered, not wanting to be dismissive after finally connecting with some of the most disconnected students in the class. "Like I said, I was sort of the safety guest, that last one who gets whatever time is left."

"You guys didn't hang out after the show?" his friend chimed in.

"No, I didn't hang out with him."

"Who were the other guests that night?" someone else on the other side of the room called out.

"Hands, please," Twain reminded the room.

The hands sprang back up. He called on a middle-aged woman who caught his eye because it was the first time she didn't look scared to be there.

"Who were the other guests that night?" she repeated the question that had just been hollered out of turn, and got a big laugh, much to her delight.

"One of the stars of that show about doctors, and a celebrity chef, I can't remember her name."

He called on a young man he hadn't even noticed before.

"Have you hung out with some other stars?"

Twain sighed and tried to think of a way to get them back into the solar system.

"I have," he said, an idea coming to him.

"Who?" the anonymous student followed up.

"I'm not telling," Twain grinned.

The class howled, most in good nature, a few exhibiting genuine anger.

"Unless you do well on your quizzes and tests," he explained.

He looked over at Alice and the gang, who were impressed with the impromptu deal he was drawing up.

"Here's how this is going to play out," Twain continued, feeling as though he was scribbling details onto a cocktail napkin late at night with an interested investor in his show or website. "Any time the class pulls an aggregate score of at least eighty percent on a quiz or test, I'll regale you with at least one tale from behind the velvet rope. Though I must stipulate that none of these stories will be lurid in nature, or otherwise impugn those who are referenced. They will, however, be candid moments, unguarded ones, from the lives of people who tend to manage their public image rather carefully."

"Can you at least give us some names?" a young woman asked who had so far spent most of her time in class thinking that nobody noticed she was constantly sending text messages on her phone.

"Yeah," one of the hat boys said from the top of the seating area, "give us a tease."

He started naming names by area, starting with some high profile current and former politicians whom he figured they would know, which elicited some intrigued sounds of recognition, then some athletes, which inspired some more enthusiastic reactions, then some A-list actors whose films he had consulted for, and finally the cast of a reality show he had hosted, which drew the loudest reactions by far with its mix of pop stars and television personalities from the periphery. The conceit of the show, called *Star Chasers*, was that the cast was training for a mission to space, without actually going into space, and had to compete to see who could best handle the exercises they were put through at the Johnson Space Center in Houston. The winner was a former runner-up from one of the singing shows, he couldn't recall which one, but *Star Chasers* was cancelled before the final episode aired.

"Oh yeah," the compulsive text messenger said. "I remember that show. You hosted it?"

"I wasn't on camera very much."

"But you hung out with them?" the other hat boy wanted assurance.

"Had many a lunch and dinner together," he nodded.

"Aw, man," the young man leaned back in his chair and adjusted the hat on his head. "I'm totally studying."

"Please do," Twain encouraged him over the giggles that rippled through the room. "I don't have any kids, so all of you can be the recorders of these stories, the keepers of the flame."

He finally noticed a few students who were clearly disgusted with the direction the class was taking. He was thankful he noticed them, however, as they reminded him of the ratio he was used to, comprising but a smidgeon of the overall attendance and satisfaction rating, while serving as a reminder to get back on course when the material was veering too far off topic.

"But since you only get dessert if you eat your vegetables, let's get back to business."

And it was as if he was back on tour, performing for a crowd who paid hundreds of dollars for their seats, eager to impress and be seen by him. He could barely complete a sentence without someone asking a question, every side comment he made elicited good-natured laughter, and on their way out of class, almost every student said good-bye as they passed en route to the door, while a bevy of the rest hovered around the lectern to ask follow-up questions, even a couple of the overgrown boys who kept their fists in the pockets of their hoodies and embodied an odd combination of listlessness with an inability to hold still. He would have liked to read the reaction of the offbeat kid who asked for a synopsis of *Huckleberry Finn*, but he had already stopped coming to class.

By the time he got through them all, the students in the next class had filled the seats and Twain swept his tote bag off the table just as the following professor entered to spread his materials across it. They passed each other with a nodding hello, and he found Alice waiting for him in the hall. He high-fived her.

"Thank you," he said.

"You would have gotten there eventually," she said.

"We are our own destinies," Twain pronounced. "Doesn't that sound like something someone once said?"

"In Kindergarten they just said to be yourself."

"Which is weird, because in Kindergarten you're years away from being yourself."

"Let's celebrate," she offered. "Did you like that place we went to after the first day of class?"

"Sure," he said. "What about Gavin and Blake?"

She shrugged. "Maybe next time."

Twain knew he should at least hesitate, if not come up with an excuse to pass, but he was enjoying the feeling of being wanted again, having glimpsed a life lacking in it. He was also confident that he was not interested in a romance with her due to his feelings for Marina, and not wanting to become a student-dating cliché in his very first semester of teaching. Of course leading her on wasn't any nobler, but claiming he assumed she was interested in nothing more than a mentorship was a very reasonable excuse. And maybe that was the case, anyway. Maybe he was flattering himself. If so, all the better. And that restaurant served really good burgers.

He tried to keep things academic when they sat down after ordering.

"I had this epiphany today," he said. "When people say they want to give something back, what they really mean is they want to be remembered well."

But Alice wanted clarity.

"So the most recent news item I could find about you dating anyone was from last year."

Twain braced himself. "News item?"

"Gossip is technically news."

"Unsubstantiated."

"Well, then verify. Are you single?"

"I don't think so," he realized it would be presumptuous to call himself and Marina a couple at this point. "We're in the early stages, but it looks promising."

If Alice was at all disappointed, she concealed it with conviction. "Anyone I know?"

"Maybe," Twain thought perhaps she was just curious, and truly had no designs. "You probably know her son."

"Wait," she shook off her expectations. "It's someone local?"

"Marina Landry. She works at the organic restaurant over by the coffee house? I don't know if her son took her last name, or her father's."

"What's his name?"

"Jesse. He graduated this past spring, so I guess he's a little younger than you. Then he moved to L.A. Maybe you don't know him."

She dropped her forearms onto the table. "You have got to be kidding me."

"So...you do know him."

"Jesse Jase is one of the biggest pricks to ever graduate from our high school."

"His last name is Jase?"

"*Cody Jase Team Motocross,*" Alice swept her hand through the air as she said it, as if spreading it on a sign. "That's what it says on the side of his dad's dirt bike trailer."

He could see why Marina didn't give Jesse the middle name James. Jesse James Jase would have been a bit much.

"Well, he moved," Twain found himself growing defensive. "Doesn't that count for something in your Get-Me-Out-Of-Here Theory?"

"No," she held firm. "Because he's not moving to start a new life. He's doing it to hide the fact he's not the golden hick anymore. He'll come back on holiday weekends and tell lies and pretend he's even hotter than he was in high school, when he's really going nowhere faster than anyone else."

"But you don't know his mother," he confirmed.

"I know who his mother decided to have a child with."

"I don't know if 'decided' is the right word," Twain said. "She told me about the circumstances leading up to it."

"Did she tell you that Cody Jase has four kids with three different women?"

"No. She skipped that."

"Which means some idiot had two kids with him. At least she's not that one. I'll give her that much credit. Unless..."

He held up his hand. "I think she would have told me about any other kids."

"Sure. You would have noticed the other name tattooed on her by now."

Twain laughed not at the joke, but in disbelief at just how much shame she carried about where she was from. "So I take it you won't be coming back on holiday weekends after you transfer."

She took a deep breath, appearing to understand she was being a bit harsh on her hometown.

"I like it here," she finally said. "I appreciate it. I appreciate what it did for me. My best friend from elementary school ended up with a couple of baby daddies before she was done with high school. Woke me up."

"So you learned from the situation."

"Big time."

"Then maybe since Marina didn't have any more kids and didn't stick with Cody, she also learned a thing or two."

"She couldn't have figured it out before unleashing Jesse Jase on the world?"

Alice appeared to use him as a point to focus on while she decided what she wanted to say. "First you don't want to share your experiences with the class, now you're foregoing the celebrity dating pool for a local single mother. If you had a fan club and I was a member, I would quite possibly renounce my membership."

Twain enjoyed the way she expressed herself. "I see none of the above includes references to my scientific abilities."

"I figured those were safe enough."

Twain bobbed his head back and forth. "Mm. Maybe."

"Oh, come on. What, you got your degree online?"

"Too long ago for that."

"You didn't major in astronomy," she concocted another possibility. "You majored in broadcasting."

"No, all of my degrees are in Astronomy, in one form or another."

The food arrived and they mixed thanking the server with their observations on how good it looked.

"All of your degrees," Alice lightly mocked his statement as a vehicle to get back into their conversation.

"They didn't come easy," Twain followed her lead as he transferred the lettuce and tomato from the side of the plate to the top of his burger, and squeezed some ketchup on the bun. "I wasn't that good at it. I fell in love with it, but there was a big difference in being interested in the universe and actually learning the mechanics of it. I should have majored in something in the Humanities if I wanted to excel as a student, that's what my talents were really suited for." He paused to take a bite and swallow. "But Astronomy grapples with essentially the same mysteries of life that the Humanities do, only with the added bonus of maybe actually solving them, so I wanted to apply whatever talents I had to this elegant field. And in order to have any street cred in a field with no streets, I needed to fight my way through some degrees. That's why I tried to avoid any cheap tricks in teaching the class. I built my business, and sustain it, on boatloads of self-promotion and a modicum of talent. I wanted to keep the class pure, prove to myself that I could base it on science. But..."

He trailed off and buried himself in another bite.

"You're not glum about what happened today, are you?" she asked. "You seemed so happy after class."

"It was great. It would have been nice to get some self-validation as an astronomer, but it's nice to know that who you are works on some level."

"So why are you telling me all this?" Alice asked.

"There's only so much I want to disappoint you."

"Okay, fine," she shirked eye contact for a short while. "So you're taken."

He had more to share. He wanted to broaden the frame, make it less about him or her or Marina and more about people, how they're not all of one thing or all of another, but really just kind of bizarre.

It would have just sounded preachy to her at this juncture, though, with the time she had available to camouflage her embarrassment running short. So he let it go, and raved about his burger, and they managed to have a civil enough conversation about how many more satellites the earth could afford to launch into its orbit before they became too dense, and if it was possible to reach a point before it came to that where we decided we didn't need any more information.

He drove home carrying a certain amount of pride in being able to diffuse the situation, mainly when it came to keeping his mouth shut when more talking would have been counterproductive, as his instincts tended toward filling discomfort with words, hoping some of them would work.

Referring to his Mom's house as 'home' also made him smile. Using the word felt like more than just the kind of verbal slip that happens when staying at a hotel for an extended stay. It felt true. He was scheduled to record some more voiceover tracks for the film the next day, and in preparing to polish the script some more, wondered how long it would take for people to consider someplace besides earth as home, and what would be involved in arriving at that feeling. Certainly more than air and water, and a definition of 'atmosphere' that went beyond the scientific entry, in light of how much deeper a home exists in the mind than it does in space.

He thought perhaps he would treat Esther and Oscar to dinner and check with them, see how they defined home having spent so much time in other people's houses.

The garage was open when he arrived. Through the back door leading to the yard he saw Oscar looking as though he was coaxing something toward him. When he saw Twain pull in, Oscar straightened and tensed up. Esther's head then popped into the door frame. She rushed out as Twain parked the truck.

"It's my fault, Dr. Henry," she waved her arms as she hustled over to him. "I wasn't paying attention."

"What happened?"

"She's in the backyard. I was folding some laundry on top of the machine and she walked out. We have her."

Twain headed for the door, and to Oscar, who would give him an honest account. Esther seemed to be trying to head him off before he reached them.

"She's just a little startled," she said in an attempt to sound calm in spite of her nerves and being short of breath.

He forged ahead and stood next to Oscar to see things from his perspective. Paget had pinned herself to the back of the house as though escaping from prison, hoping to avoid the spotlights she seemed to imagine were darting back and forth across the wall by standing perfectly still. She was unable to keep her face frozen, however, as it contorted while she hyperventilated.

"I'm sorry," Paget sobbed. "I'm sorry."

And she continued to say so over and over.

Oscar started to explain his take on the situation without Twain having to ask.

"I think in the backyard, without the bus stop, when she forgot she walked outside, she figured out she was in someone's yard instead of a public place. She just doesn't know it's her yard. I'm trying to get her in front, to the bus stop."

"I can't lock the sliding glass door," Esther continued to press her point of view while Paget kept repeating that she was sorry. "Well, I can lock it, but she knows how to unlock it, it's right there in front of her face, and there's no key, so I watch her. But she sneaked past me today. It's my fault. I should get a stick or some pipe and put it in the track of the sliding door. That should do it. It won't happen again."

Twain stepped forward and extended a hand to his Mom.

"Hello," he said. "This is my home."

"I'm sorry," she replied, a bit louder than the previous three dozen times. "Please don't call anyone."

"I won't," he assured her. "It's an honest mistake. Would you like to come inside? You look tired."

His Mom pushed a smile through her tears. "Yes, thank you."

"This way," he gestured to the back door of the garage, then he guided her through the side door into the kitchen. She took mincing, timid steps.

"Would you like something to drink?" he asked as they paused in the kitchen. "It's pretty warm out there today."

"Do you have water?"

"Of course."

"All I need is water."

He grabbed one of the plastic cups that Esther had lined up by the sink and poured his Mom some water from the pitcher in the refrigerator. She gulped it as though just rescued from the desert, and started to gag, but kept the cup to her lips. Twain helped her lower it as she spewed water over their hands.

"Easy," he said gently, while having to firmly extract the cup from her hands. "Easy does it. I'll just give you a little bit at a time."

He poured a small amount, what he estimated she could handle in one sip. She coughed up a little, but then managed to keep the rest down.

"Would you like some more?" he asked her.

She nodded.

They repeated the routine. Twain looked over at the slim opening made available by the side door not shutting completely, and noticed Esther and Oscar peering through it. His Mom thrust her cup forward and he poured her another sip.

"I have a room," he said.

She stopped drinking and glared at him.

"I'm dating Montgomery Clift," she said.

"I didn't mean it that way," he made clear. "You've been through a lot. I thought you might like to rest."

She exhaled and seemed about to cry again. "I would."

He replenished her cup one more time and they walked back to her room. He offered her the recliner and showed her how to use it.

"Stay as long as you wish," he told her.

"I don't want to impose," she replied.

They looked at each other, and for the first time since he answered the call from the doctor, he sensed a relationship. Now he felt like crying, and decided he had better leave before that happened, since it would confuse and upset her again. He smiled as best he could and let her be.

Esther was in the hall fidgeting like an expectant grandmother outside a maternity ward.

"You can decide how you want to introduce yourself," he said to her.

"She remembered that she thinks she's dating Montgomery Clift," she pitched with all the optimism she could muster.

He felt like berating her, asking her what she was trying to accomplish by pretending his Mom wasn't getting worse, but he couldn't imagine an answer that would satisfy him. She was seeing something she wanted to see, something he couldn't understand. And meanwhile, as he still felt a bit of warmth from perceiving a message in his Mom's statement about not wanting to be a burden, he understood he was doing likewise. He was sifting through all of the complexities of a life nearing its end and finding what he wanted to find. He and Esther were in a battle of emotions, so there was no forum in which to settle it: no debate panel to judge the most rational argument, no paralyzing chokehold one could put on the other to force a tap out, it was just them and their beliefs about the unknowable universe inside Paget's head.

So he did not have dinner with Esther and Oscar. He retreated to Marina's restaurant and watched her work. She was too busy to talk much, which was fine. The horny glances and playful comments in passing were perfect. They had a glass of wine after her shift in the empty dining area, and then made out in her car for a while, long enough to steam up the windows. They laughed at what they had done, proud of being able to maintain one of the features of youth worth saving.

Marina wrote "TH + ML" on the windshield with her finger. Twain looked at the world outside through the letters, the small clear space that provided a glimpse at what awaited once the kissing was over.

Chapter Ten

This is not to say I have made any definitive end-of-life decisions regarding my mother, only that in reviewing your heartfelt entries on this page of hers, it's clear that you are a group of people who mean a lot to her, at least as much as she means to you, and when the day that we all must face arrives, I would much prefer to send you all some good old-fashioned invitations to her memorial service by mail, rather than an e-invite or Facebook event. So when time permits, if you would be so kind as to send me your mailing addresses at the e-mail account linked below, I promise not to sell the list to any direct mail marketing companies. Any surge in catalogues filling up your mailbox will be purely coincidental.

Twain sat at the table in front of his laptop and debated whether he should keep the last two sentences as the cursor on the screen hovered over the "post" button. Enough of the women whose contributions he had read exhibited a sense of humor, so he decided to run with the draft on screen, and whittle down the guest list by not inviting anyone who replied in anger.

He was about to scan that day's script one more time for possible re-writes and to rehearse its tempos before heading out the door when Oscar walked in.

"Dr. Henry?"

"Yes, Oscar?"

"Can I talk to you before Esther gets here?"

"Sure. Have a seat."

He obliged, though it seemed he would have preferred to stand.

"Esther and me, we have never lost a patient."

"Okay."

"Our first job, the patient was an old man, he was very nice, but one of his daughters lost her job and decided she wanted to take care of him now that she had the time. The next one, Esther worked by herself. It was a lady in very bad condition, on a feeding tube, so she just needed to be cleaned and changed. When she died, Esther did not feel like she knew her at all."

"I understand, Oscar."

"But I want you to understand that whatever you decide to do when your Mom gets sick again is your choice. Esther has not been very professional about this. I tried to talk to her about it, but..."

"You couldn't quite get up the nerve?"

Oscar smiled. "No."

Twain recalled the moment over dinner when he first arrived that appeared to indicate Paget had perhaps unburdened herself to him, something about his father.

"Did you play this role for Mom, too?"

"What do you mean?"

"The voice of reason, the confidant. Esther is the outgoing one, the flashy one, but when Mom wanted to be real, she talked to you."

Oscar shifted in the chair.

"Your mother did not have much memory left when we started to work here."

"I'm not asking you to claim to be a better nurse than your wife. She's a wonderful woman, does her job very well."

"I don't know anything more than she does, Dr. Henry."

And Twain believed him, or at least believed that if he did know something, he was not about to tell him, not at that point. This made Oscar all the more admirable in Twain's eyes. Keeping a secret for someone who no longer knows what a secret is struck him as true dedication.

Twain was treated to a trivial glimpse of what kind of life his mother might be leading when he arrived at the local television studio to record the latest tracks. His first appointment there had been made within hours of first contacting them, but this one was booked days in advance, so the population of those pursuing careers in media who made sure they were on site that day tripled in size.

Friendly stranger upon friendly stranger greeted him as if they had known one another for years, and some claimed to have met him before at this media expo or that broadcasting symposium, but never a science or astronomy conference. They spoke to him as old friends, using television jargon they assumed he would understand, engaging him in discussions of trying to work their way up, where they had been before this station, what other small-town affiliates they had endured, and where they wanted to go next. There was no talk of news or advertising, and what either of those things meant to them, only about being on camera, as though a lens was the portal to immortality.

He was relieved to finally reach the sound studio, where an unimpressed jack-of-all trades techie was in charge, a local who found a way to stay in the area without working in the hospitality or agriculture industry. He remained seated in the control room behind a glass wall, and all he asked of Twain was to tell him when he was ready.

When he was, and the sound man gave him his cue, Twain spoke his lines into the microphone as if it wasn't there, as though he was having a glass of wine with Marina, trying to impress her.

"A kiss is a great way to end a movie, but it's only the beginning of a relationship. And we know that, so when we feel like we've experienced a kiss worthy of a movie, we don't just say how wonderful it is, but how scary it is. The menial job pays you money, the college degree costs money. Elections are exciting, governing is dull. Maybe the reason our dreams don't come true more often is because they take too long. They don't happen in a moment, and we live for moments, we're good at them.

"Is this why we stopped at the moon? Everything else is so far away: other planets, other galaxies, other life. They would take so long to reach,

the cost would be so high, the work so hard. It seems impossible at this point. But this is only a moment. And we're good at moments.

"It's why we love social networking. Moments are what we share on our pages. We present our lives in a series of them, of highlights mostly, but also of hard times if we think they will portray us as strong, or elicit a string of consoling comments. And maybe this is our destiny when it comes to interacting with other life in the universe, for if we take our bodies out of the equation, the distances are far less out of reach. The unmanned, robotic mission can go to unfathomable lengths without having to drag us along with our needs: food, water, oxygen, physical activity, medical attention, companionship, entertainment. Maybe all of this communicating we do online is the next step in our evolution. We may never meet any of our fellow life forms in person, but we will conduct business with them and form bonds with them nonetheless.

"Will those bonds be any less legitimate if we have not shaken hands, or whatever appendage they may have extending from them? Can you feel anything for someone who only touched two of your senses? And how will we manage our legacies, knowing that the afterlife of our words and expressions is no longer the exclusive domain of artists and public figures, and will continue to interact with the living after we're gone? What we lose in spontaneity, do we gain in aspirations? Will we strive to leave a greater legacy? Will it not be a legacy so much as an image? Something we construct that may not be an accurate representation of ourselves? Is that what life on the other planets will do, too? Will they seem so much better than us, tap into our insecurities, and when some of us finally reach their planet, will it have been stripped of life, decimated by an ugly streak they never shared with us?

"Perhaps this need to craft superior versions of ourselves can lift us all up, our deceitfulness ironically turning out to be a force for good. Maybe our vanity will force our hand, inspire us to live up to the façade we created just in case our new friends are able to visit and see what's behind our pages.

"Some have said that we never really grow out of the playground, that adulthood is high school with money. Maybe the universe is the same way. Maybe for all of its vastness, it's just as small as we are."

Twain held a lengthy pause before backing away from the microphone, wishing he was holding the mic in his hand so he could triumphantly drop it on the floor.

"Is that it?" the sound man asked over the intercom.

"Yes," said Twain, feeling too inflated to read anything into the question. "For now, at least. I'm still working on the finale."

"I thought this was an educational film on space exploration."

"It is."

"Where's all the information on space exploration?"

"I already recorded those parts with some other guy a few weeks ago. These are the parts designed to get the kids wondering."

The sound man shrugged.

"Just send it to the producers," Twain snapped. "They'll love it."

He could see that the sound man was doing so. Twain stood his ground for a couple of long minutes. Just when he was about to panic, thinking that maybe none of them were in a position to receive the call and listen to the track, his phone vibrated in his pocket. The text message read "Love it!" He thrust the screen of his phone at the man behind the glass and pointed to it on his way out.

The sound man raised one thumb in the air which may as well have been a middle finger.

Later, in joining Marina for a late lunch at the deli down the street from the restaurant before her shift, Twain was still bothered enough by the sound man's insouciance to complain that people aren't interested in enough of what life has to offer.

"We live in this wonderful age where we can easily learn about anything," he built on his point, "but all we do is learn everything about one thing."

"What's wrong with that?" she asked.

"Nothing, in and of itself. But why be so flippant about all the other things?"

"So those recommendations we get when we buy something online," she played off him, "they should be based on the opposite of what we just bought."

"Yes," Twain ran with her idea. "Instead of saying 'people who bought this also bought this,' it should say, 'people who bought this would be much more well-rounded if they bought this.'"

"Wow," Marina teased him. "I'll bet we could start a business with that model and be bankrupt within six months."

"You think we could make it six months?" he went along with her.

"Maybe. What do you do when a parent buys some innocent book or a video for their kid? Suggest *Lolita,* something like that?"

"I was thinking some Sylvia Plath, depending on how bright and shiny the children's book is. We'd have a lightness versus darkness algorithm."

"We can use your website for a test run," she suggested. "When they buy copies of your show, or a book. Wait...did you write a book?"

"Yes," he admitted. "It's like an *Astronomy for Dummies*, but there was already one of those, so we didn't use the word 'dummies.'"

"So when they buy one of the things on your site," she continued, "you can recommend some intelligent design books, or creationist videos."

"Okay," he said. "I get it. It's a crappy idea."

"I like what you wrote on your Mom's page this morning," she changed the subject. "That was a good idea."

"Thank you. I was afraid it might be too glib."

"It was fine. Even the sound man would have liked it."

"I'm sure he'd give me a thumbs-up."

"Did you get my mailing address?"

"I haven't checked the account yet," he said. "But what makes you think you're invited?"

She portrayed shock and offense at his jab, and they ceased fire to enjoy their sandwiches for a little while, having ordered two different specialties and traded halves.

"Can I see her?" she asked, breaking the silence in more deafening fashion than if she had screamed for no reason.

He gauged her sincerity, deemed it legitimate, then reminded her she had to work.

"I can call a couple of people scheduled for closing shifts tonight," she said. "They'll trade with me in a heartbeat, and I can go in later."

"It's not what you think," Twain said.

"And what do I think?"

"That she'll just call you by some other name, or say something off the wall that you try not to laugh at, like she's a toddler."

Now she looked seriously hurt.

"Why would I think that?"

"Because that's the way it's portrayed most of the time."

"Do you think I'm that stupid?"

"I think you got to know her enough and love her enough that you may want to believe it," he said.

Marina didn't deny it as she stared at her lunch.

"When was the last time you saw her?" Twain asked.

"I don't know. When did you hire the nurses?"

"Almost two years ago."

"Right around then."

Twain sighed and tried to think of a way to fend off her request.

"There's no adjustment period," he said.

"What do you mean?"

"You've probably heard of those studies that show how when someone undergoes some trauma, paralyzed in an accident for example, or a cancer diagnosis, the death of a spouse, they go through a period of grief, of course, when they're not themselves. But then in about a year they pretty much get back to being who they were. If they were an upbeat person, they get there again, wheelchair or chemotherapy, widowed, whatever the case may be. But Mom can't get there. She can't go back to being the person she was, since that's the very thing that's been taken. You wouldn't be visiting her. You'd be visiting a figment of her."

Twain could tell his explanations for denying her a visit were not helping her feel any less offended, so he spun the rationale back on himself.

"I don't think I'd be handling the situation very well if it weren't for being able to hire such great help," he said. "My daily visits are hard enough, and I should be used to them by now."

"See?" she finally responded. "You couldn't find nurses like that around here twenty years ago."

Twain swooped in on the opening to bend the conversation.

"You couldn't find any retired people around here twenty years ago."

"A equals B."

"But then I imagine a lot of the locals are bitter about not being able to afford that kind of care for their families," he added. "And understandably so."

"If any of the fairy tales about the past were true," she said, "then they shouldn't need it. The family members and the neighbors would all be pitching in to help."

"I've got it," Twain indicated that the next big idea was here. "This is bigger than our website that suggests things you may not want to hear."

"Yes?" Marina still seemed scorned over being denied access to Paget, but was trying to be a good sport.

"Outsourcing elder care," he unfurled his announcement. "A lot of people are opting to go overseas to have surgery done, medical tourism I think they call it, so why not ship your parents or grandparents overseas for convalescent care? End of life tourism. With the money you save, you can visit them in whatever exotic locale you've chosen."

"Might as well," she agreed. "They're just as isolated at home, it seems."

Twain slumped. She would not be diverted.

"You really want to see her," he confirmed.

Marina nodded.

"Why today?"

"How many todays are left?"

"Fine. Call someone."

The first call she made bought her the time. She knew the way to Paget's house, so after they hurried the last few bites of their sandwiches, they agreed to meet there.

Twain was just getting out of his truck when Marina arrived.

There were no signs of activity when they walked through the front door.

"It's best not to call out anyone's name," Twain noted softly. "Not with Mom being so confused."

Marina looked as though she thought maybe Twain was trying to make her feel guilty about inviting herself for the visit. She remained standing in the entryway and living room area while Twain took a lap through the dining area into the kitchen to look for Esther, or perhaps Oscar if he had arrived a bit early. He peaked through the windows to see if anyone was outside, then rejoined Marina.

"They must be in Mom's room," he said.

Now Marina appeared nervous at the prospect of finally seeing her old friend. She didn't say anything, just nodded.

Twain started toward the hallway when Esther exited from the opposite direction, holding an empty bowl with a spoon. She caught her breath and jumped, the spoon rattling in the bowl.

"Oh my God, Dr. Twain," she put her free hand to her chest. "You scared me."

"Sorry, Esther," he said. "I wasn't sure what you had going on with Mom, so I didn't want to make any noise."

"I was just feeding her," she smiled.

Twain paused, wondering if in fact Mom could no longer feed herself. He was about to ask, but noticed Marina and Esther looking at each other, waiting for an introduction.

"This is Marina," Twain turned to his guest. "She's a good friend of Mom's. They used to volunteer for the Food Bank together."

"Pleased to meet you," Esther extended her hand.

"The pleasure's all mine," Marina shook it. "I've heard all about the wonderful care you're providing for Paget."

"Oh, thank you," Esther blushed. "But she's such a good patient. It's not hard."

"Marina was hoping to visit Mom today," Twain revealed.

Esther shifted her stance. "I see."

"Is it a bad time?" Marina asked.

"She might be asleep," Esther said. "It was hard for her to eat. She's having trouble swallowing."

"Really?" Twain was intrigued to learn the answer to the question he had wanted to ask earlier.

Esther became jittery. "It happens sometimes to older people."

Now Twain wanted to see his Mom even more than Marina did.

"We'll be very quiet," he said, and took Marina's hand.

"I don't know," Esther hedged.

"It'll just be a moment," Twain assured her. "Marina's due at work pretty soon."

But it was clear that Marina was also having doubts at this point.

"Come on," he squeezed her hand. "It's not like she's in the attic."

He wondered if the short walk down the hall seemed as long to her as it did to him. When they reached the door he turned the knob with barely a noise, then nudged forward. Upon entering the room he froze. His Mom was lying on her back with her head turned in his direction. She was staring at him, but may have been sleeping with her eyes open. He was trying to figure out if that was the case when he heard Marina gasp.

She was just putting her hand up to her mouth when he glanced over at her, catching herself making noise, but tears had already started to trickle down to her jaw, and she was not going be able to stop herself from crying even harder.

"Go outside," he whispered.

"I'm sorry," she gasped, and did as he said.

Twain looked back to see if the intrusion had any effect on Paget. She wore the same vast glare, and if her chest hadn't been heaving, he would have mistaken her for dead. He checked to see if she would blink, and after what seemed to be almost a minute, she did. It startled him, and he shivered. Her mouth moved, appearing to strain to form a couple of words that he could not make out.

When she held still once more, and her eyes went back to looking at nothing and everything, in the spot he happened to occupy, he decided to leave too.

He found Marina in the driveway.

"You said to go outside," she said, still calming herself down.

"I just meant out of the room."

"I heard Esther in the kitchen and didn't want to disturb her."

"Just as well," Twain said. "She'd be upset if she saw how upset you were."

"That's sweet," Marina sniffed.

"Well…" Twain cocked his head. "it's more because she's convinced I'm compiling evidence to let Mom go. She may think I brought you here to help my case."

Marina looked down at the ground.

"I admit it," she said. "I had planned on suggesting we take her for a drive, get her out of the house for a while, maybe out to the farms we used to visit. Like that would help."

"It was a nice thought."

"Like a Coldplay song would come on the radio as we were out on a country road, or U2, and she would be overcome with the scenery and the movement and stick her head out the window, spread her arms, and feel revived or something."

She looked from the ground up to the sky.

"What an idiot," she told herself aloud.

Twain put a hand on her arm. "I love that she means that much to you. I think it's great."

That seemed to help a bit, but Marina wasn't quite ready to stop the self-admonishment. He lowered his arm back down to his side as it became clear she wasn't going to follow it into an embrace.

"It would be like a kidnapping," she carried on. "As if someone we'd never met before drove up to us right now and told us they wanted to take us for a ride out in the country. She probably would have jumped out of the car at a red light or a stop sign. I've heard about that happening. Some poor old person darts out the passenger door and by the time the driver, the son or daughter, can pull over safely to get out and look for them, they're lost in the crowd."

"Every situation is like that," he tried to console her by expanding on her point. "Aside from whatever's going on inside her head, her life is nothing but strangers offering her things. She handled it for a while, the strangers were pleasant enough, but it's wearing on her, and now she's just scared all the time. You know when you're stressed, and it's a terrible feeling, but you have the ability to understand that it will pass? She can't do that anymore. She's always in a stressed-out moment that never reaches the point where she can comfort herself that it won't last forever. It's the dark side of that old expression about living for the moment."

"Her eyes," she reflected. "Is that what the universe is like?"

He wasn't sure what she was asking.

"Cold, unfeeling," she explained. "You look to it searching for signs of life, and it just stares back. Not even stares, just…is."

"I think she was sleeping."

"Come on, Twain," she snarled. "I'm freaking out here."

"Okay, sorry. Look…" he searched for a response that could appease her without compromising his views, which he thought would be the same as lying to her. "As far as comparing the two, I'll give you this much: neither one asks 'why?' But Mom forgot how to ask, and the universe never knew."

"So it is just a big void."

"It's a bunch of hydrogen," he laid bare, "bumping into other elements. It's favorite one is carbon, and they connect and create things. They make places, and sometimes even end up with some life to live on those places."

He reached out to her again.

"I can't say why it does what it does, Marina. Only how."

She came in this time, and welcomed his arms around her.

"Thank you for the chance," she whispered.

"Thank you for caring," he answered.

They held onto each other a while longer before she groaned about having to go to work. She climbed into her car and lowered the window.

"Are you stopping by later?"

"I don't know," he fudged. "It's a school night."

"Nerd," she cracked.

"Townie," he cracked back.

She recovered some of her smile as she backed up and drove off with a wave.

Twain stood and enjoyed a perfect autumn late afternoon, long enough for Esther to open the front door and ask him if everything was okay.

"Just fine," he called back, still focused on the sharp dark red lines and soft yellow backgrounds of the trees lining the driveway and street. "Getting a good look before the leaves start falling off."

"Are you staying for dinner? We could eat outside."

Twain turned to her. "That sounds lovely. I'll treat."

"No," she gave a single flap of her hands. "I have lots of extra food we need to use. Let me cook."

"Okay. Thank you."

"You still paid for it," she shrugged, then closed the door.

Chapter Eleven

The first quiz was a disaster. It was probably more of an exam than a quiz, given its length, but Twain referred to it as a quiz to make it sound less intimidating. He also designed it to be rather easy, focusing strictly on the planets and their characteristics. He wondered what was going to happen when the next sections came along, about the many moons that revolved around the different planets, about the comets, asteroids, and meteors that breeched the boundaries of the system, and about how it all came to pass, how the celestial bodies they had studied all semester reached the point at which they now observed them. He had anticipated those units would be more challenging, so this first one was supposed to boost their confidence. Instead, Alice and her friends were part of a small handful that earned at least a ninety, while the rest scored poorly enough to pull the median well below eighty. There would be no gossip presented.

The disappointment he felt had nothing to do with being denied an opportunity to preen over his brushes with people more famous than he was, for what he had really been preening about, at least inwardly, was his teaching, thinking he had broken through his insecurities about it. He had therefore been cutting himself more and more slack about dangling bribes of shallow anecdotes in front of the students.

But now a gulf opened between how much he thought they were absorbing and how much they actually were.

And while he was sitting in the faculty conference room by himself at the head of a lengthy table, still absorbing the blow and devising a way to deliver the news to the class, he received a call that was identified as being from the college, the institution he just discovered he was letting down so badly. It was as though they somehow knew. So out of unfounded fear, he didn't take the call.

When the voicemail notification flashed onto the screen, he checked it and heard Professor Wheatley's voice, his tone matching the expression he wore at the interview. He sounded as though evaluating Twain was the last thing he wanted to do, but was saddled with the obligation. He wanted to set up their pre-evaluation meeting, and conduct it on or near the main campus, since he was going to have to come to the satellite campus to observe the class. Twain stared across the tabletop for a while before deciding to call back. As dreary as he felt, he still maintained his dislike of uncompleted tasks hanging over him.

He figured if Wheatley was still in his office, he would pick up since the desk phones had no caller ID screens. It also came as no surprise that when he did answer, there was a lilt in his voice that communicated how much he wished he could have screened the call.

After they had set up a lunch meeting for the following afternoon, Twain asked, "Is there a place you like to go off campus? My treat. I don't know anyplace other than the airport snack bar."

Wheatley named a place and provided the address, but insisted that he pay his own way.

"But if I don't bribe you, how am I going to get a good evaluation?" Twain only half-joked.

The professor must have picked up on a mordant undertone in Twain's voice, as he suddenly sounded attentive.

"Not quite what you thought it would be?"

Twain paused, debating how much he should divulge. His distress was overwhelming, however, and nudged him toward a confession, so great was his need to talk to someone who could commiserate, and maybe even help.

"At first, no, it wasn't what I thought," he admitted. "Then I thought I had it figured out, and now I'm back to feeling clueless."

He thought he heard Wheatley take in a long, quiet breath of satisfaction before he said, "I can't tell you how glad I am to hear that."

Twain was about to lash out and ask why he had such a problem with him, but Wheatley continued before Twain could find a balance between his feelings and how he wanted to articulate them.

"I'm relieved to know that you care," the professor made clear.

The mental scribbling was deleted, and Twain was left speechless for an entirely different reason, his impulse sapped, what he thought he knew extinguished.

"What is it that surprises you the most?" Wheatley asked.

Twain mulled over the possibilities, disregarding one of them out loud in the process.

"It's not the lack of motivation," he said. "I think I stumbled upon a way to address that. Though you probably won't like it."

"Something about using stories from the celebrity circuit?"

"I did so reluctantly," he asserted.

"Reluctantly?"

Twain sighed. "Nobody understands how much I wanted to avoid that."

"Well what would you think about you if you weren't you?"

Wheatley's table-turning triggered a realization.

"It's the discrepancy," Twain decided. "How they see something and how I see it. And it's not even a matter of me trying to teach something I'm really good at and not understanding why others can't get it. I honestly struggled as a student. I thought I could relate. But I can't. I can't get inside their heads."

Apparently a fan of studied pauses, Wheatley engaged in another one.

"I'm going to bring you something to our lunch meeting tomorrow," he finally said. "And I recommend a very light breakfast. They feed you well at this place."

The portions did indeed look generous as the next day Twain passed by some tables en route to his temporary mentor.

Wheatley was seated near one of the windows that were bordered by green and white checkered curtains, the same material that held together the dried flower arrangements hanging on the walls. A short stack of papers sat on the table next to his place setting.

They exchanged greetings and when they sat back down, Wheatley got down to business.

"You *were* a good student," he insisted.

"Excuse me?"

"On the phone you said you weren't a good student, and therefore thought you could be of like mind with the people in your class."

"I admit an embarrassing truth about my past and now you're going to argue with me about it?"

"You knew how to study," Wheatley explained. "You knew how to play the game. They don't."

"They...the students in my class?"

"Well, the ones struggling. Their lives are about forgetting, about not taking their work home with them, trying to ignore how great the odds are stacked against them, pretending their pasts didn't happen in order to imagine a better future. Then we ask them to remember things, analyze them, face facts and store them and refer to the past to understand the future."

He lifted the thin pile of papers. "My wife works in the Academic Support Department. She teaches some short courses on study skills, leads some workshops in the Student Success Center. There's this essay she assigns, more like a paragraph. They're supposed to give an honest assessment of their situation, whether their lives are in a place that allows them to go to college, if they're going to have the time to devote to it, what kind of obstacles may get in the way."

He handed them to Twain. "Every time she assigns it, I like to make some copies of what they turn in and read through them to remind myself of what's going on out there in my classroom, to keep from getting too elitist and condescending. Since you wondered what was going on inside their heads, I thought you might like to read the latest batch."

"Thank you," Twain looked them over, running his thumb up one of the corners of the stack and letting the individual pages fall in sequence, as though the words were pictures that would animate whatever answer they could offer. "So how do you help them toggle between the two worlds?"

Wheatley smiled. "I'm curious what you come up with."

Twain leaned back in his chair and looked up at the ceiling, playfully muttering, "Some mentor."

The professor's smile proceeded into a laugh, and after claiming he would naturally steal any worthwhile techniques Twain developed, they spent the rest of their time discussing anything but astronomy, focusing instead on movies and sports, marveling at the country-sized portions they managed to finish, which led to an exchange of restaurant recommendations for the different corners of the district they inhabited, until Wheatley had to excuse himself in order to make it back to campus in time for his late afternoon class. They set up a date for him to observe Twain's class before exiting.

"Thank you for not living up to my expectations," Wheatley said while they shook hands outside the door.

"Likewise," Twain grinned.

"That bad?"

"I thought I represented everything you hated."

Wheatley shook his head. "Sorry. It wasn't personal. It's the same concern I've had with just about any new hire. We tend to think if someone knows their subject, they can teach it. But it's not what you expect, and even when you start to understand it, you never stop adjusting."

As they walked their separate ways, Wheatley toward the main campus and Twain to the parking lot by the side of the restaurant, Wheatley said something that Twain couldn't quite make out. He stopped and turned around, and Wheatley repeated it.

"Enjoy the essays!"

The spelling and grammar posed some distractions, but not enough to undermine their authority, since the recurring theme was how far removed the authors felt from being able to complete a semester's worth of classes, much less a degree.

Twain moved from the table by the kitchen to the table in the backyard and told Esther he was working. He wanted to be alone with the sentences.

I want respect of my children, wrote one man. *They say I love you, but is hard to believe when I work. My hands are always too hot or too cold at work. My gloves are wet of fog or rain in winter, and wet of sweat in summer. I take off my gloves at lunch and my hands feel better but then I go back to work. My job pays money so I go to college, but my job too get in my way. I want my hands free, all the time free. I want to feel respect when my kids say I love you. I hope is not too late.*

A younger woman wrote, *If my husband find out I go to college, I am dead. I tell all people that help me here, do not call me. I ask to send text message then, I delete message from here after I read. My husband is mad every day, mad at everything. There is no happy in house like us. If he is mad then I only be sad, or mad too. And if to get out I need better job. I pretend to go to work in days I go to college. I have no family. I have some chance if my husband think I go to work always.*

An articulate young man wrote his essay during one of his more lucid days, apparently.

Some days I wear clean clothes, even a tie, and ride my bike to work or to school. Other days I put on the shorts I never get around to washing, and my ugly purple t-shirt with the light green letters that I won in a race on the last day of sixth grade, and I walk. I don't know where I'm walking, I just walk. Some days I understand what people are saying. Other days are just noise. I see people talking to me, but it doesn't mean anything. The sound of dogs barking is much louder than they are, and makes more sense. They are right in front of me, telling me why I may lose my job, why I am failing a class, but only the barking reaches my ears. Even if there are no dogs nearby. It is the sound of a recording of dogs barking, and the speed is too slow or too fast, the sound quality is terrible. It's just noise. I can barely hear what the dogs are saying. But I look and it is a person. Still there, still trying to help me understand. I look down at my t-shirt that reminds me of when I won something, when people cheered for me. Nobody cheers for me when I wear clean clothes, and I can't remember that race in sixth grade unless I'm looking at my ugly t-shirt.

The most traditionally erudite piece was by a single mother who clearly could have pursued a degree, possibly several, under difference circumstances. He read it several times.

I've heard from more than one source that parenting becomes more satisfying once you're done with it, she opened. *When you can look back and realize you did it, maybe even successfully. So in other words, it's pretty much the opposite of that old expression about it not being the destination, but the journey. And I'll buy that. Not because the journey is all that hard. I'm not asking for pity here. I do not want to contribute to the single mother narrative of a woman wronged, or struggling. The single mother section is dominated by that story. No, for me at least, it's not a hard journey in the sense that I had a colicky baby or my kid has severe ADHD or lights fires in vacant lots. I've been lucky enough to avoid major heartaches so far. What I wasn't expecting is how tedious it can be. The stories I remember hearing about motherhood were either scary or heartwarming. They were the highlights or lowlights. Nobody told me stories about the other 23 hours of the day, about the hours of wandering around playgrounds like a security guard making sure your child doesn't do anything that leads to a hospital room or a lawsuit, the hours of standing in public bathroom stalls waiting for them to pass a stool they insist is on the way, the hours of not being able to answer 450 of the 500 questions they ask each day as intelligently as you'd like to. And that's what concerns me about going to college at the same time. It's also about delayed gratification. It's another destination with a dull journey. It's another layer of patience I'm not sure I have. My son's father didn't have it. He wanted everything now. He was going to make a fortune in one dramatic move. Then another. And another. Then he ran out of moves, and had a hard time moving on. Not in a suicidal, depressing way. More like in an annoying, please shut up about it way. I thought having a child would help him put everything else in the past. I was an idiot. So with the ideal stereotype of the perfect family out of reach, I had a choice of living one of two other clichés, the loveless marriage or the single mother. I knew if I chose the latter, I would in fact be going it alone, because based on how he handled the failure of his bad investments, I assumed correctly that he would be terrible at handling a divorce. I went with it, though, figuring he would be better as an absent father than a present one who moped and lied about his past. I'll never know for sure if it was easier not having him around. The fact he rarely ever checks up on us gives me a pretty good indication. But I actually feel pretty good about the way I'm raising my boy. My mom tells me I've become a better person thanks to being a parent. And I feel like it's the best thing that's ever happened to me. But I wonder what my son is getting out of the deal. Am I the best thing that will ever happen to him? Have I just been using him to feel better about myself? Sometimes I feel like parenting is selfish, like all I really want to do is see how I stack up against other parents, or leave behind some sort of legacy since I can't write songs or direct films. And that haunts me more than any of the time I have to spend away from my son thanks to work or school, more than bringing him to birthday parties surrounded by dads or dropping him off at a two-parent household to play. Is he just the final judge that I need to validate my choice? Is all of this just so that someday he can tell me I did a great job? Sure, I've discovered I have more perseverance than I ever imagined, that I would do anything for my son, even go to college, which I probably would not have done otherwise. But what's unique about that? The vast majority of parents do the same, feel the same. It's what you're supposed to do. Why do I want so much credit for it? I'm afraid it's because I'm insecure, because I'll never quite be sure if I should have done this.*

Each time he read the last line, Twain wondered if she was referring to having a baby, or registering for college.

He recalled the photo albums his Mom had put together throughout his childhood, before he had moved out on his own to start his unpredictable, unexpected life, and before photographs went digital. He didn't necessarily want to see pictures of himself, he wanted to see pictures of her, and there were none on her website.

The last time he had seen the albums was several years before, during his Mom's first Christmas in her new house. She had pulled them out from a drawer in the coffee table to share with Twain's date, a staff writer for National Geographic with whom he had lost touch after the holiday season.

They weren't in the first drawer of the coffee table he burrowed through, but they were stacked to the brim of the second, making it difficult to slide open. He extracted the one off the top and sat back on the couch. The pages needed to be unstuck from one other with each turn and a loud crinkle that sounded like cellophane being unwrapped from around a plate of homemade cookies. As an old, familiar sequence of images surfaced, he was reminded of his Mom's philosophy about why she preferred still pictures over moving ones, claiming that video ruined the memories it recorded with its unflinching accuracy, leaving no space for the re-writes that come to characterize photographs. "Videos are non-fiction," she would say. "Pictures are fictional non-fiction."

At least that's how he remembered it. Maybe she said "non-fictional fiction."

And the pages did read like a book he had read many times before. The plot offered no surprises, but new discoveries were generated in some of the moments through a lens that had grown thicker with each reading.

There was the picture of him at around four years old in a petting zoo, braying back at an old sheep that had been asking for food. Twain was bent at the waist, hands on his knees, bracing himself in order to bellow so loudly. The sheep looked unfazed, and his Mom was laughing. Her friend from the Financial Aid Office had taken the picture. He was an older gay man who had lost his partner to AIDS, and would accompany them on many of their weekend day trips for a while. Twain wondered whatever happened to him. He had been such an integral part of their lives for a few years, then he wasn't. As far as Twain knew, there had been no falling out with his Mom, no new love in his life. Around the time Twain reached middle school, their old friend retired. His Mom went to the party, and mentioned the next day that he was moving to Tucson and that he said to say good-bye.

Twain never wondered before what the reasons may have been because he was a kid, then he was a teenager, then a young man establishing his career. And now he even found himself wondering about his Mom's laughter in the picture. He always assumed it was genuine, and she indeed got a kick out of the picture every time she looked at it, but in the moment, was it more of a nervous reaction? That noise coming out of him must have been excruciating. She did look a little tense, now that he was studying her in the scene more closely than he ever had before, and wasn't swayed by her jolly reaction as a fellow reader.

As the pages flopped past, he realized his Mom wasn't pictured in many of these photographs, either. More than her website, but not much more. They were mostly of him, he had just never noticed.

There he was holding that squash racquet his Mom had promised to buy him if he placed at least third in a tournament. He also held the third place trophy that led to the purchase of the racquet which he never ended up using. The mission had been accomplished. She was concerned that he was becoming too much of a bookworm, and encouraged him to get involved in a sport. Even though he enjoyed watching the more conventional sports like baseball and basketball, and almost took up golf because a couple of his friends were good at it, he chose squash because the competition would not be as heavy, and he could rise through the local ranks and appear to be adhering to his Mom's wishes beyond her expectations.

He thought back on how intent and adept he was at playing the angles, and how exhausting that must have been for her. Now as he looked at this picture he could almost hear her sighing as she took it.

When it started to dawn on him that there weren't going to be as many photographs of her as he had hoped, there was one he remembered of the two of them that he knew was somewhere in the collection, and by the third album he finally came across it.

He liked it because they didn't know their picture was being taken. It was a candid shot from a wedding reception, pulled from a pile of leftovers by the bride and offered to his Mom several months later. The bride was a young faculty member who had invited everyone in the department, which inspired a running joke that if she had just waited until she got tenure, she could have cut the guest list in half.

Twain held the album higher to guide some more light onto the page. He and Paget were seated at a table that had been cleared of plates, only coffee cups and saucers and half-filled water glasses remained. He was a little over sixteen, as he remembered being very proud of having driven to the wedding, with his Mom in the backseat and an ancient Professor of Classics riding shotgun. He served as a father figure of sorts to Paget, and about nine other people on campus who came from fractured households. So great were the demands on him to fill a variety of voids that he would often issue a lighthearted disclaimer that certain pieces of sage advice may be recycled verbatim from other conversations with similarly troubled colleagues.

But it was just the two of them in the picture, Twain and his Mom, having enjoyed a meal and the company of some interesting people, and now they were talking about something that may have revealed its own level of profundity had it been transcribed or recorded, but it wasn't. Only this soundless moment remained.

Whatever it was they spoke of, they were taking each other seriously. Twain appeared to be making a point, and his Mom was ready to interject or add something to it. They were dressed up for the event, she in a dress and he in a coat and tie, but by then they had grown a bit disheveled. Between their business attire, the coffee cups, and the pose in which they had been captured, Twain thought they looked like a couple of diplomats negotiating a treaty, or board members hashing out the details of a contract. He thought this in spite of how young he was in the photograph, because as he looked at it, he remembered how good she was at making him feel like he had a voice worth hearing. The idea he was expressing at that instant could very well have been juvenile and malformed, the product of a teenager who had just read some Camus for the first time, but his Mom was listening, and she was about to respond thoughtfully.

He closed the album. No other pictures were necessary.

Normally he found his Mom's couch too frothy, the cushions prone to swallowing up whomever sat in it. But for the moment he appreciated the feeling of sinking into its embrace, so deeply he thought maybe Esther wouldn't see him as she entered from the hallway.

"Oh, Dr. Henry," she noticed. "I never see you in that couch."

"Just taking a break from work."

"Good for you. Your Mom is ready for dinner. Can I get you anything?"

"No," he fought his way out of the puffy crevice. "But would you mind if I brought her dinner?"

"Okay," she hesitated. "But remember she needs to be fed. She's not swallowing her food very good."

"That's fine. I'll do it."

He caught up with her in the kitchen as she was adding a baby food jar of strained carrots into the bowl of mashed potatoes. She was visibly embarrassed that he had entered before she was able to complete the mixture.

"Just until she gets better," she explained. "Whole vegetables are too much for her right now."

"I understand."

She looked at the bowl for a few seconds, then pierced a spoon into the heap. When she handed it to Twain, she was near tears.

"Thank you," he said.

She nodded and swiped the baby food jar on her way to the sink, where she tried to look busy.

Twain found his Mom sitting in bed propped up by several pillows. Oscar had discovered her on the floor in front of the recliner a couple of times at night, with the chair extended to the maximum upright position designed to help someone get out of it. He concluded that she was having trouble with the recliner's control panel, and that it would be safest to move her to the bed.

His Mom looked at him as he entered, and she noticed the bowl. Her expression was no longer courteous, nor skittish. She had become weary. Twain could tell there was no need to concoct a story as to who he was or what he was doing in the room. Being bed-ridden seemed to provide a steady reminder for her that she was in some way institutionalized, though obviously not in a hospital, and she had been absorbed by the monotony. She was a prisoner at feeding time. Whoever delivered the meal was just doing their job, working a shift.

He nodded and held up the bowl, then pulled over a stool that Esther and Oscar kept in the room for just such purposes. She dutifully ate, exhibiting none of the relish that had characterized her meals just a few days earlier. The first spoonful went down easily, but the second required some coaching. She gagged and when her bite came back up, she wasn't sure what to do with it. Twain held a napkin under her chin and tried to keep her calm, suggesting she hold her breath or breathe through her nose until she redirected her food down the other pipe.

The pattern maintained itself to the bottom of the bowl, every other spoonful coming with directions. Having to keep such close tabs on her prevented Twain from indulging in the imaginary conversation he had planned on having with her.

"Perhaps after dinner," he said aloud. "During coffee."

She looked at him with irritation, as though he was overstepping his bounds as the person whose job it was to feed her and keep quiet.

When they were done, she laid back against her pillow formation and looked up at the window above the television, which was turned off. The television, like the chair, had started to provide agitation rather than comfort. She liked it quiet now, with the only movement coming from whomever was assisting her, and the occasional bird fluttering past the window and the tips of the branches that provided a place to land.

He wanted to tell her that she had a son, and deliver a message from him. And even though the message would be about how grateful he was for all she had done for him, about how much he appreciated her ability to come across as a friend without trying too hard or compromising her ability to parent, he didn't dare trouble her. At best the compliment would mean nothing to her, with no memories to make it feel well-earned. And at worst, of course, it would sadden her to think she had lost touch with a son so completely that she could not even remember him.

So he left her to the silent world outside the window. Before passing through the door, bowl in hand, he looked back at what she was looking at, and considered how different their perceptions of the same thing were. If not for the photograph, he wondered if he would have even remembered that they once had a conversation at a wedding reception, a conversation that he was sure in some way contributed to his development. All of a sudden it felt so long ago, as long as a Sunday before the first day of middle school. And then he wondered if at some point in the future it will have ever happened at all.

On his way to the kitchen he heard the faint sound of his mother's cough as he reached the opposite end of the hallway. He stopped and looked back toward her door. The small sound of her struggle for breath returned again and faded. He waited to see if there was more to come. But after what may have been several minutes, quiet prevailed, and the hallway, with her door at the end of it, seemed to extend beyond the most distant star from earth.

Chapter Twelve

Alice had grown understandably distant since he had rebuffed her play over lunch. Combined with his announcement to the class that they failed to perform well enough to earn a celebrity-flavored treat, the atmosphere was chilly in every corner of the room. Tension was still preferable to apathy as far as Twain was concerned, as it was a sign of life, but it forced him to work harder to get her attention after class.

He gently called her name as her spot came up in the indignant line that lumbered past him toward the exit.

"Could I talk to you?" he asked.

She shrugged and pulled over. He had dismissed them early, so when everyone had cleared out, there were no students from the next class waiting to file in and take their place.

"I need your help," Twain said, wincing as his voice echoed about the empty room.

Alice's stoicism was betrayed by her eyebrows.

"Turns out getting people excited about something and helping them learn about it are two very different skills," he continued, modulating his voice to accommodate the acoustics.

She formally admitted her intrigue by resting her backpack on the lectern, while Twain came upon a realization that interrupted his prepared thoughts.

"It makes me wonder about all those years on the circuit," he looked down at the tabletop. "All those interviews and presentations. They looked interested, most of them. Unlike here. But what can you tell by looking at someone? Especially if you're doing all the talking. And there was no test afterwards to see what they learned. Unlike here."

"And I'm supposed to help you with this?"

"Sorry," he blurted out a nervous laugh that filled the room for a few split seconds after it was done. "This wasn't supposed to be a therapy session. I was just hoping you and the boys could help with the class."

"How so?"

"I can't reach them," he said. "They live in a world I can't access. And it works both ways. As much as they want to hear my gossipy tales, the fact I'm able to tell them makes me all the less approachable. My promises really just separated our worlds even more. And I have a feeling that talking to teachers is already something they're not keen on doing."

"You want us to be teaching assistants?"

"Kind of," he was relieved that she was picking up on his idea. "I need someone to help them make the move from knowing the material to understanding it. I can impart the information, I can do it in an entertaining way, but I'm hoping someone like you, and Blake and Gavin and the rest, can translate it, so to speak."

"At what age do people start assuming that everyone more than like ten years younger than them are all the same?"

"Not everyone in the class is younger than me," Twain reminded her. "It's about who they are, not how old they are."

"So who are they?"

"People who don't know how to go to school," he steadied his eye contact with her. "All I'm asking is that you give them some tips on being a student, provide some strategies, be a role model, one that they can access."

She considered his proposal. "Study sessions outside of class are a tough sell."

"I'm thinking we do it in class," he came around to her side of the table. "I've got some ideas for lessons you can help me present. Then we form groups."

He ventured out toward the seating area and started acting as though the room was full and the plan was already in effect. "Each group headed by one of you to offer some guidance, explain how you would make the information sink in, while I work the room and linger by each of you for a spell and provide a ringing endorsement of what you're doing, answer some questions, and then we watch the scores rise."

He concluded his demonstration and walked back in her direction. "This stuff is too easy for your crew, anyway. It'll make the class more challenging, and look great on the letters of recommendation I'll write for each of you."

"So we do get something out of it," she smiled. "Besides satisfaction."

"Of course," he said. "But the satisfaction...oh, the satisfaction. You'll probably refuse the letters when it's all said and done."

"Nobody's agreed to anything yet," she picked up her backpack. "And I need a lot more to sell the boys on this besides a chance to interact with their fellow, um, 'colleagues'. Those lessons, the presentations you mentioned, they'd better sound good."

"Come on," he gathered up his belongings as well. "Walk with me, hang out with me. I'll buy. I need to be moving when I pitch this."

She accepted his invitation and he proceeded to foster the ideas that had been following him around since reading the Wheatley papers. The details of what he had in mind were still unfocused, but he realized that was okay at this point, since he wanted to grant Alice and her lot a fair amount of license to expand on them, so long as they adhered to the theme he established. The section was devoted to satellites, the array of worlds that were tethered to the planets, the unique characteristics embodied by each moon, and so the theme he developed was "being there". He wanted to put the students in these foreign environments as much as possible, make them feel the unfamiliar.

Twain would cover the basics of each satellite being studied: its size relative to Earth, thickness of the atmosphere, its place in orbit, surface features, and then some of Alice's team would provide a tour, give them a sense of what it would be like to stand on it.

"With certain assumptions in place, obviously," he clarified as they settled into lunch. "Like, for instance, the ability to breathe air devoid of oxygen, or withstand being pelted by winds filled with silica traveling several hundred miles per hour, or perhaps most elemental of all, not freezing to death."

And upon accepting Twain's offer, they not only instituted the assumptions, but may have had more fun with them than with the ensuing depictions of a day in another planet's shoes.

Standard practice before establishing the assumptions would be for Blake to first welcome everyone to the satellite they were visiting, and then remind them of what would really happen if they were all somehow dropped on any of the surfaces they were studying.

"Welcome to Ganymede. You're dead."

"Welcome to Callisto. You're dead."

And so on.

After a few times, all Blake had to do was announce the name of the moon, then the class would say the second part, aloud, in unison: "You're dead."

Once the back-and-forth pattern developed, Blake added a solo line of his own as a follow-up to the group chant, so by the fourth presentation the stock opening would roll out with the cadence of a knock-knock joke.

Blake: "Welcome to Oberon."

Class: "You're dead!"

Blake: "Unless..."

Then one of the team members, usually Gavin or Alice, would serve as the main tour guide while Blake and the rest carried out the performance art, which was hastily-prepared and briefly-rehearsed partly by design, in order to leave room for the unexpected.

They decided that the assumptions would be more applicable and memorable if they altered the human body in ways that would accommodate said conditions. So when they needed to be able to breathe pure nitrogen to visit Titan, which would replace the oxygen in the bloodstream, they asked everyone to imagine their blood being about 25% thicker with an imaginary layer of indestructible oxygen-rich blood that would serve as their backup supply, then produced a blender filled with strawberry milk and proceeded to add a quarter amount of flour to demonstrate. When they accounted for the temperature on Europa, they started to put on sweater after sweater, turning themselves into immobile balls of bursting wool and rayon, who then asked the class to multiply the number of sweaters they had put on by a hundred, and imagine that such protection could somehow be reduced to a layer of skin (and not just on the upper body).

The walk about the terrain would then begin, though it didn't always involve walking. Sometimes it was rolling backwards on the floor in the face of winds exceeding the wildest nightmares of an earth dweller. Sometimes it was swimming the breast stroke on top of the front table, having broken through a layer of surface ice to look for possible life that could mirror the creatures found in the deepest, darkest parts of our oceans. And in one particularly inspired bit, it was flying through the heavy air of Titan, as the boys lined up to spin and somersault Alice along the front of them. When one was done passing her off to the next, he would race down to the end of the line and wait for her next pass, creating perpetual motion.

"And flying is even better with swim fins..." Alice announced after a few trips back and forth in the front of the classroom. "...on your hands!"

And she placed the fins accordingly and mimicked flight with a bit more grace than before.

In preparation for the group sessions afterwards, the crew decided to provide some mnemonics they thought may be helpful, or at least entertaining, as often as possible. So for the ability to fly on Titan, Alice utilized its letters in the name "Titanic".

"You know how thanks to that movie, every time someone is on a boat, they find it necessary to go to the front and spread their arms and yell 'I'm the king of the world'? Well, on Titan, add an 'ic' and you've got 'Titanic', you don't need a boat!"

And the boys encircled her and lifted her as high as they could above them, like a cheerleading routine, while she spread her arms with the swim fins on them a few times as though doing the breast stroke, then held a pose with her hands outstretched and yelled, "I'm the king of the moon!...Called Titan!"

Twain found some of their science a bit sketchy, but they never strayed far enough from scientific consensus to inspire him to interrupt. He almost did on the day Wheatley visited for his peer observation, but the professor seemed to be enjoying himself, so Twain stuck to his policy of surrendering the floor for the duration of their demo. Besides, the crew's creativity was greater than their margin of error, and so infectious that he adopted their spirit for his lead-in lectures.

When trying to put the size of a satellite in perspective, he borrowed an idea he once saw at a conference that would use a photograph of a full moon at night over a desert highway, then replace the moon with an image of another planet, or for Twain's purposes, another moon. So Titan would be about double the size of our accustomed moon as it loomed ahead on the horizon with a burnt orange sheen, as would Ganymede, looking like a an even-more battered version of our moon, while Callisto and Io would be slightly larger than the sight we're used to seeing. Others were the same size, but with different features than what we grew up seeing, which prompted Twain to remark how we might not even notice at first if Europa, for instance, appeared in our sky one night instead of our moon, our moon which we had assumed for so long was the only other satellite in the sky, with which we had grown so familiar, that we didn't even give it a name. Our moon was *the* moon.

To bring life to the density of the satellites' atmospheres, he borrowed a big glass jug from the young winemaker who had given him a tour and barrel tasting, put it on the front table, and would borrow a cigarette and lighter from a student who was an injured construction worker who was going to college as part of a re-training program. Twain would then blow smoke into the jug and cork it when he estimated the smoke had reached an evocative level of thickness.

He wasn't able to talk to Wheatley on the day of his visit, as per union rules he was only allowed to stay for a fixed amount of time, but on his way out he gave Twain a thumbs-up, and sent him a text that read how much he was looking forward to reviewing the student evaluations, which would be administered by the faculty support office at a later date.

After the final moon-of-the-day exhibition, before breaking into groups to prepare for the test that would be administered next class, Twain wanted to thank Alice and her crew by explaining to the rest of the students how much more there was to be learned from their efforts, something beyond the basic information they provided. He was confident that the surface conditions of each satellite had been conveyed memorably enough to be regurgitated adequately on the test, enough so that everyone would earn a story of the time he spoke to a United States Senator who thought the sun revolved around the earth. Alice and her friends had accomplished that. But he wanted to say something about the feeling he hoped the class had noticed, and encourage them to cultivate it. He wanted to mention how in his travels, he never felt the newness of a place until he was out walking around in it. Looking out the window of an airplane while descending over it, looking out the window of a taxi en route to a hotel in the middle of it, none of that provided any sense of place. It was only after checking in, changing clothes, and emerging for a walk that a palpable feeling took over. Several steps removed from the homogeneity of the hotel, the external sensations of smell, temperature and noise merge with the internal tingle of not knowing what's around any given corner, and it starts to dawn on you that you are someplace different, and it is going to impact you, it's going to change you, if only in some small manner. He wanted to share the exhilaration of that moment with them, and his wish that the demonstrations somehow joined them to it, but thought maybe it would sound arrogant to reference his travels, that it would come across as lording his status over them, teasing them with a world they were no more likely to visit than any of the ones they were studying. So he took a different direction.

"Before I unleash Alice, Blake, and Gavin and the gang out into the seats to cover the material with you, I wanted to thank them for the great work they're doing, since I've got them lined up here already, in perfect formation for some applause."

He then jokingly gestured for the class to applaud, which they were starting to do, anyway, while the crew hammed up some bows and curtsies. As the applause subsided, he added on to his gratitude.

"One of the really interesting things about studying the moons, to me at least, is how within our solar system, some of them offer the most promising conditions for life, as opposed to the big gassy planets they orbit. And our gang here has illustrated that beautifully."

The crew was now glancing humbly in his direction. He nodded at them and continued.

"Their enthusiasm, along with your appreciation and growth that has coincided with their efforts, supplies rather definitive proof, as far as I'm concerned, that indeed the best chance at life is on the satellites."

He surveyed the room, and for the first time felt as though he had their attention for all the best reasons.

"You're going to nail this test," he added, then waved the crew into the seats to start the group work.

Wandering the aisles and rows to check in with each group, he hung near the one tutored by Alice a while longer. They made eye contact a few times as she listened to their questions and answered them the best she could, deferring to Twain a couple of times. When he moved on to the next group, he kept thinking about her, so much so that he didn't notice he was standing by Gavin's group until Gavin called his name a few times to get his attention for help with a question. He chuckled at himself and made a crack about fulfilling the stereotype of the absent-minded professor, but when the moment passed and the information had been imparted, he drifted to the front of the room to collect his thoughts on Alice, and what they amounted to.

The answer was twenty. If he and Marina and Alice were all twenty at the same time, he would be with Alice. Not because he would be any less interested in Marina, but because Marina would not be interested in him.

"So what you're saying is I would be a stuck-up bitch," Marina responded when he mentioned the scenario to her (Alice not included).

"No. I just said you wouldn't be interested in me."

"It's okay," she laughed. "I was a stuck-up bitch when I was twenty. But I was really hot, so it wasn't my fault."

"You're still hot," he said, admiring her from a seat on his Mom's patio while Marina escorted Paget around the backyard as part of a regimen to give her some exercise in the midst of being bed-ridden so often.

Marina had grown comfortable coming over to see her old friend since the initial shock. At first it was simply about confronting the situation, convincing herself she could handle not being recognized by someone she loved. Then once she proved she could face the death of their friendship while Paget was still alive, she wanted to spend more time with her, and with permission from Esther and Oscar, assisted with some of her care.

Twain never regarded his approval as permission. He had offered a warning before, then it was up to her how she wanted to respond to Paget's stare.

"Should I put on a nurse's uniform next time I do this?" she asked. "Would that be even hotter?"

Twain put a finger to his lips.

"Don't say 'nurse'," he reminded her, forming the words with overstated expressions and low volume.

Marina grimaced and hunched apologetically, but Paget didn't notice. Her expression was the same as it often was over the past couple of weeks, as though she had a cell phone plugged into her ear, the voices within holding her attention while the world in front of her was but a distraction. Her ambivalence allowed Twain to provide a possible explanation in a normal voice.

"Without a visual aid, I guess it doesn't register," he said. "Now if you actually showed up in such a uniform..."

He trailed off into an expression that perished the thought.

"I was never into role playing, anyway," Marina rationalized, guiding Paget toward the patio for one more lap around the yard.

Twain watched them with a combination of satisfaction and relaxation that he usually found hard to sustain. Either impulse tended to make him feel useless within seconds of indulging it, as though someone out there was going to catch up to him, then pass him as the new face of sound-bite astronomy, should his contentment turn to complacency.

As they swayed past him, he stood up and joined the procession, walking next to Marina so as not to crowd his Mom.

"You're a dream come true," he whispered in Marina's ear. "That's all I'm trying to say."

She took his hand and squeezed it rhythmically while the three of them sustained the circle. Drawing closer to the house, she loosened her grip and lightly touched his palm and the length of his fingers, then brushed her fingertips up and down his forearm, keeping her eyes forward.

They reached the patio and caught sight of their reflection in the sliding glass door: Twain on one side of Marina, Paget on the other. Esther materialized amongst them from the other side, a grinning apparition made flesh when she opened the door.

She suggested it was time for Paget to head back to her room. Marina directed her by the elbow toward the outstretched arm of Esther. The door slid closed behind them, and they disappeared into the image of Twain and Marina, who stood silently for several more seconds working each other's fingers before Marina finally spoke.

"Let me give you directions to my place."

"I could just follow you."

"I need a head start to make things presentable."

"Your roommate?"

"Gone for the week."

They turned to face each other, wanting to kiss, but sharing the same silent concern that Esther and Paget may still be able to see them through the window somewhere from behind the reflections.

As Marina described the route, she may as well have been reciting Shakespeare's 29th Sonnet.

"...and just after the deer crossing sign," she wound toward the conclusion, "you'll see a dirt road on the right with some mailboxes lined up next to it, and some crappy old car or truck for sale."

"You've never noticed if it's a car or a truck?"

"Right now it's a tan Ford Bronco, but that could change by the time you get there. My uncle has a whole shitty fleet in the barn he'd love to put on display, but if he dumps more than one at a time out there, somebody calls the sheriff's department."

"It's your uncle's place? You said you pay rent."

"He's a distant uncle."

"What's a 'distant' uncle?"

"Nobody in the family likes him very much."

"Well I can see why if he's charging you rent."

"My side of the family was okay with that part," she said. "The guest house is actually the nicest building on his property. I'd call it a ranch, but that would be an insult to the other ranches. And you thought a roommate was the lamest part of the deal."

She gave him a playful kiss and asked for a twenty minute head start.

"You said there were mailboxes lined up at the entrance to the dirt road," Twain remembered just as she was about to open the glass door. "Is there a number on the gate?"

"Yes, but you won't need it."

"How will I know which one is yours?"

"It's the last one you'd ever imagine yourself visiting."

He smiled. She proceeded into the house, and a few seconds later he heard the front door close.

Twain sat back down and looked up to the sky, imagining all of the violent activity churning behind the clouded blue curtain, the grand scale creation and destruction that was always there, but at a safe distance. He was grateful for his tiny corner of the universe, where someone was waiting for him to arrive at her place in twenty minutes, where he could feel as though he had the power to push the turbulence even further away.

He enjoyed watching her lie naked on her stomach across the bed almost as much as having sex, perhaps even more so. It was a chance to really see her in a most private moment. The sex was primal, the afterglow human. He drew invisible pictures of the solar system on her back with his finger, then erased them with both hands.

He tried a game where he would trace an individual planet and ask her if she could name it, but it quickly turned into a joke, as they were all just circles. "The round one" she would answer over her shoulder, with the exception being Saturn. She could name that one, since it had rings around it.

She rolled over and put her arms around him.

"And all these planets were made after a Big Bang, am I right?" she said, trying to keep a straight face, but unable to deliver the dippy innuendo without giggling.

"I was thinking of saying that at some point," he admitted. "But I just don't have your courage. Or maybe it's weakness."

"When were you thinking of saying it?"

He smiled. "You really want me to tell you?"

"Yes," she was barely containing herself.

"Around the time I was tracing Uranus."

They burst out laughing together, and as they settled down, stared at each other for a while. They traced the contours of their faces, without placing any imaginary drawings over them, and kissed some more, then made love some more.

This time there was less activity afterwards. Marina rested her head on his chest as Twain stroked her arm while they assessed the situation in silence.

Twain wondered in greater detail than before if he could be content settling down in the area. He was on the edge of sharing this idea, but thought it might startle her, or come across as afterglow talk.

"I don't think I ever really taught anyone anything before I came here," he said.

"Sure you did," she shifted her position so that she was still lying on his chest, but facing him. "It just wasn't in a classroom."

"That's what I thought," he shook his head. "But I see a big difference in what I'm doing now compared to what I'm used to doing."

"How so?"

"I'm not selling anyone anything."

"You're selling them on your subject. How great it is, how valuable it is."

"But I'm not at the same time trying to get them to tune in to my show, or tune in again so I can look appealing to advertisers, or donate money to whatever school or foundation I'm shilling for."

"You're getting them to show up to class next time."

"But that's in their best interests."

"Well, a tax write-off is in people's interests," she kissed him. "So is expanding their minds for pleasure, not just to get a grade."

"It's the questions they ask," he said.

"Who?"

"There's a difference between the questions I get from the students, and the questions I get from people at events, or people who recognize me."

She rested her head on him again, but now looked more interested than gratified.

"Students want answers," he continued. "Most of the others think they know the answers. They ask me about things they already have an opinion on, and they want that opinion validated, or they want to throw it at me. Like the existence of God, or how old the earth is. And they've imagined how that conversation is going to play out, because they think they know me, and therefore know what I'm going to say."

"That's because they only ask you about astronomy," she sat up next to him. "If they asked you about other things, you could have some really great conversations with them."

He overplayed a weary sigh and put his arm around her.

"There's so much more to me," he managed to say with a straight face into the distance.

"So much more," she patted his chest.

"From now on I'm going to devote whole sections of my lecture tour to Super Bowl predictions and stock tips," he kept staring ahead of them, as though he could visualize this new future if he looked hard enough and made decisive hand gestures. "Maybe on the show, too. A closing monologue about finding a good red wine at the right price. Or travel tips, movie recommendations..."

"Love."

He looked at her.

She was waiting for his gaze, ready to hold it.

"Love," he agreed.

They had a gentle stand-off, each waiting for the other to say something more on the subject. Neither did, but they kissed with much more confidence and less hunger than before.

And this time instead of making love, they fell asleep together.

Chapter Thirteen

The harvest became more apparent, and not just because of the banners hanging from the downtown streetlamps and signs in the storefront windows proclaiming the festivals devoted to it. Every time Twain was on the road, he seemed to encounter a truck hauling two massive trailers stacked high with grapes, or on its way out to the vineyards for loading, the empty trailers bouncing and rattling. The wide boulevard a couple of turns from his Mom's house that led to the countryside was streaked with splattered bunches that had fallen from the tops of the passing heaps.

He followed one such truck along the highway for a while on his way to meet Professor Wheatley for their post-evaluation conference. They decided to meet half way this time, since each had crossed into the other's territory for the previous encounters. Besides, the Dean of Sciences was going to join them, and there was a restaurant she wanted to take them to in the one-intersection enclave that sat a couple miles off the highway at roughly the midpoint between the two towns.

Twain had ample opportunities to pass the truck, but the trailers were filled and he had become engrossed with how all the grapes managed to stay on board in spite of the speedy, bumpy ride, as though the bunches were clinging to each other.

The truck stayed on the highway as Twain exited, the grapes on their way to be processed at some operation that was larger than the approaching little hamlet could handle, for while the village was trying to get attention by hitching its fortunes to the burgeoning wine industry nearby, it did so in a strictly touristy fashion.

Of the dozen or so buildings other than the post office, half were abandoned, and the other half were businesses that appeared to be operated by avid readers of Sunset magazine who retired early to realize their dreams: a couple of tasting rooms, a couple of restaurants, and a few boutiques that also had small restaurants or tastings rooms inside them.

He found the café recommended by the Dean easily enough, as she was standing in front of it waving at him. Within minutes Wheatley joined them, and they were seated at a table bathed in natural light that highlighted how well the owners had achieved the balance between rustic and modern such places often strive to capture.

While Twain and Wheatley looked over their menus, Stevie provided a curtailed history of the area, a familiar story of a farm town trying to find a way to survive with fewer farmers in need of its services. After ordering, she maintained control over the conversation.

"First off, Dr. Wheatley and I want to provide full disclosure," she said. "I should not be here, according to the union contract. Your post-evaluation conference is strictly between you and your peer evaluator. But given the unique circumstances, Robert approached me with the idea of making this meeting something more than your average wrap-up."

Hearing Wheatley's first name made Twain smile, for while he had grown to know him a little better, he still couldn't imagine calling him anything other than Doctor or Professor.

"The student reviews were fantastic," Wheatley picked up where Stevie left off. "Which confirmed what I saw on the day I visited."

He produced two several-page documents and slid one across the table.

"Outstanding," the professor continued. "Especially in consideration of how you felt things were going during our pre-evaluation meeting. The fact that you made genuine efforts to improve in mid-stride, and that those efforts paid off in spectacular fashion, turned any fears I had about hiring you upside down. You refused to coast on your past, and those students are receiving a world-class education because of it."

Twain was humbled to a degree with which he was unfamiliar. His voice nearly cracked as he thanked him. Wheatley sensed what was happening and stalled by having Twain sign one copy for the school, and instructing him that the other copy was his to keep.

Stevie spoke again once the signing ceremony was complete.

"We were hoping that your copy doesn't end up just being a souvenir," she said. "We're in the process of scheduling for the spring semester, and would really appreciate your consideration to stick with us. I know that wasn't the plan when you first signed on, and probably still isn't, but we thought it would be foolish of us not to at least try to make a pitch, and that perhaps your experience so far has maybe, just maybe, inspired you to reconsider."

And while Twain's agent usually did most of his negotiating for him, his years of salesmanship nonetheless stirred him to hide the fact he had already been pondering such a move.

"Will I be putting you in a bind if I say no?" he said. "I'd hate to think the class will be unstaffed once again."

"That's not really at issue," Stevie answered. "We have a couple of names in the part-time pool we can tap. Even though you're the only one who got a class this Fall, we actually hired a couple of other people as well, knowing that this Spring we have a full-timer in the Physics Department going on sabbatical leave, and a retirement at the end of the year."

Twain assumed one of the new hires was the young man who was so crestfallen upon seeing him in the hall on the day of their interviews. He was glad to think there would be a job for him after all.

"And no," Wheatley cut in. "The retirement is not mine."

They shared a laugh and Stevie proceeded with the bidding.

"But the even better news about the retirement is that it makes lobbying for a new full-time hire in our department much easier. The prioritization meetings are under way, and if ours is one of the positions that gets funded, which I'm sure it will be, we'll advertise this winter and hire in the spring for a start date of next fall. You'd of course have to apply. As I've said before, we're a state institution and can't just offer you the job, but nobody's going to challenge our decision if we follow procedure. I mean, c'mon..."

She gestured toward Twain as though he was a vintage car restored to mint condition, or a swimsuit model on a billboard.

"That's if you want to teach full-time," Wheatley added. "If you would prefer to remain in the part-time pool and continue to pursue your business opportunities, we can make that work."

Twain took a deep breath, and almost confessed to having already considered the same options, when something occurred to him that he couldn't help but sincerely express.

"I don't think what I did this semester is repeatable," he doubted aloud. "I can't imagine having another group of students like the ones helping me out with presentations, and leading the study groups. Not to mention the name-dropping. I only have so many years before the names I know will mean nothing to them. That carrot will fall off the end of the stick."

Wheatley shrugged. "Circumstances always change. You'll adjust, just like you have this semester. Real talent knows how to adapt."

The ensuing pause would have lasted even longer had the food not arrived.

Their selections were serviceable dishes made to look more photogenic thanks to sauces squirted into designs from squeeze bottles and side offerings shaved into colorful medleys. Stevie raved over her meal long enough to goad them into compliments on her restaurant recommendation.

Wheatley drastically changed the subject.

"How is your mother?" he asked.

Twain wanted to answer honestly, but the silence that attended his musing over the perfect answer quickly became uncomfortable, so he cut it short.

"I don't know," he said.

It came out more offhanded than he intended. He was relieved to see his colleagues looking more confused than put off.

"She has Alzheimer's," he explained.

"I'm sorry to hear that," Wheatley offered.

"Pretty advanced, then, I take it?" Stevie asked.

"Yes," he answered. "It was when I applied, and now even more so."

There were consoling murmurs and nods for a few bites. Now that he had moved past the opaque "health problems" statement provided at the interview, Twain felt a rush of liberation at being able to assess the situation with people who had no emotional connection to his Mom.

"For a while she was still interacting with the world," he contemplated out loud. "Even though she didn't know who I was, or anyone was, we were still there. We were trespassers, but she dealt with us. Now even that seems to be fading. She's somewhere else entirely. She doesn't just see things differently, she sees different things."

He realized he had lost eye contact with them. When he corrected himself, they looked intrigued. So much so that he felt obligated to give them more.

"But it's her physical health that we're waiting on. That's the line in the sand. I guess there's no point in visiting another world if your body can't handle it."

"If there's anything we can do, let us know," Stevie said.

"What's the process for getting a substitute?" Twain asked. "In case something happens before the end of the Fall."

"If it's just a class or two, just cancel them," Wheatley answered.

"Anything beyond that, contact me," Stevie added.

"I don't think it will be more than a couple of classes, if any," Twain said. "Work has always been a source of security for me when times are troubled. And even though this is new territory, I can't imagine feeling any different about it. Does that sound harsh?"

Wheatley shook his head. Stevie looked less sure.

"Do you have anyone you can talk to?" she asked.

Now Wheatley looked unmoored.

"Friends," Twain shrugged.

"Someone more professional," Stevie followed up, "who has experience with this sort of thing."

"Oh, Stevie..." Wheatley groaned.

Twain realized where this was headed.

"A pastor?" he guessed. "A priest?"

"A rabbi," Wheatley snarled. "A mullah."

"I'm sorry," Stevie defended herself. "I just think burying yourself in your work sounds depressing."

"That's because you're an administrator," Wheatley said.

Stevie couldn't help but appreciate the zinger.

"You're lucky I'm still paying for lunch," she chuckled.

"Writing off meals is the only good part of your job," Wheatley was on a roll. "Why forsake that?"

Twain interceded, feeling like the referee in a staged wrestling match.

"I appreciate your concern, Stevie," he assured her. "I really do. Mom's nurses are religious. At least the wife is. And I'm sure the husband is, too, if for no other reason than to make his wife happy. So if I need a little more faith, I'm sure they have some people I can look up."

"Your mother didn't go to church?" Stevie asked.

"Not when I was growing up. And I haven't seen much evidence since. Some of her friends type on her website that they're praying for her."

"Standard fare," Wheatley interjected. "Might as well be commenting on the weather."

A discussion unfolded about intent, and how difficult it can be to convey the tone of a statement online, especially when trying to be sincere, as throwing a smiley face or LOL around a piece of sarcasm is workable enough, but when it comes to grief, the words have to matter, and that's when it's hardest to find the words.

Later as they stood on the crumbling sidewalk and exchanged farewells, Stevie added something unpredictable onto her predictable reminder to consider their offer:

"And if you decide not to teach with us, I hope you'll teach somewhere."

Wheatley concurred with a nod, and Twain was certain it was the nicest professional compliment he had ever received.

He thought about how proud his Mom would be to know he had finally made an impression in what she would lovingly, jokingly refer to as "the family business."

When he arrived at her house, he told her about the meeting and the complimentary grand finale. She stared out the window for the duration of his report, glancing over at him near the end of it, roughly around the moment he borrowed her phrase about teaching being a family business. The timing was close enough, and her expression enough of a blank slate for him to decorate it as he pleased, to dress it up as a response if he ever decided to turn it into a story.

The stories he told the class after announcing the results of their test were every bit the reward he had hoped they would be. He had grown concerned as the day drew closer that maybe the stories would be a letdown after all the anticipation. So he reveled in the relief of hearing their laughter and seeing the appreciation in their faces.

And their reactions, and his need to experience them, altered his telling of the stories. He did in fact meet a senator who thought the sun revolved around the earth, but did the senator approach him with this belief, or did it come up in conversation? And how far did Twain pursue the matter? Was he speechless, or did he pelt the senator with disbelieving questions in as diplomatic a tone as he could muster? The choices Twain made as he told the story were inspired by the audience, what he thought they would like best. Each burst of approval led him farther from the truth. Likewise with the story of the aging former boy band member who included an appearance on *Star Chasers* as part of his comeback. Did he really think the Johnson Space Center was named after Magic Johnson? Or did he just not know who Lyndon Johnson was? And was he the one who would bring his own box of pasta to a restaurant and ask the chef to use it in his order, or was that the wide receiver from the Miami Dolphins? For the purposes of the class, it had to be him, because he was already telling the story about him, and the students deserved their reward.

He met with Alice, Gavin, and Blake afterwards to plan for the next section, as the rest of the crew went to their next classes. Twain dubbed the upcoming lesson plan "Visiting Objects", as the theme would be the various bodies that we associate with our solar system but which sometimes arrive from beyond the orbit of Pluto; the comets and meteors characterized by more elusive patterns, that don't stay very long, but burn brighter and tend to make a bigger impression than the ones that are always around, the ones we take for granted.

They met at their customary burger haunt, ordered the usual, and exchanged ideas. Riding a comet or meteor was an inspiring concept for the trio, and they had to stop themselves from nabbing all the good ideas on how to make the journey come to life before the rest of the crew had a chance to contribute their designs at a meeting they arranged for the next day at Gavin's house.

Twain watched, listened, and ate for the most part, occasionally confirming or correcting some of the scientific parameters they ran by him. It was always either Gavin or Blake who would ask. Alice rarely made eye contact with Twain until the meeting started to wind down, at which point she would glare at him when the boys weren't looking. Twain tried not to react. The crew was doing such good work, and he wanted to maintain harmony. When Blake excused himself to head back to campus, and Gavin needed to get home to get ready for work, Twain thought perhaps Alice would stick around and explain. But she claimed that she also had to go.

Twain stayed at the table and watched them walk to the door. Alice was last in line, so he figured there was still a chance she would give him some sort of signal that she wanted to talk. She did take a melodramatic pause in the doorway, but only to give him the meanest look in the series so far. He slumped his shoulders and bugged out his eyes for an answer, but she swept through the exit before his reaction was complete.

He sighed and took stock of the situation, deciding it was fruitless to try and find motive for the impulses of someone half his age. As he got up from the table he felt his phone vibrate. It was a text from Alice:

We would be together if I was better-looking.

He pocketed his phone and trotted to the door, reverting to a full sprint once outside, circling the parking lot, hoping Alice had not left. He spotted a car backing out of a spot. She was at the wheel. He ran over and waved through the passenger window. She turned and flinched, startled to see him, then exhaled and rolled the car back into its place.

Popping out of the car, she looked at him from across the roof, arms folded on top of it, waiting for what he had to say.

Twain caught his breath and used the time to think of how he wanted open this case.

"Thank you for being so professional about everything in class," he decided to say. "I had no idea there were still any hard feelings."

"Maybe I'm being professional," she had calmed down. "Maybe you're just oblivious."

"I'm trying to spare you," he said. "I'm doing you a favor."

"You can spare me the excuses," she got snappy again. "You would disappoint me once I learned more about you?" she referenced their last conversation on the subject. "That's what love is about. People accept each other's faults and love them anyway."

Twain joined her in putting his arms on the roof of the car and clutched his forehead, resisting the urge to say something condescending.

"You have things you need to do," he measured his tone. "Goals, accomplishments, decisions to make that should not in any way depend on what someone my age is doing with his life."

"Age is relative."

"Thank you for not saying it's just a number."

"But it is."

"And when you're stuck taking care of me at the same time as your parents, tell me those numbers don't matter. Come over to the house sometime, meet my mother, glimpse the future."

"In sickness and in health…"

"That's assuming people get married young, knowing they've got their whole lives ahead of them. You buy a pet knowing you're going to bury it, a spouse is supposed to a toss-up."

"You're so pessimistic."

"And you're so idealistic. But you'll get here. And if you hitch your life to mine, the pessimism will kick in right around the time widowhood does. That'll be a delightful combination."

"You're not that old."

"But I have a death coming before I die. I have the slow fade from the public eye. I'm going to lose my relevance before I lose my life. Everyone does, but mine will be one of the severe cases. You want to nurse me through that, too? Take time away from the exciting things you're destined for to watch me become a has-been?"

Alice slid her hands off the roof and onto her hips. "This is all bullshit. You still haven't dealt with my original point: we wouldn't be having this talk if I looked like Marina."

Twain stood up straight on his side of the car as well. She had somewhat of a point. But there was more to his attraction to Marina that he wanted to explain, and he wasn't sure how to express it without sounding as though he was disparaging the woman he loved. He needed to try, though.

"Marina's looks have a certain something to do with it, sure," he admitted. "But partly because they're fading. In her own way she's been knocked off the top of the mountain. She's already been where I'm heading."

He leaned back onto the roof between them.

"Please don't tell her I said that," he added lightly.

Alice would not be lured into an upbeat conclusion.

"She can still turn heads," she maintained. "And it's going to take a while for that to completely stop happening. She has that privilege."

"You're a lovely young woman, Alice."

"You didn't say 'beautiful.'"

"There's a difference?"

"If you say 'lovely' too fast or don't listen carefully, it can sound like 'ugly'. The word 'beautiful' leaves no doubt. Beautiful stands apart."

Twain couldn't call her beautiful now, maybe never if they stayed in touch.

He thanked her again for compartmentalizing her emotions and her work ethic.

She ducked back into her car without responding, and Twain was relieved to see her separate her feelings from her driving as well. There was no angry accelerating or squealing tires.

On his way home he started to feel as though he made his point all too well regarding the inevitable dimming of his star. The ephemeral nature of prominence, particularly the kind that dawdles on the outskirts of fame, was something he never denied, but apparently had been keeping at a great distance.

He arrived home and scrolled through the responses he had received from Mom's friends. Very few provided just a mailing address. Most went on to include messages that described the tears on their keyboard, how many boxes of tissue they had gone through and would have to bring to the service, how suddenly their tears ran back and forth between grief and delight as they remembered the past with her and a future without her. Some mentioned how surprised they were at the emotions inspired by seeing the words "memorial service". They hadn't seen Paget in over a year, and knew the end was near, but had been comforted unaware by knowing she was still there.

All of which made Twain proud to be her son, and even more insecure about his own legacy. He envisioned the kinds of comments his impending death would elicit, along the lines of "seemed like a nice guy", "felt like a friend", and lots of Rests in Peace. But no one would know him well enough to be truly distraught, to talk to his memory in their quiet moments, and keep him alive in their thoughts, not just on YouTube.

He spent a quiet dinner with Esther and Oscar, feeling a sense of finality in their relationship, wondering if they shared it, and suspecting they did thanks to their preoccupation with things they preferred not to voice.

After exchanging reminders with Oscar, Esther kissed him good night, and gave Twain a hug.

"She had a good day," she said, then hugged him again before she left.

Twain accompanied Oscar to Paget's room. While Oscar took her to the bathroom, Twain changed the sheets on her bed. The ones he removed smelled of immobility, the stale perspiration of existence rather than exertion, and he wondered what constituted "a good day" at this point.

The sheets weren't soiled. Perhaps that was the standard.

He was just finishing as his Mom was escorted back into the room by Oscar. Twain glanced her way as he folded back the top sheet, then looked at her again.

She was concentrating on him.

She even took a couple of steps toward him, brow furrowed, trying to place him. She studied his face as though his identity may be revealed in a single pore or a hair in his eyebrow. Twain had never been so pleased to have someone not recognize him. Unlike the previous blithe or fearful looks she had given him, this one was rooted in acknowledgement. And though he was certain the answer she was trying to recall was wrong, he was grateful to see that he had once more inspired something in her.

When she stopped searching, she appeared to look through him, into a horizon where she could barely make him out as he sped away into the distance. If he kissed her on the forehead, it would strike her like the first drop of rain in an unexpected storm over the invisible plain on which she stood, watching that mysterious figure who had just passed her by grow smaller.

So he said good night instead, which still startled her.

The script offered some diversion. He would strike up a few sentences then delete most of their content, and lean back to regroup, trying to ignore the audio from the television as Oscar watched Sports Center.

Twain wanted to utilize the origins of our solar system as the theme of the film's conclusion, the theories that proposed a chaotic beginning, an early existence filled with rage and debris, with orbits destined to change thanks to relentless rocky bombardments, unruly planets that danced together until they flung each other into their own paths, with no sense of the order that would eventually find its way. He wanted the students who would someday watch the film to imagine that if our space exploration could take us to emerging solar systems, then we could learn more about our past, that by trying to escape present circumstances, we could run into younger versions of them.

He managed to compose an acceptable stream of sentences, then went outside to take a break. He had always been dismissive of the idea floated by some of his contemporaries that time doesn't really exist, at least not in a straight line, that everything is happening at once, and what divides a sequence of events is space. But tonight he was more receptive.

Looking up at the stars, he wondered if there was a part of the universe where he was sitting with his Mom in the sculpture garden at the university, eating peanut butter sandwiches, about to attend his first astronomy lecture while on spring break from his elementary school, and meanwhile some light years away, marked by another constellation, he was back on the road, or back in front of a class, maybe with Marina, maybe without, in a part of the universe inaccessible to his Mom, who would love to be there instead of trapped in those spaces reserved for her childhood.

He placed several more memories in various parts of the cosmos. His break from the script had turned into his project for the night.

He lost track of time as he filled in the heavens, and went to bed later than he had in years.

Chapter Fourteen

Twain had never heard his mother scream, so he wasn't sure if it was her when the walls first rattled with the sound. It came from her room, but didn't seem to belong to a human being. It sounded like someone had started to scream, but the screams had quickly taken on a life of their own, and no longer needed their host.

He shot up from his work post at the dining table, grabbed his phone, and ran down the hall. He threw open his Mom's door and saw Esther leaning over the opposite side of the bed, clutching her hands to her chest, vomiting out the screams.

His Mom didn't seem capable of making any noise. She was shaking as though being electrocuted, wearing the terrified look of someone who has lost control of the vehicle they're driving.

"Call 911!" Esther managed to form some shrieks into words. "Please Dr. Henry! Call!"

The helpless expression on his Mom's face matched his feelings. He stood paralyzed for a few moments until Esther ran around to his side of the bed and bellowed the demands into his ear.

"Call, Dr. Henry! Call 911!"

His Mom's eyes had followed Esther's path, and now she was looking at Twain, holding his gaze while the rest of her shook. He returned her stare and reached for his phone. Rather than unlock the screen, he tapped on it and pretended to dial.

"Hello, I need an ambulance," he said to the imaginary dispatcher while maintaining eye contact with Paget. "My mother needs to go to the hospital."

Her eyes bulged even larger, and started to twitch as though she was trying to send a message via Morse code, like a hostage forced to read a statement from her captors on camera who was trying to communicate her location to the viewing audience. She struggled to make sounds of her own. They came out at a lower volume than Esther's screams, but with greater intensity, gurgling noises reminiscent of the first moments of a geyser, a hint that something much more powerful was underneath the surface. But she couldn't carry out her cries. All she could do is try her hardest to break through the surface, but her broken body wouldn't let her.

Twain unlocked the screen and found the number for Dr. Walls.

The receptionist put him through and the doctor picked up immediately.

"How is she?"

"Shaking violently."

"Did you call an ambulance?"

"Not yet."

"Good. Let me move some things around. I'll be there in ten minutes."

"Is she going to make it that long?"

"Do your best to comfort her."

Dr. Walls hung up and Twain lowered his phone to prepare himself for the longest ten minutes of his life.

"Who was that second call?" Esther asked.

"Dr. Walls."

"Is he coming too?"

"There was no first call."

He and his Mom kept looking at each other.

"There will be no ambulance," he said. "No hospital."

Her body still convulsed, but her relief shone through. Her eyes relaxed, she stopped trying to shout at him, and as she reclined back onto her pillow, her shaking almost gave the impression that she was lying in a very high-powered massage chair.

"What!?" Esther shattered the moment.

Twain remained calm, confident in his decision now that he had witnessed his Mom's reaction.

"You're killing her!" she brayed.

"She's hardly reacted to anything in weeks," he reminded her, while staying focused on his Mom. "Then I mention the hospital..."

"Maybe it's because you called her your mother!"

He felt her fists slam into his side. He turned to face her and she kept coming at him, pounding on him like a locked door.

"So now she knows her own son is trying to kill her!"

He grabbed her wrists and guided her out of the room.

"Take the day off," he said once they were in the hall.

She stopped resisting his grip and fell into his arms, crying as uncontrollably as she was screaming a few minutes before.

He joined her and they held each other as though their emotions may reduce them to nothing if not for the ballast each provided, and all they could do was lash themselves to one another and ride out the threat.

Within a couple of minutes the fury passed, and only exhaustion remained. They went from clutching each other to hugging, and Twain echoed his offer to take the day off, in a tone far less intense. She nodded and went to the kitchen to call Oscar.

Twain went back into his Mom's room.

She had forgotten the serenity of a few minutes earlier, and was once again struggling for breath amongst the tremors. He stood by, unsure how to follow through on Dr. Walls' orders to comfort her.

He sat down on the side of the bed and rubbed her arm, trying to settle it down without being too forceful. He leaned over and put his hands on her shoulders, still searching for the right touch between firm and gentle.

She sat up and let him hug her. He was baffled as to how such a fragile body could produce such tremendous quakes. He decided to embrace her like a bird, like the dove they used to have in his fifth grade classroom. Whenever they took her out of her cage, the teacher would remind them to hold her strong enough to keep her from getting away, but tender enough not to hurt her.

It seemed to work. She continued to shake, but no longer felt as though she was in the throes of death. Twain even detected a sense of peace. But that was probably just him. It was the first serene physical contact between them in over two years.

He held on and waited.

Chapter Fifteen

Dr. Walls had something for Paget to calm her down, and some information for Twain, who sat on the other side of the bed to give the doctor room to work. Dr. Walls gave him a phone number for the local hospice, and a sense of what was happening to his Mom.

He stood and explained aspiration while Twain remained seated as though attending a class. The doctor described how her difficulties in directing food and liquid down the right tube had caught up with her, how enough had headed for her lungs instead of her stomach to cause pneumonia. He bent her arm slowly back and forth at the elbow, encouraging the medicine he had administered to flow, and said pneumonia used to be called "the old person's friend" for its ability to cut through other health complications and end suffering back when there were so many ways to suffer, and so few ways to pacify it.

Twain caught his breath every time the end was referenced, as though having an allergic reaction to his decision. Dr. Walls noticed.

"You're doing the right thing," the doctor assured him.

"She isn't that much of a bother," Twain gulped some more air.

"Neither is a plant."

They glared at each other, Twain to see if he was joking, Dr. Walls to show he was not.

"Her wishes were clear," the doctor continued.

"Easy for her to say."

Twain was surprised to hear himself say that, but looked at his Mom and indeed experienced a spasm of resentment.

"I have to get back to the office," Dr. Walls reached over to shake his hand.

Twain stood and obliged. Their hands fastened above his Mom.

"Thank you for coming, Doctor."

"Thank you for calling. Now please make the other call."

They both looked down at her. Twain crossed his arms and covered his mouth with one hand.

"What's the alternative?" Dr. Walls asked.

Twain looked at his Mom resting peacefully and had no answer.

Within a half hour of making the call, a woman in scrubs appeared at the front door with a thin three-ring binder of information on what would happen over the next several days.

The cover and the pages were unadorned with any pictures of the elderly being cradled by their loved ones, or of hands clasped together, or of doves. The wording was unsentimental and straightforward, the font standard. In describing how someone dies, it may as well have been explaining how to place a work order with an office manager.

Twain was grateful for the approach. He was supplying enough of his own personal gush. He didn't need generic, contrived attempts by a committee of authors who had never met his Mom.

The woman at the door had said another volunteer would arrive soon with some meds to alleviate any discomfort his mother may experience during the process, and indeed such a woman did appear, holding a paper bag of comfort.

The operation was distinguishing itself as clockwork so quickly, Twain put plenty of stock in the timeline laid out in the binder. It claimed that she may take a few days to slip into unconsciousness, but when she did, she would talk loudly in her sleep for about a day, then become quiet for another day or two, her breathing growing progressively labored, until at last it ceased.

The last few pages were a list of mortuaries. Twain wasn't looking forward to hearing Esther bray at him over cremation. He considered firing her. He was cancelling class for the upcoming week after all, so he would be around, and once his Mom was gone, Esther's services were no longer needed, anyway. But he couldn't seriously consider it. They had come too far together. And then there was Oscar. Twain couldn't imagine firing him, too, and he wouldn't stay if his wife was let go.

Twain decided to ask Esther for a recommendation on a pastor to administer some last rites, and perhaps offer some words at the memorial service. There were a lot of messages passing through his Mom's website that invoked God and prayer, so a lack of faith in the service would be conspicuous.

He wouldn't have been surprised if Esther had a separate suggestion for each, a pastor with good death bed manner and a pastor good with crowds. But she stuck with one, Pastor Dan, and glowed at having been asked. She said she would make the arrangements, noting that she would tell Pastor Dan to come and administer the last rites when time was clearly drawing to a close, just in case a miracle happened before Paget reached that point.

Twain thanked her, and kept her enthusiasm up his sleeve in case she came at him hard over how to handle the body.

Aunt Grace was the only family member he needed to call. As usual, she let her voice mail pick up. Twain recited the situation, concluding with a reading of Grace's mailing address, and a request to call him back if it needed to be updated.

After e-mailing his class about the cancellation of the week ahead, claiming he had to leave town for a conference, he debated posting the news about his Mom's condition on her website, but decided to wait until she had taken her last breath. He wanted to keep the next few days private.

With the exception of Marina, of course. He told her she could come by any time she wanted. When she did, Twain found he was able to play the role of stoic, supportive male easier than he expected, since he had purged so much of the emotion attached to his decision in Esther's arms on the day he made it.

He would stroke Marina's hair and rub her back when she would weep at her friend's bedside, and Twain discovered that his own efforts regarding self-control mainly had to do with trying not to make a move on her, as aroused as he was at his ability to be the kind of man he had hoped he would be when the opportunity arose, and as inappropriate as it would be to make such a move under the circumstances. Besides, revealing his horniness would totally undermine the image he had happened upon.

He set a date for the service, one month from the following weekend. The autumn weather would be battling winter, but he wanted to give people time to make arrangements to attend, and he could rent some tents and heat lamps for the backyard if the forecast dictated.

He bought some invitations at a precious-looking boutique downtown and started addressing them, while Esther changed the sheets one last time and dressed his Mom in a nightgown she insisted on buying her that looked like it should come with a four-poster bed. Twain asked her if she was sure she wanted to risk soiling it, but she reminded him that Paget wasn't eating anymore, so there was nothing left to digest.

He wrote letters of recommendation for Esther and Oscar, who were going to spend much of the week interviewing for new jobs.

He tried to work on the script. He brought his work into her room and sat in her recliner. But he ended up looking at her most of the time. She would scan the sky outside the window, the bobbing branches catching her eye every so often. She rarely noticed Twain was in the room. When she did, she would shudder with a mild start, mutter something apologetic, then go back to looking out the window, as though they were strangers who accidentally bumped into each other at an airport while looking up at the departures screen. Writing about the challenges of exploring deep space failed to inspire him, as there was so much right in front of him he didn't know, could most likely never know. There was less than an inch of flesh and bone that separated him from his mother's secrets. Billions of light years weren't necessary to obscure the mystery.

Eventually he settled into something of an impersonation of his Mom's last few weeks, sitting in her recliner, unacquainted with the world outside her room, his mind distancing itself from speculation and commentary and centering instead on images, moments he just remembered without applying any meaning to them, insignificant memories he was surprised to have stored somewhere, unless of course he had just made them up: leaning back against the chain link fence surrounding the deserted outdoor basketball court at his elementary school while sipping the overflow off the top of a can of soda all by himself on a Saturday, riding his bike down a hill with his jacket unzipped and the sides flapping out behind him like a cape, surfacing from under the churning hot water of a Jacuzzi to see a nondescript façade of hotel rooms surrounding him with the smell of chlorine burning his nostrils, walking past a booth at a street fair hung with clay wind chimes that together sounded like a wooden xylophone being bonked on by several people at once who don't know how to play it. There was a limitless supply of these discreet visions, and they proceeded without any analysis from him. He and his Mom sat in the same room separated by a distance for which there was no unit of measurement.

Occasionally he got up to feed himself, but then lapsed back into his trance when he got back into her room. He finally snapped out of it when she started talking to herself.

Initially he thought it was just her spotting him again in her field of vision and mumbling an acknowledgement, but she was unconscious, and her voice didn't stop. Words were attached to every breath she took, the volume rising on the exhale, lowering on the inhale, a stream of words that were hard to recognize, that sounded more like an extinct tongue being chanted around a fire, her breathless tempo adding to the effect, as though she was dancing around that flame in a ritual before the dawn of recorded language and history, when the only goal in life was to survive.

Periodically a word or phrase would distinguish itself. She would warn someone to stay away from that tree with the beehive in it, or wish she could pitch instead of play left field, or recommend adding basil to the mayonnaise. Twain would lean forward when such a signal would emerge from the noise, listening for something he could identify. He thought he heard her sister's name at one point, something about Grace and a pack of dogs. He definitely heard the name Darcy, but he wasn't sure whether it was the cat Mr. Darcy or an old friend with the first name Darcy, as she moaned plenty of names he could understand but did not know.

And as night fell and they approached the midpoint of the day or so that the hospice binder said she would talk like this, he had yet to hear his name, or a moment that sounded familiar. He would chastise himself for being so egotistical, then consider it a legitimate worry to wonder if he had really left no indelible marks on his own mother's life, and finally he would conclude that his name and his moments were simply amongst the many that were not being annunciated along the fevered stream of tales.

By the small hours of the morning it was becoming difficult to make out any of the words charging from her. Twain wasn't sure if it was due to his exhaustion or hers. He shook himself and leaned forward one more time, managing to focus for several minutes before his eyes started to deaden again.

It was hers. She was no longer speaking clearly even in short bursts. Her voice still intoned and lilted in a way that suggested something was being said, but any connection between her mind and the muscles needed for speech was severed. He decided to believe that one of the noises being made was his name.

Twain used the remote to recline the chair, and fell asleep before reaching the most horizontal position.

He was startled by silence a few hours later.

His mother had stopped talking.

She was breathing deeply, so the room was not completely quiet. Her mouth was open toward the ceiling. The air would go in bubbling and come out wheezing, as though it was entering a cauldron inside of her where a potion was brewing that would hold all of the answers to what lies beyond once it was finished.

Twain ordered the recliner back to its upright position, and as it slowly completed the transformation, he rose from it at the same mechanical pace, drawn to her bedside as if still asleep. He sat down and leaned over to study her in profile, believing for an instant that maybe he could see the air entering and exiting, and that maybe the air was visiting some place past her body and arriving home with some signals.

He shot back up, fully awake, and realized she had two more days at the most. Seeing her fight for air made him want some of his own. He pushed his way out of her room, then out of the house. After breathing in a big, fresh batch of air, feeling every bit of it work through him, he looked around with no purpose until he saw the mock bus stop. He had never sat at it.

It was reassuring to sit someplace where you couldn't imagine anyone wanting to sit. A car passed by from a few houses down, occupied by a woman dressed for a white collar work day. Twain waved at her, and she seemed to think being inside a vehicle somehow obstructed her face, which glared back at him with more bafflement than necessary. Twain felt a twinge of the kind of rebellion that he used to feel in high school, in college, and the early days of his career, the kind of rebellion that had no great purpose, other than to make you feel as though you thought of something no one else thought to do, as unimportant and silly as that something may be.

The longer he sat there, however, the more normal it started to feel, like he was part of a commute, waiting for a bus on a street deserted because it was early in the morning, not because it was lightly-traveled. He looked up and down the street, and on the downward glance away from the driveway, saw a gray cat sitting several feet from the bench, in front of some bushes from which he must have emerged. It looked complacent, staring out at the street just as Twain had been doing.

"Mr. Darcy," Twain nodded.

The cat turned his head and made eye contact, slowly blinking every so often, not interested in the staring contest cats are supposed to be known for.

Twain lowered his hand near the ground and gestured for him to come over.

"I think I rubbed your chin once when you were sitting in Mom's lap a few years ago. Whaddya say?"

Mr. Darcy stayed put, close enough to indicate trust, but still out of reach.

Twain gave up and resumed his commuter hunch. They sat there for a while, somewhat side by side. Another car set out to work, and Mr. Darcy held his ground. The passing motorist looked at the odd couple, focusing mainly on the unruffled cat.

Seeing another person leave reminded Twain there were people he needed to call. He reached into his back pocket for his phone and started with Esther, who said she would bring the pastor, then Oscar, who had already started a new job and said he would stop by sometime after Esther and the pastor had been there, and finally Marina, who asked if she could come after her shift later that night. Twain assured her that was fine, as he was not expecting to sleep much, if at all, during these final hours.

When he finally got off the phone, he looked over for Mr. Darcy, but he had disappeared. With the bench that much more lonely, he stood up, scanned his surroundings for the cat, and walked back inside.

He returned to the chair in his Mom's room and listened to her breathe. It provided a surprising sense of calm. He was so determined to be there when she stopped that anything could have happened around them—an eagle bursting through the window, a meteor through the roof, and armed mob through the door—and he would still be focused on her breath, sitting staring at her like a cat over a gopher hole.

So when Esther and the pastor let themselves in, it didn't startle him at all. It even took him a few seconds to acknowledge their presence. Esther was more composed than he would have expected, perhaps since she was with her pastor, who was dressed in a Hawaiian shirt and introduced himself as Pastor Dan. Twain thanked him for coming and cleared out of their way, standing in a corner of the room he had never stood before.

Pastor Dan sprung into some words that were familiar to Twain, even though he had rarely attended church and had not much studied the Bible. Esther took great comfort in the words, but to Twain they sounded like habit, a crossover hit song played so often that even someone who didn't own it could sing along, to the chorus at least, though without the emotional strap that bound it to the true fans. Regardless, he was glad the pastor came. He considered it good science, for while he leaned toward the idea that there is only here, not a hereafter, the scientific method demanded that he exhaust all other possibilities.

Twain was certain his Mom would be okay with Pastor Dan's contribution. He even had this vision of her coming to for a few seconds, taking stock of the situation, then looking over at him with a shrug that said, "Sure, why not?"

She knew the Bible well thanks to its influence on literature, and always encouraged Twain to know it better as a scientist in order to "know his enemy". She was under the impression that creationists would start to frequent his appearances and interrupt by screaming scripture, and that having some reasonable responses prepared would carry him through.

"Have you been praying?" he found Pastor Dan asking him.

Twain searched for a way back to the present moment. "I've been thinking a lot," he arrived. "About life, and death, about relationships."

"Then you have been praying," Pastor Dan smiled.

Twain was certain he had been lured into a scripted exchange, but as someone who had developed plenty of his own fabricated spontaneous moments that came in handy while working a room, he admired its quality and told Dan he looked forward to having him at the service in a few weeks.

Esther joined them in his corner, and gave him a hug before they left. Then Twain spent the rest of the day watching his Mom breathe.

As the sun set and her room gradually rotated from orange, to gray, and then dark, he remained seated, with no urge to turn on any lights. He listened to the fluid in her lungs babble, and started to feel like he was sitting beside a river on a moonless night. He imagined the river overtaking her, welcoming her as a permanent voice flowing from its rocks and lilies, her empty bed bubbling to the surface, which Twain would set on fire and send down the current in memoriam.

A faint series of knocks failed to break the image, as it reminded him of a woodpecker chopping a hole in a tree trunk in the woods by the river bed. The next wave of knocks reminded him that Marina had planned on coming over after her shift.

He rose from the chair and needed a moment to achieve balance and remember how to get to the front door. The outside of the house was as dark as the inside. He had failed to leave on the outdoor light to welcome her arrival. She was lightly touched by the glare of the street light up the driveway, enough so that he could see her face: she was not demanding answers, she was hoping for one, and the questions had nothing to do with the courtesy of leaving a light on.

She hugged him without a word. They held their position in the doorway for some time, then continued through the darkness, down the hall to Paget's room. Rather than turn on the light switch by the door frame and ignite the room, Twain felt his way over to the recliner and turned on the reading lamp that stood next to it.

The dim glow unveiled Marina already sitting next to Paget, holding her hand. She massaged Paget's arm with her other hand, caressing it up and down, letting her know everything was okay.

When she let go and stood up, Twain made a move toward her, expecting to receive another hug and then escort her to the door. But Marina made her way around the foot of the bed to the other side, and crawled onto the mattress beside her friend, snuggling up next to her, draping her arms around her.

Twain looked at the two of them. No such scene would ever take place between him and any of his friends.

Marina's breathing was just as heavy as Paget's, her tears and sniffles creating a strong tide of her own as well. She settled down after some time, more fatigued than composed. The sounds coming from Paget were once again the only sounds in the room. Marina rolled onto her back and stared up at the ceiling, long enough so that Twain started to assume she was spending the night there. He sat down and tried to craft some way to remind her that he was hoping to keep the decisive hours private. At a certain point, though, he wasn't sure he wanted to anymore, right around the time she finally got up.

He rose to meet her, but found himself catching up to her as she walked past him toward the door. He followed her down the hall and when they reached the front entrance, he turned on the outdoor light. They embraced, and he was going to open the door for her, but then they kissed.

Twain wasn't sure who initiated it. The intensity rose so quickly that details had a hard time holding on. Sensation carried them. One moment, a detail that he would recall later, was when they stopped and looked at each other. It may have been about propriety, if what they were doing was in poor taste, or at least weird. But then they ended up in the backyard, absorbed in one another, shivering with need and from the chill, so their pause could have been a silent agreement to take it outside. That was as far as his memory could jog, though, with regard to the initiation, as things grew even more primitive in the open air. Each stripped down the other on the lawn, which had just started to moisten in the moonlight, so it wasn't too scratchy, wasn't too wet. He noticed this when they were done, and he was the one whose body was most in touch with the ground, as Marina laid on top of him. He had wanted to stay inside of her until the end, at first because he wanted to stay a part of her for as long as he could, even if it only amounted to a few more seconds, then later, just before he pulled out, because he imagined it would force her to finally say something, even if it was in panic or anger. He had snuck in some laughter as he moaned and grunted, masking it with heavy breathing when he was finished, not wanting to explain his notions of their silence as a contest that he was willing to win by playing dirty.

As their breathing normalized in unison, he stroked her back and identified constellations, making up a couple of new ones by re-drawing the traditional lines that formed the ones memorized for generations. The originals were all inspired by a need to find order amongst the overwhelming, anyway, so he was in familiar company.

The quiet game continued. Twain had some ideas on how it might play out if someone lost. If it was him, he would ask aloud if they should have done this. If she broke first, she would have answered his question before he asked it, stating that Paget would not only approve, but think it was fantastic. And Twain would then claim it wouldn't be the first time his Mom took delight in something that embarrassed him. But it would be the last.

Marina stood and inspected the clothes that had landed across the lawn and patio, gathering up an article when it proved to be hers and tossing it on the table. Twain sat up, cross-legged, and watched her as she hunted, imagining her as a constellation, a star marking each of her feet, knees, hands, elbows, and breasts, with a cluster of stars to suggest her head. When her pile was complete, she approached the table and got dressed. He didn't get up off the ground until she was done. They hugged and he had never felt more naked in his life.

She looked as though she wanted to say something, then stopped short. He nodded, trying to let her know he understood. Then they both smiled and kissed good night. She let herself back in the house and out the front door. Twain stood in the yard for a long moment before gathering up the remaining clothes and putting them on.

He returned to his Mom's room and reclined in the chair. She sounded more like the ocean now than a river. He teetered along the water's edge between consciousness and unconsciousness, and each time he tripped from sleep back into the room, the roar was louder, as though a storm was coming and the waves were curling higher and crashing harder. Then as the noise reached a crescendo, it became muffled. He was underwater, engulfed by the surf, going neither up nor down, just hovering. The roar became a growl, low and rumbling all around him. But he wasn't drowning. There was no struggle. Until he heard the knocking. Then he spluttered for breath, had a spasm, and was back in the chair.

Morning sunlight bathed the room. His Mom was still breathing, and the knock was coming from the door next to her bed. It slowly opened and Twain's pulse spiked with panic.

Oscar's head peaked in. Twain exhaled as his heart rate plummeted.

"Nobody answered the front door," Oscar apologized. "I wanted to make sure everything is okay."

"That's fine," Twain continued to wake up. "I'm glad you did. I don't want to miss anything."

He stood up and Oscar proceeded into the room. They shook hands.

"I was afraid it was the Grim Reaper," Twain said.

Oscar was usually a good audience, but this time he didn't respond to Twain's quip. He was preoccupied with an envelope he held. It was a standard letter-sized envelope that appeared to have a several-page document folded within.

"What's that?" Twain asked.

Oscar seemed interested in performing some sort of introduction, but wasn't sure how to. So he just said it:

"A letter from your mother."

Twain's nervous system caught fire.

"I don't know what it says," Oscar handed it to him. "It's been closed since she gave it to me."

"Oscar..."

"So when you asked me questions about your father or anything like that, I wasn't lying when I said I don't know. I knew she was working on it, I saw her, but that's all."

"I would never accuse you of anything."

Oscar took a deep breath and looked over at her.

"She wanted me to wait and give it to you when she was gone," he said. "I thought you would like to read it before. But I didn't want to go against her wishes."

"This seems like a pretty good compromise," Twain ran his hands around the edges of the envelope. It said "Twain" on the front, in his Mom's handwriting.

"It makes perfect sense that she would trust you, Oscar. Thank you."

Oscar shrugged.

"I hope it brings you some comfort," he said. "Maybe some answers."

They shook hands again.

"See you at the service?" Twain asked.

"Of course," Oscar nodded.

He turned to leave, then paused as he faced the bed. He knelt down on one knee, took her hand, and kissed it.

"It's been a pleasure," he whispered.

He touched her hand to his forehead, laid it down next to her, and stood back up, taking one last look at her before he left.

Chapter Sixteen

This is not an easy letter for me to write, and not because I'm losing my mind and can only sustain a coherent thought for a few minutes at a time. I have to find a different pen each time I sit down to write, because I can't remember where I put the one I was using before. I'm sure it was someplace perfect, someplace I wouldn't forget. I'm sure that's what I told myself as I put it there. Sorry for the changing colors, back and forth between black and blue, every few sentences. This is about my tenth draft, and I've given up trying to make it look smooth. Even when I happen upon the same pen, my handwriting looks a little different each time. So here it is, in all its messiness, and it is a messy situation, isn't it? I'm not trying to be dramatic, speaking to you from the grave, that sort of grandstanding. I would have made a video if that was my intention, because I look like I'm in the grave already. I have that vacant expression that will only get more abandoned as this thing moves along. I still know who I am, but the face in the mirror doesn't seem to know. It would have been a great affect, actually. Made for quite a show. But then again, I would have required so many takes to get things right, to straighten out what I want to say, that all the editing and cuts would totally undermine my appearance. Besides, I would need help to splice it all together, and this is between you and me.

Before we get to the main event (and we both know what that is), I want to thank you for the decisions you have made concerning the end of my life. I know my living will may have been a bit ambiguous for a lawyer's or doctor's taste, but as a lifelong literature lover, I couldn't help myself. I had to leave open some room for interpretation. And I trust your reading of it aligned with my intended moral of the story. I also want to let you know that I never for one minute resented your decision to hire in-home care. Even if you hadn't found such a wonderful team as Esther and Oscar, I understood and agreed with you. I'm pretty certain I expressed this to you in person, or over the phone at some point. Those are the kinds of moments that have been the first to leave me, so I just wanted to be sure I got it in writing. Sure, some people perform the care on their own, but I didn't want you to forego your career. I'm very proud of you. I know I've said that many a time, even if I can't remember any of them. But I can't say it enough, and I want to do so once more before all avenues to feeling that pride and expressing it are cut off. And besides, being at home with nurses beats being in a nursing home. Plus you continued to visit me often. Right? Right? (Kidding.)

Okay. So here we go. Let me cut to the chase about your father (now that I've stalled for days and paragraphs), then backtrack and explain why I would rather die than tell you about him in person.

He was not a famous academic, nor even a competent one. He was nothing. And I don't use that term loosely. He really was a zero. He was a big man on the last high school campus I attended, the last of several schools strung together thanks to my family's nomadic existence. I managed to stay at that one for most of my senior year, graduating from it after a late start, after Thanksgiving break, when my father moved us yet again following a stint on a turkey farm where he claimed to have set a record for most birds killed. Or maybe that was the claim he made about the slaughterhouse, and it was cows. Could be. Anyway, I don't want to turn this into a saga about my father, or my mother for that matter. I was only slightly less tight-lipped about them, of course, than I was regarding your father, but all you need to know about them is the same thing I've told you before: they out-Dickens the most vile guardians Charles Dickens ever created. Their crimes against parenting will die with me.

So anyway, I made a couple of friends at that school who never got suspicious as to why we could never go to my place after school or on weekends. Or at least they were kind enough not to pry. Meanwhile your father, the big fish, was the paragon of all that I had wanted my entire childhood. He had everything. He had lived in that community his whole life, was a gifted athlete, a local hero, stunningly handsome, and his family owned a successful business, making them wealthy by the standards of their small town. And that town was the extent of their vision. Not that I noticed back then, back when I worshipped their son. In fact, he liked to speak of the "real world". He spoke of it when he failed to turn in yet another assignment. His dad's business was the real world, so he didn't have to deal with being "book smart". He was "street smart". But the streets were very narrow.

And later on, when I had finished my bachelor's degree and returned for an informal class reunion at the banquet room of a local hotel over summer break, he was well on his way to losing that business. The town was growing, and competition arrived that the family didn't know how to handle. They foolishly thought their son, simply by being younger than them, had some sort of insight into modern business. But all he knew how to do was spend money. Unwisely. Which was not a skill any other employers were looking for, either. He had already gone through a couple of side jobs he had taken in preparation for the inevitable. His bosses were fans of his from his heyday, but even they could only stand so much.

I, on the other hand, was swelling with pride. I had secured my job at the university and was planning on going to graduate school there. I was on my way. I was lifting off, soon to be soaring above him, the former object of my obsession. He still looked good, he was just starting to bloat, and he was suddenly interested in what I had to say. I was no business major, but I sounded smart, and was acting interested in his problems. No one else wanted to hear about them, because the people who were always around him could not come to grips with what was happening to him, they could not process it, and so they pretended his problems didn't exist.

Dammit, Twain. I had it. I was a breath away. The circle of trash I was chained to from birth had been broken. All I was going to do at that woozy little reunion was allow myself to preen for a few minutes, then have a drink and reminisce with some people I genuinely liked. It was the only childhood pit stop where I had made any friends. There was nobody else I could celebrate with who would know where I had come from. Grace said she was proud of me, but she was far away, having escaped from Mom and Dad long before I could, and she was hardly the merrymaker, anyway. So it was off to the Homewood Inn for some jug Chablis in plastic cocktail cups. And it was as if I had walked into a time machine, and there I was at the spring dance, and that arrogant, beautiful son of a bitch who had no idea how special I was had finally figured it out. He wanted me. Even more proof of how far I'd come.

I decided to lie to you out of embarrassment, really, but covered over that reason with something that sounded more rational, as liars tend to do. My upbringing had been saturated with contaminated men, and I had let another one in. I wasn't about to tell him or his family. Putting you in a basket and floating you down a river would make more sense than allowing those people into your life. So I invented the great and mysterious professor. I wanted you to grow up thinking your circumstances were something you could take advantage of, rather than something you had to overcome. It takes an exceptional person to achieve the latter, and I didn't trust my gene pool. I needed a new one.

Or so I thought. You proved me wrong. I knew by the time you were about five that the ruse was unnecessary. But I told myself you were too young to handle a change in the story I had raised you on. Then later I told myself that adolescence is a confusing enough time without having to hear the truth. Then when you were a teenager, I didn't want to risk disrupting all you were on your way to accomplishing. And finally having lived with that lie for so long, I may have started to believe it.

I'm certain your father has killed himself by now, though not in a way that would allow him to leave a note or inspire the medical examiner to declare it a suicide. You're welcome to look him up and check. In this envelope on a separate sheet of paper, I've left his name and the street I would walk a dozen times a day. I don't imagine he lives there anymore, but plugging the two names into a search engine will probably get you to a recent contact, or an obituary.

I hope you can forgive me. I have this dream that some wonderful things are happening during your stay here, and all that wonderfulness is lightening up the trip, distracting you enough to put you in a forgiving mood. I imagine you meeting some of the delightful, down-to-earth women I have befriended here, many around your age, and pursuing a relationship with one of them. I worked in the Literature Department, after all. I love a good romance. If that hasn't happened yet, would you please try? Check my web page, or hang around downtown and drop my name. And bring her around if things are going well between you two. My head will be empty. Perhaps some new, pleasant memories can seep in if your connection is strong enough.

I feel better each time I sit down to write this, oddly enough, considering that each time I sit down to write I'm closer to never being able to do so again. I wish I had confessed sooner, for it's my only regret at this point. I did everything I was supposed to do to keep my brain nimble. Not that I was aware of any family history. Few on my side lived long enough to provide any sort of sample size, and most lived off the grid, so there would be no record of them, much less a medical record. I was just so happy to have started the process of deleting them, and to watch you complete the rebellion, that I embraced life out of unabashed joy, not because I was looking over my shoulder.

So I volunteered for more charity organizations than I realistically had time for, read voraciously, did crossword puzzles and Sudoku, watched cutting edge television, and in general lived a life fit for a movie trailer starring me, riding a bike on a sunny autumn day down a tree-lined street filled with gold and ember leaves, my happy head tilted up toward the sunlight filtering through the branches, Vivaldi playing in the background, maybe a voiceover narration dropping in a line about drinking deeply from the cup of life, that sort of thing.

But I was an outlier, an exception on the wrong side of the curve. It was going to get me no matter what I did. And I would have made a great old lady. I was going to be one of those fantastic weathered broads whom people describe as spry, full of vim and vigor. I was bound to be young at heart because I wasn't afraid of being old.

I'm not complaining, though. I'm sure I made a vow not to complain about what's happening to me. And if I made no such vow, I'm making one now. Of my six-plus decades on earth, almost five of them were magnificent. I have lived a life that for most of human history would be considered royalty, only better because people aren't trying to poison me or marry me off to a cousin. I have lived a life more fulfilling and rich than nearly one hundred percent of the billions who have come before me, and surround me now. For me to inhabit such a small fraction of less than one percent and have the gall to envy an even smaller fraction would be shameful.

It just took me by surprise. I have been so strong throughout my life. (If I can't complain, then let me brag.) Marching into old age was a foregone conclusion. But maybe I needed so much strength to get through my younger years that I didn't have much left when I reached this point. Which is complete drivel, of course. But this is what we do with our lives, right? Turn them into stories with motivations and patterns and themes and much better dialogue than we actually muster. And not just literature lovers. No wonder we claim to be made in the image of God, someone whose character and very being are endlessly debated. We don't know ourselves any better.

So if I may leave you with something on the way out, let it be something outside of myself, let me focus on the exterior and take the interior with me, where maybe once and for all somebody can explain myself to me.

Regardless of what's been happening and what's to come, the most striking thing about facing death is how stunning everything is as I bid it goodbye, how vivid and spectacular it all seems, all of the things that will still be here when I'm not, from clouds to weeds to the swirls in metal and the grain in wood. I thought I already had a deep appreciation for my moment on this planet, but there is another level, and it has nothing to do with ourselves, and everything to do with what surrounds us. Don't wait to adopt this perspective. Photographs from deep space are lovely, but everything in them is deadly. Anything with life on it can't be seen, if it's even there. It's not even a single pixel in one of those lethal masterpieces. Meanwhile there I was this spring, the cherry blossoms being blown off the tree by a gentle breeze, the yard turning into a warm snowstorm of pink petals.

Look closely, always.

I'd like to say I'll be looking closely after you when I'm gone, but I believe I've already glimpsed heaven, and it kept me pretty busy. Who wants their mother hovering over them all the time, anyway?

The universe may be expanding, but it will never catch up to my love for you.

And thus, with an ellipses...

Twain remained standing and read the letter three more times. Only then did he look at the sheet of paper that had his father's name and address on it and nothing else. It resonated about as much as an afterthought can.

He put him back in the envelope and read her letter again. This time when he finished, he walked over to the empty side of the bed and laid down next to her, like Marina had, like he never had, and rested his head on her shoulder and read her words again. He started to hear her voice when he read them.

And when she stopped breathing, when he put his ear to her chest and heard nothing, the silence was the same one that fills the heavens.

Chapter Seventeen

The house felt even more empty than it was. There were no family heirlooms, of course, but it finally dawned on him that none of the old furniture from the modest rental he had grown up in had retired with his Mom, either, aside from a few photographs and some elementary school knick knacks he had made for her. The lack of material threads tying him to the property allowed the succession of human departures to completely hollow out the rooms of any sentiment. Everything seemed like it should have a price tag dangling from it. He spent as few of his waking hours there as possible, conducting his work in coffee houses, restaurants, and on campus. If he did take the full-time job at the college, he would put the house on the market and get a place of his own. It already came across to him as being staged and ready for showings, anyway, so listing it would be a formality.

It was as though he had been walking ahead of her on a bridge, having a conversation with her over his shoulder, and when she stopped responding, he had turned around to find her gone, with no ripples on the water, no sign of her in either direction, no hints where she may be.

The job in its current state was providing a helpful distraction. He was grateful for the opportunity to get off the bridge for a while, and feel certain about something. When lecturing, he effortlessly found the sweet center between energetic and calm. When fielding questions, his focus was pinpoint, his answers concise. He allowed the teaching assistants even more freedom in planning their presentations and leading the group study sessions, while managing them even more effectively with just the right word or phrase to guide them in a more productive direction, strictly when needed. The assistants picked up on the subtle increase of his intensity since he had taken that week off. During a quick follow-up meeting with the crew after class, Alice finally asked him if that week was due to his mother.

"It was," he told them.

After a moment of debating whether to keep playing it coy, he decided he owed them some honesty.

"She's gone."

Each of the young men, starting with Gavin and Blake, lined up to shake his hand and wish him condolences. They weren't very good at it, unsure how much they should try to lighten the mood or how somber they should remain. Twain at first attributed the disquiet to their youth, but based on recent experience, concluded that few people respond to death very well at any age.

Submitting his Mom's obituary to the local paper and posting it on her website had provided his first clue. Names that he had previously associated with eloquent and apt passages on her site suddenly overdid it, or became conspicuously mute. Most of the others relied on pat contributions invoking thoughts and prayers, but Twain started to sympathize with them, since the template provided safe passage for their unsteady impulses. Besides, such standard fare was far better than the frowning faces that some tossed onto the screen.

Alice was the best. She just gave him a hug and left it at that.

Finishing the script and tending to his other business interests, unlike the classroom, offered anxiety rather than relief. They were isolating, and the last place he wanted to be for the time being was alone inside his head. The final monologue of the film started to sound like a eulogy every time he got rolling on it. He wasn't necessarily worried about the words being too self-referential, as long as they were relevant to what needed to be said. So he would put it aside, and plan on reexamining it once he had achieved some separation from recent events. In speaking with his agent about upcoming engagements after the semester was over, he had a nagging sense that those appearances would not be as calming as teaching was proving to be. Yes they would involve interacting with people, but in a much more presentational manner. They would be about the product rather than the process.

Marina still preferred not to let him sleep at her place. She didn't want to address any questions about him that her roommate would ask, or her uncle the landlord, who liked to find reasons to knock on her door. But she was also leery of spending the night at Paget's house, more so than Twain, so they were somewhat back to where they started, finding places to fool around before or after her shift, like a couple of teenagers with disapproving parents. It was as exciting as it was frustrating, but just as in the teen years, their frustration was not simply sexual. It carried a relentless wondering if they were still going to be together when the world got real. And this agitation was hard to articulate without resorting to asking the same questions of one another over and over, so instead of asking them, they held on tighter, kissed harder, and when the coast seemed clear, humped recklessly.

Twain couldn't tell who was being more distant. Talking to her was difficult, but he didn't feel like talking much. He appreciated being quiet together, but theirs was not a relaxing quiet. If there was such a thing as closure, and he had his doubts, he was relying on the memorial service to provide it.

The weather was just the kind of day his Mom loved, cool temperatures under sunny skies. He followed through on renting the heat lamps, but the tents weren't necessary, and the rental outfit didn't charge him a cancellation fee because someone in the office knew his Mom from the many charity events she had helped coordinate. Likewise, the catering company tried to cut him a significant discount in tribute to their dealings with her, but he insisted on paying the full amount. They still arrived with a few complimentary cases of wine, filled with a collection of bottles donated by a variety of winery employees who wanted to pay their respects.

Over a hundred people showed up, and he recognized very few of them, just a handful from his childhood who managed to make the trip. As fun as it was to see them, he was more taken with his Mom's new wave of friends. They weren't any more charming or witty than her older friends, but Twain was invigorated in knowing she had met so many of them later in life, which in turn allowed him to imagine there were still people out there he had yet to meet who could end up being very dear to him. He basked in a kind of well-being that had been elusive for the last month thanks to this idea of a new life always being possible.

"So this is what it's like to have truly lived," an old professor from her old university proclaimed for Twain's benefit as they found themselves standing together surveying the crowd. He said it in honor of her, but Twain perceived a sliver of contrition in his voice, perhaps because the professor had mentioned he still lived near campus and taught part-time in retirement.

With a month to draft their feelings, his Mom's friends had come up with some brilliant and touching tributes. Some shared them in front of the audience when the program called for it, after Twain thanked everyone for coming and introduced Pastor Dan, who couched some scripture with some kind words about Paget. Others kept their accolades at the table, amongst the group sitting with them, while still others passed on their memories to Twain as he conversed with them one-on-one. So many stories and character witnesses came forward that Twain had to admit to himself he would not be able to remember each one. But as a whole, it was their affinity for her that left the most unforgettable impression. They really knew her, or at least felt connected to her. The stories were between them, the person telling it and Paget. The only time she was referenced singularly was when a guest described her, what they loved about her. As soon as they launched into their story, it was all about the interaction: the time they decided at the last minute that foliage would look good around the podium at a Boys and Girls Club event, so Paget found a truck in the parking lot with the keys in it and they drove down a tree-lined street pulling off the smallest lower branches and throwing them in the back, returning before anyone noticed anything was missing; the time they trained her to take over the most challenging Meals on Wheels route, and the mystery lady in the residence motel who had barely cracked her door for decades finally opened it all the way and let them in on Paget's first day; the time they were organizing a benefit for the police department, and Paget wanted to see what the job was really like, so they went on a ride-along with some officers one night and Paget convinced a woman in a domestic dispute to come with her to the women's shelter, and took the man to his first couple of AA meetings.

Aunt Grace was even inspired to contribute.

She said she was the only one there who knew Paget before her son was born, which was true. She said there was good reason for that, which was also true. She said she grew up being jealous of how unaffected her sister seemed to be by all of the things they would later keep to themselves as they got older. She said back then she was convinced it was only thanks to her that Paget had the opportunity to be so cheerful, that she was shielding her sister from the worst, providing a ring of innocence for her little sister to play inside. But she always knew this wasn't the case, that Paget had something more than a crabby big sister watching over her. There was something enchanted about her. She lived in a world apart.

This was also true, but Grace had never admitted it before. And now that she had, there was nothing else she could say. She tried, but could not.

Twain almost got up to give her a hug and escort her back to her chair, but one display of emotion was one more than she was used to exhibiting, and he didn't want Grace to go from feeling humbled to humiliated. He regretted his decision for a moment as she still struggled on her way back to the table. But as soon as she sat down and some nearby guests leaned over to offer their compliments and sympathy, each contribution helped to rebuild her usual self, until she was once again fully armored by the time the next person started to speak. He caught her eye at one point and gave her a nod, which was all she needed.

When the testimonies were done and the audience reverted back to a crowd, Twain managed a break from shaking hands and hugging people, and found an empty chair at one of the tables, away from a heat lamp, and turned his face to the sky with his eyes closed, taking in the warmth of the sun while the air around him remained chilled.

As he turned to face the earth again, he found himself in eye contact with Marina. She smiled bashfully, as though apologizing for peeking in on his private time. Twain volleyed a smile back, but a much more broad one, as he finally fell into the direction he had been leaning: he wanted her to be a part of his privacy, and he wanted it to happen here, in this part of the world. She looked away, and he decided that the reason their bond had been so apprehensive lately was because he had not established his plans with her, since he wasn't even sure of them. Now that he was ready to eliminate that limbo, comfort would reign. And someday when his funeral took place, there would be fewer people in attendance than if he stayed on his current trajectory, but the quality of the relationships would make up for the quantity.

"May I have your attention, everyone?" Twain stood up and tapped on a water glass with a butter knife. "Just one more group hug and then you can go back to doing your own things..."

The crowd quieted down in a trickle of chuckles and cut-off conversations.

Twain thanked them and walked over to a corner of the yard where some decorative ceramic pots stood empty amongst the shrubs bordering the lawn, the annuals that had bloomed in them over the summer having withered and been pulled out weeks before. One of the pots had a cover, and Twain reached down and held it up for display as the people migrated closer to him.

"Well, here she is," he announced.

He intended it to be a light moment, but he had to gather himself before proceeding. Some of the guests indeed laughed heartily, which helped him capture the tears he could feel cooling off along his lower eyelids. Some laughed uneasily. Esther scowled at him, visions of an open casket still shading her outlook, which made him chuckle as well, a couple of the cold tears breaking free and heating up as they rolled down his cheeks.

"I wasn't sure where to put her," he continued. "I barely have a fixed address, and it's a dingy little apartment at that. This house will be on the market soon…"

He wished he hadn't said that. He looked for Marina to see how she reacted, afraid she would assume it meant he was leaving town, but he couldn't find her.

"It was truly her home," he added. "And as I seriously consider moving here, to this town, I need to forge my own space if I do."

Twain hoped that would put Marina at ease, wherever she was.

"Besides, the most important reason Mom loved this place was not the house or the surroundings, though they are obviously persuasive points in its favor. The biggest reason she loved it here was because of you, all of you. Which is the same reason she loved the university, and our old hometown. You provided the foundation upon which she was able to build this next chapter. She loved where she lived, where she was working, where she retired. She had no special vacation spots or bucket list places, because she was so content with where she was. They were her special places. She was already there. So if you don't find it too morbid, I'd like to see to it that she winds up all across the areas she adored, delivered by the people who made them adorable."

He took out a small Tupperware container the size of a shot glass.

"There will be stacks of these containers next to the urn, and on your way out this evening, if you'll indulge us, please take one and take a little bit of Mom with you."

Twain demonstrated the procedure, dipping one side of the Tupperware into the urn and scooping out a small portion of ashes.

"Then cast her where you'd like to remember her."

He gently scattered his portion at the base of an evergreen tree a few steps off the grass, then turned his attention back to the guests.

"Any spot you love, she'll love it, too."

Some of them clearly had their doubts.

"And if you'd prefer to pass, don't feel guilty. It was my idea, not hers."

His disclaimer soothed most of the holdouts. Except for Esther.

He fielded a few compliments and some good-natured barbs as he made his way to the kitchen to fetch the containers and stack them on the table by the urn. Once the spread was complete and he started to mingle again, people shared their ideas on where they were going to bring her. Some mentioned places out of town she had traveled with them, places Twain never knew she had gone, places they were going to re-visit thanks to her.

He glanced at the urn every so often and was pleased to note that the containers were dwindling at around the same rate as the guests. Occasionally he managed to see someone taking their turn, hesitant at first, then quickly getting used to the idea. But he couldn't find Marina, even as the attendance faded. He started to wonder if he had actually seen her, or if it was an illusion made of sunlight and his thoughts, with a dash of cool air.

Esther and Oscar said their good-byes. She had a container in her hand, and Twain asked if she was going to put it in a casket and bury it. Oscar laughed before she did to try and prompt her, but it wasn't necessary. She didn't laugh. But she did kiss the container, then kiss Twain. They embraced almost as long as they had on the day his Mom started to aspirate. Oscar watched them through misty eyes, and when Twain shook his hand, he made sure Oscar still had his cell phone number.

"I do," Oscar nodded.

Then he and Twain embraced, too.

Twain assumed they were the last people to leave whom he knew well, and in allowing himself to therefore take another lap in search of Marina, was surprised to see Grace exchanging hugs with some guests as they all prepared to go. The guests thanked Twain for a beautiful day as they passed, leaving him facing Grace.

"Potential clients?" he asked.

"You don't hug clients," she shook her head. "Not professional."

"So you had a good day, then?"

Grace untightened her smile.

"You did a fine job, Twain. Thank you."

He stood there curious as to whether she was going to hug him. None was forthcoming.

"The ash ceremony?" Twain asked. "Not too weird?"

Grace shrugged. "It's the kind of thing your mother liked."

He nodded and smiled in agreement, then decided to force the issue. He opened his arms to her.

She accepted his invitation with a civil nod, as though her number had been called at a service deli. And though Twain felt he had wrapped his arms around bags of groceries that exuded more warmth, he appreciated the novelty of the moment.

Grace extracted herself from his hug.

"Look at it this way," she said, acknowledging the frost. "At least there won't be any fights over inheritances. The line between my side and your mother's side has always been perfectly drawn."

"True," he agreed.

And as he watched her go, he thought of how stark his side of the line was. It was just him. Unless he tapped into this father's family.

But that wasn't the answer.

The catering company was just starting to clean up, and the truck had yet to arrive to pick up the tables and heat lamps. He couldn't bear to wait any longer, so he asked the head server to let the party supply people in when they arrived, and to leave the door unlocked if he wasn't back by the time they were done.

He took a few steps toward the door before remembering something. Marina had obviously left a while ago, if she had been there at all. So he trotted to the backyard, grabbed a Tupperware container, and gathered up a share of ashes for her.

Once outside the city limits, the sun peeked over the hilltops at the remaining leaves of the vineyards, illuminating even the crunchiest leaves with a postcard autumn glow. Most of the vines had gone dormant, but there were still some red and yellow patches lingering along with the brown, holding on until the next flurry of wind blew them into the past.

As Twain slowed into the turn that ran to Marina's place, he noticed a large pickup truck towing a horse trailer heading his way, also slowing down to make the turn in the opposite direction. It drew closer and he saw that it wasn't a horse trailer, and then saw the writing on the side: *Cody Jase Team Motocross.*

He had a couple of miles to go before reaching the dirt road that led to her uncle's ranch, so he used those miles to calm himself down. Where there was an ex, there were times that required conversation, especially when kids were involved. He took himself through that logic enough to lower his pulse, but there was only so low it could go. He was essentially going to propose to her, after all, so he changed the name of his 'anxiety' to 'excitement' and sped forward.

The current vehicle for sale that her uncle had on display by the mailboxes was a filthy dirt bike, which helped the uneasy peace of mind he was negotiating, as he decided to assume it was the reason for Cody's visit. Then he saw the curtains swinging in the front window of Marina's rental as his truck popped along the gravel road that veered into the ranch, which he interpreted as her being excited to see him.

He managed to rise from his pickup and take a few tingly strides without wobbling. He felt more strength return to his legs with each step. Then with several paces left to go, she opened her door.

He saw her face, and he forced himself to smile and proceed forward so he wouldn't collapse onto the ground and howl. All that was left was to find out the reason why. He took what seemed to be a very long walk across the dirt, hoping it was anything but her choosing Cody over him.

She eked out a "hi" as he arrived.

Twain nodded.

"Are you here to sweep me off my feet?" she asked.

"That was the idea."

She looked away and sniffled a few times, then wiped her face with the back of each hand, one at a time. She took a deep breath, and as she turned to face him, opened the door wider so Twain could see inside.

A baby sat in the room, facing the couch, dressed in a girly pink jumper. She was clutching the seat cushions, trying to pull herself up, grunting lightly.

Twain stared. The baby succeeded in standing and looked over her shoulder at the two of them, announcing her accomplishment with a squawk.

"Cody's latest bimbo left her with him," Marina explained. "She said she wasn't the mother type and bailed."

"And how involved are you?"

"Cody's Mom is done raising his kids for him, and I don't blame her. I'm the only one of Cody's baby mammas who even tried. So he came to me when his Mom said not this time."

The baby was smiling now, quite proud of herself. Twain was inspired all over again.

"Okay," he professed.

"No..." Marina waved him off.

"She's so young," he pursued his case. "It will be like raising our own."

"You don't understand," she kept waving. "That's sweet, Twain, and I appreciate it. But no. I can't hold you back."

"I was going to stay, anyway," he said. "That's the plan. I've got an offer from the college. I'm tired of being everywhere and nowhere. I'm a ghost, popping up on some people's screens now and then. I want to be here. With you. I want to teach people about the universe and get to know earth a little better."

Marina looked even more frustrated. She clutched her head, then let her arms fall.

"I cannot subject you to the Jase family," she said.

"Screw them," he shot back. "We'll find a way to get custody."

"Oh my God, Twain..."

"What?"

"You're really not thinking this through."

"C'mon, look at her."

"Yes, she's been a perfect angel for the forty-five seconds you've known her."

"Give me a little more credit than that..."

"I'm giving you all the credit in the world, sweetie. I love that you want to do this. And she really is a great kid, so far. But Cody, and his Mom, and that crazy bitch who gave birth...you have no idea."

"I have some idea."

"But you haven't lived it. Cody will ignore her because she's a girl, his Mom will change her mind about taking care of her at least three dozen more times, and the mother, well, the only thing worse than her leaving is her coming back, and she will come back, every so often, somehow even dumber each time, but she'll have rights, and some judge will be like, 'well, she's the mother, and she didn't leave her in a garbage can or anything'..." Marina glanced skyward. "Oh God, Twain. Get out while you can."

She took a break and looked over at the baby. Twain wasn't sure how to resume his defense, so he watched the baby too. She plopped on the floor, and was just as proud of that as she was about standing up.

"Poor kid," Marina narrated. "I wish I could protect her from the family tree that's going to fall on her."

"All this 'I' stuff," Twain said. "Think in terms of 'we.'"

"You're just as innocent as she is," Marina scoffed. "At least I know I can protect you."

"Why are you so sure I won't be able to handle it? Why won't you give me a chance?"

"You're a lifelong bachelor with a lucrative career. Forgive me if I'm a bit skeptical that you're ready for this."

"That's not fair."

"This girl needs stability, any little bit of it she can get her little hands on. I can't risk another person checking out on her."

"Now you're being mean."

"I'm being realistic, Twain. You're always so brutally honest about your career, knowing your shortcomings and working around them. Can you please be just as honest about this?"

Twain watched the baby crawl away from them, toward the corridor leading to the bedrooms. Her breathy squeals caught Marina's attention. She darted over to re-direct her, and the baby was not happy about it. The happy sounds of discovering something new changed to cries of disappointment. Marina bounced her around and whispered in her ear while looking for something to distract her.

His appeal was over.

He wondered if she had presented all of her reasons for why she didn't want him around. He was about to check. He was about to say "I love you" and see how she responded. But he decided to keep their love mysterious. He said "good bye" instead, and closed the door behind him.

When he reached the driver's seat, he noticed the container full of ashes on the passenger seat. He looked back to see if the door was open or the curtains pulled to the side, but neither was. As he drove away, he imagined everything behind him softening and falling to the ground like curtains cut from their rods.

There was still a trace of light across the countryside, a dim touch that made the vineyards appear much closer to hibernation than they seemed on the way over. He had spoken with many a winemaker during his stay who claimed this was going to be a very good year. The grapes that were gone had grown beautifully, now fermenting across the country in a thousand different bins, slowly revealing whether the optimistic predictions would be true.

Twain imagined the wine labels in the future that would be imprinted with this time and this place, and what sorts of feelings may surface when he read those numbers and those letters, when he looked back and tried to define this year based on more than what was inside the bottle.

Some rows of vines just ahead were sound asleep, not a single leaf left on them, saving their strength to spring back in a few months. They sloped down a hill facing east, away from the sunset, the shorter days allowing moisture to accumulate along the base of the twisted boughs that leveled out from the bottom of the grade. He pulled over and grabbed the container of ashes.

He sprinkled her around an old vine whose roots were clearly very deep, and watched her mix with the water and blend into the ground. He thought of how a great bottle of wine doesn't last. It has its time, its reputation grows, and holding on to it for too long turns it into a memento, rather than what it truly was, and the only way to really know its greatness is to rely on the stories people tell.

There once was something beautiful, an incarnation. You should have been there. Let me try to explain.

Chapter Eighteen

All that was left to do was to try not to ruin Alice's life.

There were other tasks, but none were as difficult. Teaching was fun. Finishing the script was satisfying. Refusing the Dean's offer was neither, but it was brief. Trying not to call Marina was a more drawn out challenge, as was organizing the sale of the house. Spending time with Alice, however, was everything: fun, satisfying, and challenging; drawn out and all too brief.

His Mom's death, according to Alice at least, had rendered Twain as vulnerable as she had been after laying out her feeling for him. And though he wasn't sure he agreed with her analysis, they did find themselves on familiar, flirty ground that made it hard to uphold the platonic vow he had sworn for her sake. Assisting her in preparing her university applications helped to remind him why it was so important to resist. The letter of recommendation he composed for her laid out all of her qualities in writing, all the talents she would be squandering by attaching her goals to his. Maybe not all of them, but enough of them, and the ones sacrificed would not be by choice, but by conditions that he created.

He never dared mention he was having second thoughts about her, or that Marina had left him for a one-year old, and Alice never brought her up. Except during the week before Finals.

He was taking the gang out for one last meal, a dinner this time so everyone could make it. They went to their usual grill, which they practically had to themselves since it was regarded as more of a lunch stop. While everyone was still gathered around the table, Alice asked Twain if Marina was going with him when he left.

As much as her question put him on the spot, it was still preferable to having her bring it up when it was just the two of them, if she had to ask.

Oohs and catcalls sprang from the guys. Twain reckoned their reactions were primarily out of relief at getting confirmation that he and Alice were not an item, rather than any genuine interest in his other relationships. Regardless, the hoots bought him some time to consider how he wanted to answer, so he fielded them with good cheer and plotted a response.

"She still has some family obligations," he said as the noise subsided. "She decided to stay."

"So you did ask her to leave with you?" Alice followed up.

"The situation became clear before I had a chance."

"Did you consider staying?"

"I did..." Twain decided to leave it at that. Now the males were interested.

"Who are we talking about?" asked Blake.

"Jesse Jase's mom," said Alice.

Blake smiled and nodded, as did a couple of the others, including Gavin.

"If anyone calls her a MILF," Alice warned the table, "I'll break this ketchup bottle over their head."

"It's a plastic bottle," Gavin noted.

"People still say MILF?" Twain asked no one in particular.

"Idiots do," Alice offered.

"I just figured if I knew what it meant, it must be out of date," said Twain.

"See?" Gavin pounced. "If you would just keep teaching, you could stay up to date on things like slang and music. It keeps you young."

The gang started pelting him with pleas to stay. Twain appreciated their efforts, but had a decent explanation that was partially true.

"The college can't just offer me a position," he told them. "It's not that kind of an institution. And even if they could, if they fudged the rules to give it to me, I wouldn't be comfortable with that. Now come on," he changed the subject. "Who's old enough to drink? Somebody have a beer with me."

A couple of them were, and he bought the rest non-alcoholic brews so they could have a toast.

"To all the bright futures around this table," he proclaimed. "May you seize them and make yourselves proud."

They clinked their bottles and drank.

"I wish I could remember a good quote that fits the situation," Twain apologized as they finished swallowing. "I never seem to be able to do that."

"I've got one," Blake smiled. "It's from the astronomer Twain Henry, who once said, 'Don't you know who I am?'"

Everyone enjoyed the dig, including Twain, who in his defense claimed he never actually said that, he just thought it.

More playful barbs flew across the table as the melancholy realization set in that something unique was coming to an end, something that didn't need to be acknowledged out loud. They were together, aware of how valuable their time had become, and were content to let the meter run.

One by one they fell away. Twain was relieved that Alice didn't hold out until the end, that she left in the middle with a friendly hug.

But after they were all gone, and Twain bought one more beer that he drank alone at a smaller table while he watched an old man clear their last meeting place until it looked like they had never been there, he left the empty dining room with a wave to the cashier, and found Alice waiting for him by his truck.

They kissed for a moment that would always follow them.

"It's a good-bye kiss, isn't it?" she asked as they stayed in each other's arms.

"I'll wait for you," he said. "And if you don't find anyone while you're pursuing your dreams, I'll be there."

"I don't believe you."

"Nothing in my adult life has been permanent, aside from what I study. And even that may be gone by now. The lights in the sky may be from stars that died years ago. You're going to be my last chance."

They kissed again.

"Just remember," he reminded her. "The deal's off if you don't earn at least two degrees and make at least one discovery that changes humanity for the better."

"And all you have to do is wait?"

"I have to try and not get too old."

"Good luck with that," she teased.

"It won't be as hard as keeping my promise to leave you alone. But I'm determined to feel good about this."

She smiled for a moment, then looked down for quite some time. She finally broke through her surface and gave him one more quick kiss good bye.

"I'll be watching," she said.

"I'll be waiting," he said.

As her footsteps called across the parking lot, Twain knew she would meet somebody well before he had a chance to get much older. And though he wished nothing less for her, he was barely able to stop himself from chasing her down and telling her to forget everything he said.

He distracted himself by sending Marina a text, the first contact he had dared since the last time he saw her, cradling a baby she had not imagined.

Thank you for giving me a chance even though you're so familiar with what men can do.

He wasn't expecting a reply, but as he watched Alice drive away, he felt his phone quiver and checked the screen.

A round, yellow, cartoon smiling face looked back at him, courtesy of Marina.

He smiled back at it, and then in the direction of Alice's tail lights as they grew smaller in the dark.

Seeing Alice in class on the day of the final was difficult, too. But he had an audience and a job to do, which helped to keep him in the right direction.

He asked if they would indulge him one last time before the exam, if they would listen to the ending of the script he had been working on so that he could get their feedback and perhaps make some changes before he recorded it. They agreed, and as he read it, he tried not to focus too much on Alice.

"Do people really fear the end of the world? Or are they curious to see it happen? It would be satisfying to know that life will not go on without us, that our end is the end. But the actual end of the world will not be so sudden or shocking. The drama will play out over generations, our expanding sun slowly making life on earth less hospitable, until by the time it finally swallows our home, we will have been long gone from it, either because we left, or faded away.

"Finding a way out will also not come quickly. There will be fits and starts, failed experiments, broken contracts, lack of investment, of political will, battles over rights, over who gets credit, who gets to go first, frustrations over the speed, at not being able to see the results of our work, at not being able to participate in the end. We all want to be there when it happens, but we can't be. We want to walk on the sidewalk, not pave it.

"But we have no choice. We're getting kicked out eventually, by the very source that gave us life."

Twain couldn't help but turn his attention toward Alice a little more frequently, and found he barely needed to look down at the words.

"It's hard to think about. We went through so much chaos to get here: planets switching orbits, pulling each other into their gravitational fields, flinging one another like a game of crack the whip,

jockeying for position in the swirling wake of our sun as it, too, struggled to mature. Each body faced a constant pounding in the process of finding its place, a barrage of rubble that both wounded and shaped it. Some ended up outside the circle, shunned from our system, relegated to the Kuiper belt and the Oort cloud, pockets of its members occasionally breaking free to fly through our space and remind us of the old, tumultuous days.

"Those days are easy to look back on when we're in a peaceful place, a prosperous one, when we're enjoying some well-earned complacency. But the sun that juggled our roots in its arms will extend its reach again to take it all back. We need to find our own way."

He abandoned the script and addressed Alice as squarely as he could without staring, adding some lines that would not make it into the final product, that were just for her.

"And there's beauty in that ride. Hard-earned beauty that makes the naturally lovely even more beautiful."

Alice looked away, turning her head to the side.

Twain still imagined her in profile as he watched a rough cut of the film in a screening room with the producers weeks later.

His voice came through speakers in the ceiling, and as usual he was surprised at how foreign his voice sounded, how different it seemed when he listened to a recording of it, rather than hearing it at the same time he was speaking.

"And when we arrive at these new places," he heard himself say, *"we will learn more about the places we've been. We will get glimpses into where we came from, what we were. But the only way to get there is to fight through the frustrations and withstand the hard work required to make it possible. Only then can we find a new home, and maybe discover why it was always so difficult for us to understand that while we may not live in unique times, we can make our time unique."*

A familiar view of earth from outer space filled the screen, then the perspective gradually widened and gained speed as it passed by a succession of earth-like planets, each apparently capable of hosting life, but none looking exactly alike, and none revealing what that life may resemble.

One of the producers then piped up about this being the point where the musical score would swell, and the credits would roll.

"Well done," Twain complimented them as the lights came on. They were all sitting behind him, and he was still getting used to the light, so he addressed the emptiness in front of him.

"Really?" another producer asked.

"Best I've seen on the subject," Twain added.

"It wouldn't have been the same film without you," yet another producer said. "You gave it an identity."

"It was my pleasure," Twain replied, still facing forward. "The offer came at a very good time."

The collection of producers grew quiet. Twain had a feeling they were glancing at each other, deciding which one should speak next.

"And...speaking of time," one of them finally said. "We were wondering if maybe you had some time to attend a premiere we're putting together. Maybe a couple of them, actually, at some education conferences coming up."

"If it's premiered a second time, is it still a premiere?" he teased.

They fell silent again and Twain felt guilty. He turned around to face them. They each had a pad of paper and a pen for taking notes.

"Of course," he said. "And I'll promote it as much as I can on my own."

The producers were relieved.

"We really appreciate that," the one sitting closest to him said.

Twain shrugged. "It's what I do."

He turned back around and looked up at the blank screen. The producers talked amongst themselves about the logistics of the premiere. Twain considered his promise to them, his assurance that this is what he does, and doubted that doing something else would have really worked, and questioned how much of where he now found himself was choice rather than circumstance. The empty screen appeared to expand as he stared at it, and he asked himself if there was anything he had that was not given to him.

When there was an opening in their conversation, Twain turned in his seat again to join in.

"May I ask you a favor?"

"Sure," one of them decided to answer on their behalf.

"Would it be possible to include a dedication somewhere? The beginning, the end, before or after the credits, wherever you see fit?"

They exchanged looks and none seemed to have a problem with it.

"Okay," one said.

"What would you like it to say?" asked another.

"May I borrow a pad of paper?"

The one closest to him tore off the top sheet that had some notes on it, then passed him the pad and a pen.

Twain turned back toward the screen and wrote down what he imagined seeing on it someday:

To my mother,
Who lost her way on one path,
But found happiness on another

Also by Sean Boling

The Current Mr. Orr
Devin's Best Afterlife
Once in Two Lifetimes
Revenge and Wellness in the Sweet Hereafter

Standalone
Cut Flowers
Abraham the Anchor Baby Terrorist
Pigs and Other Living Things
The Summer of Our Foreclosure
Satellite Campus
A Charter to That Other Place
The Latest Version of My Love Story
Show Them What They Won
The Name Field
Should
Moral Adjacent
Over Here We Have

About the Author

Sean lives with his family in Templeton, California. He teaches English at Cuesta College.